Promo~~tional Copy~~

This copy of *Marie's Nutcracker* has been distributed FREE to many dance schools and dance companies in the United States as a promotional program from SES Publishing. Please distribute to dancers at your school. The promotional copy of the book is a FREE gift to you and not for resale. We hope you enjoy it.

We appreciate your feedback. If you want to make comments, please send an email to info@NutcrackerLtd.com. If you write a review in your newsletter, please send us a copy of the document.

Please visit Amazon to purchase additional copies.

Product Details

Paperback | $17.00
Published by SES Publishing
November 15, 2022
| 259 Pages | 6 x 9 |
ISBN 9798356738111

Available at <u>Amazon</u>
To locate book at Amazon, please search by:
      <u>Title:</u> "Marie's Nutcracker," or
      <u>ISBN:</u> 9798356738111, or
      <u>Amazon product number</u>: B0BKYHMGD1, or
      <u>Amazon link</u>: https://a.co/d/egrgDHA

Marie's Nutcracker

Written by Margaret Marie Klenzing
Illustrations by Rori Alexander

SES Publishing, November 2022

Contact:
Chuck Stewart, Director SES Publishing
Email: info@NutcrackerLtd.com
323-327-1299

Available at Amazon:
ISBN 9798356738111

To locate book at Amazon, please search by:
        Title: "Marie's Nutcracker," or
        ISBN: 9798356738111, or
        Amazon product number: B0BKYHMGD1, or
        Amazon link: https://a.co/d/egrgDHA

Table of Contents

Illustrations

Introduction

Maire's Nutcracker shares personal insights about my first love—classical ballet. The story revolves around a fictional character named Marie and her involvement in the production of the *Nutcracker Ballet*. But really, it was my journey to understand what classical ballet is and my relationship to dance. Most of the situations and discussions in the story come from my personal experiences or those of my children, both my daughter and son, who took ballet. The events really happened. Some experiences were fun, some lovely, while others were terrifying or lonely. I think the physical and emotional challenges faced by professional ballet dancers help give insight into life's deepest questions. What is art? What is dance? Why do I dance? What is the meaning of life? Eventually, all ballet dancers face these realities and must find ways to cope. But through it all, there is the *Nutcracker*, always there and always fun. Tchaikovsky wrote a masterpiece that inspires joy and beauty and will last forever. I hope this book is not only a fun romp through *Candy Land* but may inspire deeper reflections on the meaning of dance.

I believe ballet is for everyone. I am pleased that the ballet world is slowly diversifying. To that end, most of the characters in the book are not physically described leaving it up to the reader to imagine the kind of person they want in that role. Ballet should be open to all who are attracted to the majesty, beauty, finesse, and athleticism of dance. I hope this book speaks to the hearts of all who want to dance.

I was introduced to Rori Alexander through a mutual dance friend who was her ballet teacher. I'm honored to have met Rori. She has a keen sense of ballet positions and is skilled as an illustrator. She also worked closely with me to include racial and ethnic diversity in her work. It is important to make dance accessible to all people. I believe her illustrations enhance the telling of Marie's experiences in the production of the *Nutcracker Ballet*.

I want to thank all those who reviewed the rough manuscripts and gave helpful insights: Sandra Bell, James Cabral, Michael Crane, Edward Frederick, Jasmine Gagnier-Katz, Susan Hall, Cathy Ludwig-Haworth, Debbie Saliba-Leeper, and Jane Wallace Cherry. To the women, we were sisters in dance. Wonderful memories and life-long friends came from our ballet experiences.

Enjoy.

Margaret Marie Klenzing 2022

Prologue

  Just as there is that moment when the heat of summer gives way to cool nights and warm days announcing that fall has arrived, there is that moment when we know winter is close at hand; and that is the first time we hear melodies on the radio or at the mall from the *Nutcracker Ballet*. From *Dance of the Sugar Plum Fairy* to *March of the Toy Soldiers*, *Waltz of the Flowers,* and the *Russian Dance*, Tchaikovsky's songs are etched in the collective memory of every child and family throughout the land. The *Nutcracker* symbolizes the gaiety of family gatherings for winter holidays with an abundance of food, dance, and merriment. Decorations are lavishly placed in malls and stores, converting them into winter wonderlands.

  No winter season would be complete without attending a performance of the *Nutcracker Ballet*. From the northeastern reaches of Maine to the southern Gulf States, to the Great Plains and the Rocky Mountains, and to the Golden Coasts of the Pacific, large and small ballet companies mount their annual *Nutcracker* productions. Regardless of budget or expertise, the magic of the *Nutcracker* shines with every marching soldier, dancing flower, waltzing snowflake, scurrying mouse, and pas de deux.

WINTER WONDERLAND AT THE MALL

1 — Opportunity

"... five... six... seven... eight... "

Barbara slapped her hands in rhythm to the music.

"... and... *tombe´* ... *pas de bouree´* ... "

Jasmine and I began executing the combination down the diagonal in the dance studio. As the two lead dancers at my mother's ballet school, we always started combinations for the other dancers to watch and imitate.

Barbara looked pleased and continued, "... that's right... *glissade assemble´* ... now prepare to jump high and not out... "

I dreaded the next step, the very difficult *gargouillade*. We had worked on it all week. It combines a jump where one foot then the other inscribes circles in the air, what we call *rond de jambe*, with both feet making a clockwise motion. At one point, you are supposed to look like you are hanging in the air with the feet and lower leg making circular motions. Very tough. I didn't like it. It reminded me of a crab wiggling its legs while flying through the air. It wasn't very feminine.

"... excellent Jasmine." Barbara smiled and always praised Jasmine's dancing. I often felt jealous.

"... and Marie, remember to jump higher next time... not out."

I was a good turner, so I added a *pirouette* with two *fouetté* turns at the end of the combination. It was a great flourish. I nailed five turns on pointe, something most girls on pointe could not do. I looked over to see if my mother noticed. She didn't. She concentrated on the next group of girls following us down the diagonal. I knew I shouldn't have felt bad, but I felt her snub.

The dance studio contained four separate rooms of varying sizes. Being located in a mall was a marketing decision by my mother. Studio A was the largest room, with mirrors lining one full side and ballet *barres* lining the other side of the room. We held most group rehearsals in Studio A. Portable *barres* were regularly used in the center of the room. Barbara had spared no expense with the floor, covered by imported vinyl that could be used on stage floors. The vinyl floor covering made the surface consistent even when wet from sweat and was much appreciated by the professionally bound dancers, especially the girls wearing pointe shoes.

The vaulted ceilings were accented with floor-to-ceiling French windows at one end looking out to the sidewalk and trees of the mall. Anyone walking by could look in. I didn't like being exposed like that, being on display, not while trying to improve my ballet technique. But I chalked it up to learning to perform in front of people. Still, having random faces peer through the front plate windows at random times was disconcerting. I guessed it was all right, especially since the store spaces were so cheap that the dance studio could afford many practice rooms. I was thankful mother started a local dance company. It gave me a chance to perform. I dreamt of dancing someday with a large ballet company like American Ballet Theater in New York.

Early evening darkness encroached through the arched windows. Some were fogging up from the warm moist air in the studio. People from the outside could look in while we had difficulty looking out. Plus, the sweat from our exercises and breaths fogged up against the cold glass windows, obscuring them into poor mirrors that distorted our images. It was best to ignore the windows.

Mother founded the Classical Ballet Society in a suburban mall as the professional arm of her ballet school. She had been a renowned ballerina in her day, but those days were long gone. Being in her mid-fifties, she still taught daily ballet classes and was thin and elegant. Her long hair was streaked with gray that helped soften the somewhat angular and harsh nature of her cheeks and jaw. She could be an imposing figure. Life had become routine, filled with her family and ballet. And mounting the annual *Nutcracker* took its toll.

I walked over to the *barre* affixed to the wall.

John nudged my arm. "You are soooo good... no one really does the *gargouillade* any more... its old school... but your turns are spectacular... only a few professional ballerinas in the entire world can turn as well as you... you are so balanced."

John was my best friend and confidant at ballet. He was also seventeen, a serious student, and very athletic, excelling at jumps and *batterie,* and hoped to be hired as a ballet dancer once we graduated high school in a few months. Because we were the same height, he found partnering with me to be difficult. Once I rose up on toe, I was taller than him, and it was a challenge for him to reach my hands for finger turns and certain lifts. He hoped to grow a few more inches.

Jasmine stood on the other side of the large room, leaning against the ballet bar with one arm. A few girls from her clique encircled her, and they laughed. I was sure they were telling her how good she was. And she was good. We often competed against each other in regional dance competitions. Sometimes she won, whereas other times, I would win first place. But I found her personality difficult to be around. She was self-centered and full of herself. If she ever complimented me, I did not believe her. There was always an air of conceit in her condescending voice.

While the class of twenty advanced dancers finished up the traveling combination, a distinguished older woman dressed in an expensive tailored business suit and hair pulled up into a French bun entered the room. She was very thin and walked like she belonged on stage. I wondered who she was.

Barbara acknowledged the woman's presence by nodding her head in her direction. The mysterious woman stood back, out of the way, by the piano. I would have guessed that she was a classical dancer at some point in her life.

John and I returned to the center of the room along with all the other students. Strong but soft music filled the room. *Rêverie* was taking place. It was a simple routine that closed the class and honored the teacher. We stepped to our side with arms spread out to acknowledge the audience. With a step back into the fourth position *croisé,* the girl dancers would make a long sweep down the front leg. The boy dancers would make a short upright bow, gently shifting weight toward the front foot, planting it down, extending one arm forward to compliment the *derrière* leg; then a quick step sideways to repeat the routine on the other side; simple yet elegant—a time-honored tradition. No ballet class seemed finished without the *rêverie*.

The music ended, and we clapped earnestly, honoring our teacher, my mother. We broke rank and walked over to our dance bags lined up along the wall. As usual, we dancers were flush-faced and chatted happily. Dance class always made me feel better.

The mysterious woman walked over to Barbara and shook her hand. I couldn't tell if mother actually knew the woman.

"Attention... attention, everyone. Please don't leave yet I have several important announcements to make." Barbara surveyed the room to see if everyone was paying attention.

Just then, a young man dressed in a heavy hooded jacket walked in. He pushed back his hood revealing short stocks of hair in complete disarray. He was cute in that California surfer kind of look. I immediately noticed that some of the other girls in the room perked up at the sight of the good-looking young man.

Barbara and the other woman shook the young man's hands. They exchanged a few words, not audible to the rest of the room.

"Quiet down," said Barbara, who took an authoritative stance at the front of the room. A few of the dancers stood at the *barre*, whereas others sat on the floor, some with their legs sprawled into splits. Most grabbed their dance bags for a sweater, water bottle, and cell phone.

"You know that we have been in preparation for our annual *Nutcracker*. We have started work on some of the *corps de ballet* scenes and are finalizing the solos and *pas de deux*. With only a few weeks left, we are focusing on all the special roles. Let me introduce Peter Blair."

Barbara extended her hand toward the tall young man. He gave a short wave to everyone in the room. The room broke into applause. I was unsure that I should have known who he was.

"Many of you may recognize Peter, he is this year's winner of the annual New York Metropolitan Ballet Competition, and he has so graciously agreed to be the *Prince* in our production of the *Nutcracker*. We are honored to have him here."

The room broke into another round of applause. Many dancers made comments to each other with full attention on Peter. Now I recognized him. He was truly outstanding and an up-and-coming new star. A few of the students took photos with their cell phones. It was exciting to have such a quality dancer in the program.

"He will be dancing with Jasmine as the *Nutcracker Prince* and in the final *Pas de Deux*."

A few heads turned and looked at Jasmine with envy. She smiled smugly as she already knew she was going to dance the part of Clara in this year's production. Jasmine was my same age and attended my same high school. Unlike so many of the other girls who wore their hair in a classic bun, she tended to leave it hanging free or in a ponytail. It was her act of rebellion against the strictness of the classical ballet world. The softness of her hair contrasted with the strength of her well-toned body. She walked with great authority, if not excessive pride. She knew she was good, an attitude that sometimes came across as arrogance. Although she was liked and had a small cadre of close friends, her streak of ruthlessness tended to put those around her on edge.

"Jasmine is one of our finest dancers and will help make this year's *Nutcracker* memorable," Barbara added.

Everyone applauded—a few of the girls whispered to each other.

"I also have some very exciting news to give. For the past few months, I've been in contact with a New York company named *Nutcracker Limited* about their filming of a brand-new *Nutcracker* for television and film. I want to introduce to you Ms. Sandra Bell, director of *Nutcracker Limited*, to talk about this new alliance."

The woman dressed in the expensive suit walked up regally and stood next to Barbara. You could tell she was an ex-dancer by the way she carried her back and by the way she moved her arms. She embodied ballet elegance.

"Thank you, Barbara. *Nutcracker Limited* is a new company brought together to produce a totally new *Nutcracker Ballet* that will speak to the young people of today. We are collaborating with many dance companies in the United States who are sending their best dancers to perform specific numbers from the beloved *Nutcracker*. We've been in discussion with Barbara about using this dance studio as a center of operations during filming in the mall. Barbara has been so gracious to offer us your studio over a few weeks for rehearsal spaces for the visiting stars. For some of the smaller parts in our production, we will be hiring a few of YOU from this dance studio to participate."

The word *YOU* swept the room and rattled through my brain. I, we, could be in a movie, and a dance movie at that. The students gasped at the prospect of being hired to be in a ballet movie.

"Barbara is allowing me to watch your classes the next few days to select those individuals whom we will hire."

Barbara clapped her hands, followed by applause from everyone in the room. The room buzzed with excitement. I was as surprised as the rest of the girls. Mother hadn't spoken about this at home. It must've been a big secret.

"This is very exciting," said Barbara to the group, "and *thank you*, Ms. Bell. It will be an honor for those girls to earn their first paying job in ballet."

While Sandra was talking, Peter removed his jacket and heavy sweatpants, revealing light gray tights underneath that showed off the shredded muscles in his legs. He was sitting on the floor, changing out of his tennis shoes into ballet slippers. His tank top showed off his deep tan, something unusual for someone who just came from New York. Obviously, he lived someplace else. He stretched easily into full splits, a necessary attribute found in all great male dancers of today.

Barbara shook Sandra's hand and walked to the center of the room. Just then, a small boy walked in carrying a toy drone and controller. He swung open the door that hit the door frame hard.

BANG.

The door stayed open. All eyes turned toward his direction to see what the commotion was. It was Nick, my brother and eleven years old, and he didn't notice that he was the center of attention. Too many years of being at his mother's business made him indifferent to what was happening.

Barbara turned toward the young boy with a quick look. "Nick, please be quiet," and then returned to Sandra. "Sorry, Sandra. That's my son, Nick."

A group of younger girls in dance clothes followed behind Nick and poured through the doors. They were curious about the good news that was spreading fast through the studio.

Barbara surveyed the room of her student dancers and said, "Now that we are all warmed up, we are going to begin work on the *Pas de Deux*. Peter has consented to teach the Russian version of the dance. Not only will Jasmine and her understudy, Marie, prepare the part for the stage, but all the rest of you will learn an important *pas de deux* in the ballet repertoire."

Barbara began to bark orders. "We need all the older dancers to partner up and the younger girls to wait out in the hall."

Barbara turned her attention to Jasmine and me.

"Girls, please come up. I want you to meet Peter."

Jasmine strode confidently up to Peter, shook his hand, and moved in closer to embrace his arm; in some ways, it was an overt act of ownership. Peter smiled and made a small bow.

I followed closely behind and gently shook Peter's hand. I was never confident about my dancing. Too many things added to my insecurities. I always felt that my mother was much more critical of me than the other girls. I also felt that my mother expected me to follow in her footsteps to become a great ballerina. Sometimes it was overwhelming.

Again, Peter made a cursory smile and took a small bow.

Barbara continued directing the room, "John, please come up and partner Marie… and Jasmine, you will be here with Peter. The other three couples… take positions at the back of the room."

Barbara and Sandra sat on chairs with their backs to the front mirrors to watch the rehearsal. The other couples spread out in the large room. Peter took the center of the room.

"Well, thank you," Peter said. "I really like teaching this particular version of the *Nutcracker Pas de Deux*. I feel it's the best one out there. The *Variations* and *Coda* will be worked on later this week." Peter reached and took Jasmine's hand. "OK, men, stage left, women stage right."

All the dancers moved to their respective positions. Jasmine let go of Peter's hand and walked stage right.

"Take a few steps in, bow… third arms. Walk towards your partner and take hands." Peter clearly knew how to take charge. He demonstrated with Jasmine as she walked in to take his hand. Peter and Jasmine continued marking the steps.

"*Promenade* downstage, women take a right *arabesque en pointe*. Men… take a low third using both hands; now a slow *arabesque penchée*. Women, really stretch it out… and, men, look at her with love."

I noticed that Peter looked like he was in love with Jasmine, really in love. That was a revelation for me to see a professional dancer be able to emote, on the spot, with a new partner; and make it look genuine.

Peter and Jasmine stopped and stood up. Jasmine hesitated a moment, smirking. She was pleased with Peter and that she was the star. Both of them walked to their respective offstage position.

"Now everyone, do it together… five, six, seven, eight… " Peter called out the count, and all the dancers marked along.

I had danced with John many times over the years. Unfortunately, he was about my same height making it difficult for him to partner me. John also had not matured enough to be able to lift me with ease. Often, the choreography was changed to accommodate his limitations.

12

"Great! Let's do it with music." Peter walked over to the music player and pressed play. The opening *Intrada* harp music to the *Nutcracker Pas de Deux* gently lofted through the room. The dancers began to move.

"That's the way… continue walking towards your partner… now listen for the swell, and that's your bow." Peter looked left and right across the room and praised, "Good, everybody."

The girls stepped into *arabesque*, holding onto the boy's one hand. Slowly they leaned like a teeter-totter, stretching their leg higher into the air while their chest lowered to their knee in a deep *arabesque penchée* with the boys stretching out in a low third position. This was a difficult position for the girls to hold while on pointe. The deeper a girl *arabesque penchée*, the more unsteady she becomes and the more she relies upon the strength of her partner's hand to keep steady.

Peter and Jasmine looked exquisite and effortless. Her *arabesque penchée* became a full split. Peter looked steady as a rock.

But I found it difficult to hold my *arabesque* with John. I grasped at John's hand, which was unsteady. Although my *arabesque penchée* was equal to Jasmine's, I couldn't hold the position and, to my chagrin, fell off pointe.

THUD.

I quickly stood up and retook the position. I looked around the room and saw everyone looking at me. I was embarrassed.

Peter was aware of the stumble but ignored my misstep and did not comment. Peter and Jasmine stopped. He walked up to the front of the room to turn off the music.

Peter smiled. "Good, everybody. A few more times, and you will have an elegant beginning."

Sandra reached over to Peter and took his hand. Peter leaned down to better hear her. A few words were exchanged that were inaudible to the rest of the room. Sandra gave a short laugh while she glanced toward me. I could not hear what was said but immediately jumped to the conclusion that they were talking about my flub. Peter stood up and walked back to the center. My heart sank.

"In the next hour, I'm hoping to get you through the first half of this *Pas de Deux*. All the big lifts occur near the end, so we'll work those on another day. Remember, the man is a prince, and the woman is Clara or the Sugar Plum Fairy. You are elegant, strong, and will show off your tremendous technique during the solo work... but always remember to have fun."

*

2 — Not A 'Boy' Again

The hour rehearsal flew by quickly. Peter was teaching a truly exquisite form of the *Pas de Deux*. Unlike much of Tchaikovsky's *Swan Lake* set by Marius Petipa and Lev Ivanov in the late eighteenth century, the *Nutcracker* choreography is not set in stone. Every company can play with the steps and, in fact, the very storyline. I could see that the choreography Peter was teaching was better than others I had seen. It was regal, had elegance, and was built to spectacular lifts at the end. Still, I was worried I was not fully qualified to be Jasmine's understudy.

All the dancers gathered up their dance bags and filed out of Studio A. Before leaving, most dancers shook Peter's hand to thank him for the rehearsal. Sandra and Barbara congratulated Peter and Jasmine on how well they looked together. Jasmine sashayed out, feeling smug. I smiled but tried to leave quickly without speaking. I didn't feel up to the expectations for pleasantries.

"Marie. Marie. Please... come here," Barbara spoke up.

My shoulders dropped. I had no choice but to walk over and speak with my mother within earshot of Peter and Sandra.

"Take Nick home... and, if you would, please start dinner. I'll be home in an hour... Nick and your father will be hungry." Barbara barely looked at me while giving directions. Thank goodness no one mentioned my fumble.

I walked out of Studio A, leaving Peter, Sandra, and Barbara to talk. Making my way down the hallway, I could hear the other girls gossiping about Peter. I sat momentarily on the bench near Jasmine. The three older girls from rehearsal couldn't resist.

"He's cute... and he can dance!" said Carol.

"Cute? He's hot," squealed Nancy while twisting the ends of her hair.

"Did you see his ass?" gushed Madison, "and I'd like to climb his candy cane."

All the girls giggled. They could be so immature.

Jasmine jumped in and added, "and he doesn't have a girlfriend... or boyfriend." She squared off her shoulders in triumph, "I checked online."

That got a second laugh from the girls.

"I'm going to show him around town one of these nights," said Jasmine with a smirk. Jasmine gloated while squinting her eyes toward me. I looked away, feeling very uncomfortable by the conversation. I felt it was unseemly to speak that way, especially about someone I had just met. Jasmine gathered her things, flung her hair back, and walked to the dressing room.

Nancy joined in, tossing a glance toward Jasmine. "I wish I had a Prince charming. You think she'll get him?"

As the oldest girl, Madison spoke from years of palling around with Jasmine. "When she sets her sights on a guy, there is no hope." Madison fiddled with her pointe shoe ribbons and closed the conversation. "She'll snag him for sure."

All this talk upset and confused me, and I didn't want to think about it. All I wanted to do was get out of there. I gathered my things and walked briskly down the hall toward the reception area. I paused in front of the mirror that was visible through the doorway of the dressing room. I stood firmly in front of the mirror, straightened my clothes, and checked my profile. Feeling ugly, I swayed my back, stuck out my stomach as far as it would go, and frowned. I hated my image in the mirror. I couldn't imagine anyone finding me attractive.

In the reception area, I saw Nick holding onto his drone. "Nick... come on. Mom wants me to take you home."

"Goodnight," waved Tom, the receptionist, but no one responded.

Nick jumped off the chair, put on his heavy coat, and rushed for the front door. I ignored Tom and quickly followed behind Nick out the door into the wintry night air. The cold air on my face was a welcomed relief from the oppressive and humid air of the ballet studio.

Then I remembered my coat. "Nick," I said, "go to the car... I'll be there soon." I turned and walked back inside the studio reception.

As the door closed, Barbara walked up to Tom. Behind the reception desk hung an imposing poster of Barbara in a tutu from her glory days as a world-class ballerina. While standing there, the poster framed Barbara's profile.

"Oh, Barbara," said Tom while handing her some notes, "these calls came for you while you were in rehearsal... There's one from a man named 'Roland.' He simply said to let you know that he's 'going to be in town.'"

Barbara was exhausted and didn't want to consider returning phone calls this late at night. Most dancers had already left. A young girl and her mother sitting on the nearby bench stood up and approached Barbara. Sheila was a lanky thirteen-year-old with messy hair and glasses whose hands and arms stuck out of her costume jacket conspicuously. She wore an 18th-century formal children's costume used in Act 1 of the *Nutcracker* that she had obviously outgrown from the year before.

"Barbara, Barbara," demanded the mother, who looked as unkempt as her daughter, "I have to speak to you about my daughter's costume." The mother tugged at the fabric and said, "Look at it... just look... there's no way *my* daughter can dance the same role she did last year."

Barbara was overly tired. She just wanted the day to be over and said, "Let's go to the office and try to straighten this out."

As Barbara passed the reception desk, she leaned into Tom and asked, "Is Beatrice still here?"

Tom nodded his head. "I'm sure she's in the office."

Barbara waved me to join her.

Sure enough, when we arrived at the tiny office, Beatrice was busy at work tearing out seams from other costumes. The office was cluttered with pieces of fabric everywhere, and the desk was strewed with paperwork and newspaper clippings. An old couch was shoved against one wall. It was so old that the cushions had permanent indentations from years of sweaty bottoms lingering on them.

With her rumpled hair, glasses parked on top of her head, and tape measure draped around her neck, Beatrice was the image of the quintessential costume designer.

Barbara handed Sheila off to Beatrice and said, "Sheila has outgrown her costume." Sheila was looking very ragged.

Beatrice pulled down her glasses and looked over the costume. "Hmm, hmm, maybe we could let it out a bit here or add a ruffle there... but really, Sheila, it does not fit."

"Well, find her another!" the mother jumped in with a demanding voice.

"Sorry, but this is the last dress we have for this act," clarified Beatrice peering over the edge of her glasses and sighing with exasperation.

Barbara had witnessed this scene too often over many years and pitied the poor girl at that awkward age. "Then, she'll have to be one of the boys. We are always short boys," Barbara stated matter-of-factly.

"No... NO. It'll fit." Sheila cried as she tugged even harder at the edges of the costume. At that moment, Tom entered the cramped office, making the space even smaller and claustrophobic. Being a retired dancer, Tom had witnessed this same drama with young dancers growing up.

Barbara carefully took Sheila's shoulders in her hands with a no-nonsense hold and looked directly into her eyes. "We're always short boys and men. It's not so bad. Why you can even play a mouse in the battle scene, that's fun."

"No, no, no. I don't want to be a boy," Sheila whined and slumped.

"Come on, Sheila... we need you. Unfortunately, you're at that in-between age where you're too tall for the little girl parts but not big enough to dance in the *corps de ballet*. Most of the older girls have gone through the same thing. They survived... they made the most of it and had a fun time. Why even my daughter, Marie, has been a mouse at one time."

Barbara and Sheila turned to look at me, putting me on the spot. I quickly nodded and gave a weak smile.

Barbara tried making it all seem fun and normal and used her most convincing voice. "Besides, the boys get to be on stage more minutes than the little girls. Wouldn't you like that?"

Sheila burst into tears. The mother was flustered and did not know how to respond. She just stood there, catatonic.

Barbara placed her arm around Sheila's shoulders and signaled Beatrice to come over and take the little girl out of her arms. "There, there. Beatrice will take care of you. Why next year, you may be able to try out for the *corps de ballet*... Won't that be fun?"

Sheila nodded weakly and sniffled some more while Beatrice escorted the girl and the mother out the door. Beatrice signaled with her hand to Barbara that they were going down the hall to the costume-fitting department.

"Every year... at least one or two of the girls are at that awkward transition," sighed Barbara as she lifted her head toward Tom and me. "How are we doing this year for men and boys?

"Not good. I think it's time to contact all the fathers with a *full-court press.*"

Barbara guffawed at the sports analogy used by Tom as if anyone in the ballet arts would know anything about sports. "Wouldn't it be great if we could ever grow large enough to have real professional men and boys in the company?"

Tom nodded in agreement.

Barbara fiddled with the phone notes and said, "Well, Tom, make the arrangements for a meeting of the parents so I can get a few of the fathers involved... and maybe a few of their sons."

Tom pulled down the calendar from the wall. "Saturday is open. Just before the 9:30 *Snowflake* rehearsal."

Barbara sat in the office swivel chair and looked distracted by the phone messages handed to her by Tom. She rocked the chair back and forth while fingering one message in particular; she seemed a million miles away.

"Barbara... Next week? Saturday?" Tom pressed.

Barbara snapped out of her daze. "Oh, yes. That's fine. Make the arrangements. Oh, and I assume you heard the word about the film? I would have told you about it earlier, but it was finalized only yesterday. Nutcracker Limited will be using a couple of our studios for last-minute rehearsals before they film here at the mall. I know it will be a bit cramped considering that we are rehearsing for OUR annual *Nutcracker*, but I thought it was an opportunity we couldn't pass up... and they will wrap up in just ten days."

"How exciting!" exclaimed Tom.

"They will mostly need Studio C and D during the week while we need the rooms on the weekend. Besides, they may need to hire additional dancers or extras. Wouldn't it be great if some of our dancers got paid to be a part of a feature film? It would so much help them feel like real dancers. Anyway, I think Ms. Bell and Peter are in Studio A. If not, I'll put you in touch with her so the two of you can work out a schedule. If we have to combine some of our classes or rehearsals to make space, then do it. I don't want to miss this opportunity."

"Great, I'll coordinate with Ms. Bell."

"Very much so," added Barbara with a satisfied smile on her face.

Tom got up and walked out the door to find Sandra leaving me alone with mother.

Barbara looked back at one particular phone message. A knowing smile crossed her face as a wave of memories flooded her mind. She picked up the phone and dialed.

"Hello, Roland? Yes, it's Barbara... Yes, yes... Yes, it's so good to hear your voice... it's been too long... You're in town?... Well, that's wonderful... Sunday, dinner? Sunday's good... Can't wait to see you. Do you know the address?... Well, of course... We'll all be glad to see you. It's been too long... Bye."

Barbara chuckled to herself. It was always wonderful to talk to her favorite ballet partner.

In walked Peter. "Howdy, Barbara." Peter spied me sitting on the couch and gave me a wink. "Again, I want to thank you for hiring me to dance in your production of *Nutcracker*."

Barbara was distracted but turned to Peter. "You are most welcome. Winning the New York Metropolitan Ballet Competition is a real accomplishment, it will open many doors for you. We're lucky to get you before you become a huge star and too expensive for our little company."

"Well, thank you. My agent is working on getting me a soloist position with one of the larger American companies, but I'm also open to going to Europe." Peter was eager to talk more about his plans, but it was obvious that Barbara was dead tired from a day of teaching and rehearsals and wanted to end the conversation.

"Are the hotel arrangements we made for you acceptable?" asked Barbara matter-of-factly.

Peter could see that Barbara was all business. "Fine... Fine. It's close and will be OK for the five weeks that I'm here."

Barbara gave a deep sigh of weariness that Peter noticed.

"Are you OK?" Peter inquired.

"Just tired. When you mentioned five weeks, that made me so aware that we have only three weeks of rehearsals left before two weeks of performances, there is so much more to do."

"Well, you know I won't be dancing all the time. If you need help with anything, just let me know," Peter offered. "I may be a Prince, but I'm not a prima donna."

Barbara didn't pick up on the play on words.

Peter danced a little soft-shoe, "... just a joke. I'm a California boy who likes to keep busy, including teaching ballet."

Barbara stood up and reached for the light switch. Peter got the hint and turned and walked out the door.

Barbara scooted us out the door. "Let's all get out of here before we die from exhaustion," Barbara said in a voice that was both frustrated and tired at the same time.

*

3 — Prima Donna

My family lived in a suburban two-story house close to the mall and dance studio. Located in the Northeast United States, we experienced the four seasons in all their glory. Fall was always a special time for me when trees lose their leaves in anticipation of heavy snow and frigid conditions. This morning hinted at a very frosty winter. Outside the kitchen window, the sky was gray with menacing storm clouds, and dried leaves in bright orange and yellows blew across the browning lawn.

Friday morning breakfast was always rushed in our household. Mom and Dad took turns driving Nick to special classes at the Natural History Museum. The kitchen's center island provided the perfect place to prepare small meals. Barbara and I were cutting apples to add to the plates of muffins and eggs. My Dad, Bill Stahl, was sitting at the small kitchen table in the dining nook, reading the news on his iPad. Although he was in his mid-fifties, he had all his hair and only streaks of gray.

Nick played on the floor with the family's dog—Prima. It was an odd name for an odd dog and was short for 'Prima Donna.' Prima was a very pregnant gold and silver Yorkshire terrier.

"Nick, not so rough with Prima," cautioned Barbara.

Nick often ignored our mother.

Bill noticed Nick playing and raised his voice. "Nick put her back in her basket in Marie's room. She's due any day now."

Nick was in one of his robot moods. He said, "As you command," very stiffly and electronically. Nick stood up and carried Prima out of the kitchen to her nearby bed basket. He walked stiffed legged like a robot making clicking sounds as he went.

Barbara was excited to share about the new Nutcracker Prince and said to anyone listening, "You should have seen Peter yesterday. He's an excellent dancer."

Bill was busy with the news and did not comment. I was also busy. No one spoke.

23

Barbara, exasperated, continued, "I'm sure he's worth every penny we pay him. He'll draw a good crowd this year." Barbara was miffed that no one seemed to be listening. She walked to the table and plunked the food down in front of Bill and me. Small trails of steam floated above the eggs and warm muffins.

I looked at the food and picked up just one slice of apple. Glancing over the edge of his paper, Bill noticed me not eating.

"Marie, come on honey, eat everything your mother has prepared," pleaded Bill. "The eggs are just the way you like them."

I had been down this tiresome road before. "Sorry, I'm not hungry." I apologized, attempting to control the discussion away from how much I ate or didn't eat.

Barbara chided Bill. "Don't force her. She is learning self-discipline... something every dancer must have."

Barbara gave me an affirming smile and sat down with the rest of us at the table. Just then, Nick marched back in like a robot without Prima and sat at the table. He immediately pulled out a hand-held video game to play and used a fork to stab at his food.

Barbara gazed first at Bill and then turned to Nick with her best motherly face and said, "Honey... Nick... I need your help again this year."

Bill knew something was up from the tone of her voice. He looked askance, trying not to make eye contact with her, whereas Nick was oblivious to the world playing on his electronic game.

"We need more men and boys for the *Nutcracker*," pleaded Barbara.

"What, again?" asked Bill. He looked over to Nick to see his reaction.

"You copy?" Nick said quickly without looking up.

Barbara continued, "We just don't have enough men or boys for Act 1."

"Again?" repeated Bill.

Barbara was exasperated. She thought that, by now, Bill and Nick were used to her need for more men and boys for the ballet and for them to participate willingly. Yet, each year it was becoming more like a sparring match to cajole them into the show.

Barbara shook her head. "I've had Tom set up a meeting tomorrow to solicit more of the fathers."

"Saturday?" Bill questioned.

Barbara truly needed their help. Maybe pleading would work. "We have only three weeks of rehearsals left and then two weeks on."

"But Saturday is when Nick and I go to the football games," Bill whined while fiddling with his food and still looking at the news but not really reading.

Bill's whine got to Barbara. She thought that by now, she would not have to beg the men of the family to help with the annual business ritual. "It's only football. This is my business... and every year, we put on the *Nutcracker*. You know that. I need you two," Barbara said with agitation.

"Every Saturday?" repeated Bill.

"Just five weekends. Just like last year," said Barbara sounding serious.

Bill wanted to get out of it and gain Nick's support. He turned toward Nick and said, "You'll get enough fathers. Besides, that's Nick's and my time... right buddy?"

Nick was still immersed in his video game and increased the rate at which his fingers danced across the controls.

Barbara took a stronger strategy and focused her attention on Nick since it was obvious that if she could win him over, then Bill would agree.

Barbara tried her pitch to Nick. "Honey, wouldn't you like to be in the show this year. You had fun last year."

Nick continued to ignore everyone.

Barbara used her sweetest voice. "You're bigger this year. That means you can also be in the Mouse King battle and be a Christmas tree. It's a lot of fun." Barbara hoped he might be drawn to the bigger parts.

Bill wasn't going to be outdone and tried his best father-son strategy. With a lowered fatherly voice, Bill said, "Come on, buddy, it's our time to do guys things."

Nick stood up and placed both hands on the table in a commanding stance. His action surprised everyone, particularly when he looked both parents in the eye.

Nick spoke very formally, "Mother. Father. I'm eleven years old, and we need to come to an understanding... I want to be an anthropologist."

Barbara and Bill were taken aback by Nick's formal speech. I giggled and rolled my eyes. Nick was often nerdy, but he seemed to be on a roll.

Nick turned to Bill and said, "Father, I respect your desires to spend time with me, but I detest the mindless brutality of human violence that is football. I've made the best of the situation by analyzing through the lens of conflict theory the tribal rituals of sports, but, alas, I've become bored with the repetition of artificially constructed hormonal driven interaction."

Nick turned to Barbara and continued, "... and Mother. You bring joy to many each year with your theatrical presentation, but I have ethical conflicts with the premise of women needing men to save them from chauvinistic hegemony."

Barbara and Bill were stunned silent. I couldn't contain my giggles, got up, and walked to the refrigerator.

Bill was the first to speak, "Where does he get all that?"

"Who's the academic in the family?" Barbara said slyly to Bill, who held a doctorate degree.

Bill was defensive and said, "But that's different. I'm a therapist, not a technical egghead."

Barbara tired of the chase and asked Nick directly, "Will you be in the show this year?"

Nick turned to Barbara, "For you, Mother, yes."

Nick then turned to Bill, "And Father... perhaps we can explore other forms of male-bonding activities once the show is over."

Bill was incredulous. "What did he say? He's only eleven."

I walked out of the kitchen and back to my room. I heard small moans coming from Prima's bed on the floor. She was giving birth. One small puppy had already emerged. I was surprised and shrieked.

Bill, Barbara, and Nick ran to my room. When they entered, I was kneeling on the floor. I turned my head and put a finger to my lips, shushing everyone quiet. I signaled with my head to make everyone look down at the floor at Prima's bed. More puppies were emerging.

Barbara cooed, "Oh, how cute."

Nick piped in. "How gross... all the blood, everywhere." Nick's eyes were wide open.

Prima licked the newly born puppies. I reached out and stroked Prima's head. The family shared a quiet moment watching the miracle of birth.

I said tenderly, "They're just in time to be our Christmas puppies."

Nick became aware of the time. Watching Prima disrupted and delayed the family's usual routine.

"Time to take me to the Museum. One of you has to drive me," piped in Nick.

Bill spoke up, "That... that's what's making him into an egghead."

Barbara was distracted and said, "Oh... um... Bill, could you take him? Marie and I have rehearsal later this afternoon."

Bill felt sarcastic and looked over to Nick. "Oh, yes, to make him an anthropologist. Come on, buddy. Get your bag, and we're out the door."

Bill and Nick walked out of my bedroom, leaving Barbara and me with Prima and her newborn puppies. I gently picked up one of the puppies and took a selfie with my phone to post online. "They are so precious... so fragile. I'll love them forever."

*

4 — More Opportunities

Saturday morning brought together all the dancers and parents to the studio. As each person filed through Studio A doors, Tom handed out instructions. Chilly air burst through the front door each time it was opened. It was a large group of sixty people. The *Nutcracker* has a large cast. Not only are there families and children in Act 1, but there are the mice and soldiers during the battle scene and then, of course, all the skilled dancers for the specialty dances in the second half of the ballet where Clara and the Nutcracker are entertained in the *Land of the Sweets.*

Parents and siblings are often called upon with small productions to fill the stage in Act 1. Here, families gather together to light the Christmas tree, give gifts to the children, dance, and be merry. It is also in Act 1 when the mysterious Godfather Drosselmeier gives Clara a Nutcracker doll.

Barbara took control of the room, raised her voice, and said, "Please quiet down... May I have everyone's attention."

The room settled down. Many children sat on the floor, whereas most parents stood against the ballet *barre*. The heaters had not caught up with the room's chill, and most people kept on their heavy coats. Everyone faced Barbara. Next to Barbara stood my father, Tom, the receptionist, and Ms. Sandra Bell from Nutcracker Ltd. Some of the older students, including Jasmine and me, and dance captains, stood nearby. Peter seemed unsure of what to do or where to be and sat by himself off to one side, surrounded by strangers.

Barbara spoke up, "I want to thank all of you for coming today. We have been preparing for our annual *Nutcracker* these past few months. We are down to three more weeks of rehearsals. I'm pleased by the progress made by all our dancers in learning their parts. Let's give applause to all the girls and boys."

Barbara extended her hand and acknowledged the crowd. They gave a roaring approval, and many of the children turned to smile at their parents.

"As you know, Act 1 is held in a Victorian home. We need about eight couples to play the part of parents. I'm glad to see so many returning parents this year, which will make this easier. Your experience and insight will help the newer parents learn their parts. We also need a few more boys for the mime sequence. That is why we have called all the families in today."

"You all know Bill, my husband," Barbara took Bill by his hand, "will be organizing the families. Don't worry; you won't have to jump or turn or do fancy dance steps... just mainly walk to the music. Tom handed you some instructions that will help."

Barbara turned toward Tom. "Tom, will you raise your hand so everyone can see who you are."

Tom waved to the group.

"He is responsible for teaching the steps and getting you moving around the stage. So, don't worry. You are in good hands. He has done this for years and danced professionally. If you have any questions about scheduling, he's the man to see."

Barbara paused to give a small applause. "We also need a few of your sons to be in Act 1 and, in particular, the Battle against the Mouse King. We need both mice and soldiers. Again, you don't really need to dance, just walk, and follow the music. It is a lot of fun."

A few of the boys perked up, but most just stood there stoically, looking more like captives forced by their sisters to be in a ballet.

Tom stepped forward to rally the troops and said, "Come on, boys. You get to be on stage in a soldier uniform, using your sword to fight the mice. It doesn't get much better than that." Tom mimicked fighting with a sword. His actions got the interest of a few of the boys, but most were still apathetic. Tom ignored the lack of response and attributed it to the early frosty morning lethargy.

"Thanks, Tom, for that pep talk," said Barbara trying to build upon Tom's enthusiasm. "In a few minutes, Bill will be taking you all to Studio B to work out the details. I want to give some more details about Nutcracker Limited. You may have heard that they will be filming an exciting updated version of the

30

Nutcracker right here in our mall, and they will be hiring some of you as extras plus other parts. Here, I'll let Ms. Sandra Bell explain what is needed."

Sandra stepped forward. Even early on a Saturday morning, she exuded grace and class and said, "Thank you, Barbara, for the use of your studio and personnel. Next week, many world-class dancers will be flying in to shoot their specific numbers. In one scene, we will need a crowd to perform a simple dance as a flash mob. You will wear regular warm clothing. We need all ages of people... so it is open to parents, teenagers, grandparents, and children. We will pay union wages for all these parts. For children under age 18, we will need a waiver form signed by your parents. Instructions for this shoot are given on the paper in your hand. Are there any questions?"

The room buzzed with excitement. Many hands shot up. People quickly lifted the instruction sheet that they initially ignored to read the details.

Barbara stepped back in and calmed the room down. "Alright. Alright. Please quiet down. I know this is very exciting to be in a movie and a paid position at that. Ms. Bell will approach you if she is interested in having you in the movie. And, of course, we have our own *Nutcracker* performances starting in just three weeks. Right now, I need all the parents and boys to follow Bill and Tom to Studio B, where they will assign positions, discuss costumes, and set the rehearsal schedules. Ms. Bell will come to you in a while. All advanced dancers... please stay here. We are holding a rehearsal of the *Pas de Deux*."

Tom raised his hand high and yelled, "Follow me. All the parents and boys, follow me to Studio B."

The room bounced with energy. Performing in the *Nutcracker* and acting in a movie was just overwhelming for the people of a small-town ballet school. Quickly the room emptied, leaving only the dancers in Studio A. The older boys and girls took off their sweats and began to limber up.

A small table and chair were set up near a corner of the room where Sandra would work. The younger dancers sat around the table's perimeter, waiting to be called for the movie part. They giggled with excitement.

I was also caught up in the excitement and jabbered with the girls nearby and said, "I think I want to be part of the movie. Should be fun."

Barbara took control of the room. "Shush. You younger students, please sit quietly. Ms. Bell will talk with each of you individually about being in the movie. Come up to the desk when Ms. Bell calls your name."

Barbara turned her attention to the older dancers. "Peter has told me that you have completed learning the *Pas de Deux*. We'll run through it first with music— just a quick run-through. Then we'll change partners. The understudies need to work with the other partner to be prepared in case we have an emergency."

I felt anxious. I had never danced with Peter and was in awe at how good Jasmine looked dancing with him. Even though I had learned the part with John, it just never gelled. John was trying his best, but I was too much for him to handle. I feared that I was too fat. I worried I would be inadequate, no, worse, a failure dancing with Peter and how embarrassed I would be.

The dancers took their positions. I was with John, Peter was with Jasmine, and the other three couples were in the back of the room. Barbara pushed the start button, and music filled the room. The boys entered from stage left, whereas the girls entered from stage right.

The dance went well but not perfectly. A few rehearsals that week had polished the number. One significant modification Peter made to the choreography was to take out all the one-hand and difficult lifts, replacing them with simpler, sit-on-the-shoulder or fish catches. That made it much easier for John and the less skilled male dancers. Still, I was afraid to stretch my extensions for fear of pushing John over.

Barbara stepped in and said, "OK. We'll do the solo work later. Change partners. Marie with Peter, Jasmine with John, and the other couples switch around... Take position."

Barbara began the music.

I was very anxious. My shallow breaths accented the knots in my stomach as fear overcame me. I walked in and bowed *en croix* with third arms as regally as I could while looking directly into Peter's eyes. I walked toward Peter and *promenade* downstage. On cue, I stepped on pointe in *arabesque*. Immediately I was struck by how much stronger and more confident Peter's arm was compared to John's. I slowly stretched into an *arabesque penchée*. Unlike with John, I felt I could stretch it out into a full split. Although there was a slight wobble, I did not feel restricted. Instead, I felt entirely supported.

PLOP!

The sound swept the room.

"COW... YOU COW!!!" yelled Jasmine at John.

Everyone stopped and turned to see the commotion. Jasmine was flat on the floor at John's feet. She obviously had fallen out of *arabesque*. He extended his hand to help her up.

"You weakling. You're ruining MY dance!" said Jasmine while she pushed his hand aside and stood up. "You can't even hold your hand still."

She turned to Barbara and demanded, "I can't dance with him. This is MY dance, and I'm the star. I'll only dance with Peter."

The room went still. All eyes turned to Barbara, waiting to see what she would do next. Barbara paused, turned, and reached over to turn off the music. The room echoed with silence. After a long moment and through clenched teeth, Barbara calmly directed the students to "Do it again... from the beginning... with your current partner."

"What! I refuse to be treated like this," yelled Jasmine.

Barbara had no choice but to confront Jasmine. "There is always the chance Peter will be injured during the run. We must have an understudy. John is our best male dancer, and he is the understudy. You will practice with him. As a professional, you understand this." Barbara stood her ground.

Jasmine was undecided about what to do. It was a standoff between two strong personalities. She rocked back and forth, began walking away, and then returned to John. She refused to look him in the face.

Barbara spoke up, "Everyone, calm down. Let's begin again. Take opening positions."

John was devastated. He slumped and walked to stage right. It was not unusual for Jasmine to be cruel, but this time it went too far and completely unnerved him.

"No, no, you ignoramus," yelled Jasmine to John. "You enter stage left. You are so incompetent." Jasmine could be so vicious.

John turned around and did a run-skip combination to get to the other side of the room as quickly as possible, trying to avert everyone's stares. The room was tense. The other dancers wanted Jasmine to act professionally and cut the shenanigans.

Barbara waited an extra moment to allow people to compose themselves. She began the music.

Everyone was on edge, but they made it to the end of the *Pas de Deux* without major incident. Even Jasmine and John made it to the end without her falling or calling him names. It was a struggle for most of us. It is always a new experience dancing with a new partner. Each dancer has slight variations in how he or she holds hands, supports turns, prepares lifts, and more.

I found dancing with Peter very enjoyable; actually, the best partnering experience I had ever had. It wasn't so much that John was a lousy dancer as he was a little guy without much strength. On the other hand, Peter was four to five inches taller than me, a few years older, and with more muscle development. He could really hold a position; that helped me push to my limits—and being lifted by Peter was a revelation. He was so strong and flawless. I felt I could fly. I found myself relaxing when I danced with Peter. He gave considerable eye contact and reassured me with every move. In fact, a number of times, he made complimentary comments to me while dancing. No partner of mine had ever done that before, and it worked. His compliments calmed me down. Dancing with Peter was a joy, and, yes, he was handsome.

While the rehearsal was going on, Sandra met with the younger girls and their parents. She quietly discussed what was involved and presented a release form and contract for them to sign to participate in the filming. After signing, they left through the hallway. Eventually, Sandra was done processing all the younger dancers and was left alone at the table to watch the rehearsal.

"Excellent. Excellent!" said Barbara. "From now on through the run of the show, we will rehearse the *Pas de Deux* with both your assigned partner and your alternate. We must always be prepared for the understudy to fill in." Barbara turned to Sandra, "Do you have anything to add, Ms. Bell?"

Sandra stood up and added, "I only have to discuss parts in the film with your older dancers. I still need some crowd people to participate in a simple flash mob dance, some of the men for soldiers in the Battle, and either boys or girls to play the mice. We are looking for a handful of people who could do some simple gymnastics in the mouse costume... simple things like cartwheels, handstands, or backflips. Please come up if you are interested."

Most of the dancers walked up to the table. Jasmine and Peter stood next to the ballet barre. I also hung out by the barre, holding back to the last. The other dancers were processed, leaving only the three principals to consider. Finally, I walked up to Sandra to enlist.

"Oh, good, Marie. I was hoping you would want to be in the film," Sandra said. "I could use you in the crowd flash mob dance. I have enough men for soldiers, so that leaves being a mouse. Understand no one will see your face because you would be wearing a costume with a headpiece. But I could use your height. Can you do gymnastics?"

Jasmine pushed away from the *barre*, strolled past the table but close enough for me to hear, and said, "Flash mob? Mouse? Are you kidding? I'm a real ballet dancer. I'm DEVOTED to my art and not this trash." She raised her voice with sarcasm when she said, "*Devoted* to my art."

I hesitated. What Jasmine said made me feel little and cheap. I loved ballet. It was my entire world. I viewed ballet as the highest art form that took a lifetime of devotion to master and appreciate. For me, ballet transcended reality. When the music was just right, and the moves were just right, my body and mind became beauty. *Beauty*, what an admirable goal! What more could I want from life? I didn't want to cheapen my convictions for a bit part in a movie.

Sensing my hesitancy, Peter rushed forward to the table, picked up one of the forms, and said, "I'll do it... I'll be a mouse and dance in a flash mob."

Both Jasmine and I turned in disbelief. Jasmine's face changed to disdain.

"I expected more from you, Peter," Jasmine's words dripped with icy condescension.

"It's a paying job... and in a movie." Peter turned directly to Sandra, "Of course, I'll have to check with my agent. But I would love to work for you."

I was surprised and asked, "Really?"

"When did working a legitimate job become something to look down upon? I have time on my hands for the next few weeks. Class and rehearsals do not consume every minute of my day. It will be fun. Besides, a movie credit would be good for my resume. A paying gig is a paying gig. No shame in that," said Peter as he reached to touch my arm to reassure me.

Sandra spoke up, "OK, Peter, I'll put you down. But have your agent contact me immediately." Sandra turned to me and asked, "So, what will it be, Marie?"

I looked at Peter, turned to Jasmine with her sour face, and back to Sandra. In an impulsive moment, I picked up one of the forms. "I'll do it... and thanks."

Jasmine quickly left the room with large arrogant strides letting the door slam behind her.

Sandra and Barbara entered into a quiet conversation, reviewing the sign-ups for the movie. Peter and I packed up their dance bags and spoke privately.

I quizzed Peter and asked, "Did you mean what you said? I mean, a mouse? Why, you're a star!"

"Every word." Peter seemed happy. Actually, Peter seemed happy all the time. "I've met many Jasmines in my life. They can suck the joy right out of dancing."

I covered my mouth to muffle a laugh. *Suck* was the right term.

Peter was sincere in what he said. "We all started to dance with joy. It was fun. It was great to fly when you jump or turn. At some point, it can become frightening and emotionally painful. Then the joy goes away. That's when dancers begin to hurt themselves or abuse themselves with painkillers, alcohol, anorexia, or drugs... and lash out at other dancers. What a shame. It started so innocently."

I was silent. His words had deep meaning to me.

"So, let's have some fun," Peter laughed, "and be a mouse, dance, and get paid for it. What could be better?"

Barbara walked to the doors. She cupped her hands and yelled down the hallway, "OK, dancers. Time for all the specialty dances and then *Waltz of the Snowflakes.*" Barbara turned back into Studio A and addressed Peter. "Thank you, Peter. We won't need you until late this afternoon when we run through the Battle scene. Just check the schedule posted outside." Barbara turned to me. "Marie, we'll be needing you for the *Snowflakes.*"

"Would it be OK if I stay and watch?" Peter inquired.

"Of course," responded Barbara.

Just then, a flood of dancers entered the room, filled with all the excitement of the upcoming performance and movie shoot.

*

5 — Roland Comes for Dinner

Nighttime comes early during the winter in the Northeast. Although it had not snowed yet, it was very cold. My family lived on a typical suburban street of brick homes, brick being the material of choice for homes in the Northeast. With less than a month before Christmas, most houses were decorated for the season. Some houses were draped with small LED lights. Others had a mixture of large old bulbs with smaller pin lights. And there were always the show-offs who installed an elaborate set of lights and props, all synchronized to music.

Roland drove up to the house in a rental SUV. Roland was a tall, thin man in his fifties, wearing a long coat, a knit hat, and leather gloves. He was prepared, no, more accurately, *overdressed*, for the cold. Being from California, he was neither accustomed to the cold nor able to accurately determine the layers of clothing needed for the weather. He walked to the front door between the rows of colored lights defining the walkway. A holly wreath embedded with dancing elves circled the doorknocker Roland used to announce his arrival.

KNOCK, KNOCK.

Roland heard the commotion of running feet and dropped items from behind the door. Nick answered the door. He wore a Sherlock Holmes-style hat and carried a pipe— which looked cute on the eleven-year-old. You could tell he had run to the door. Breathlessly he turned to yell down the hall, "It's him." Nick unexpectedly ran away down the hall, leaving the door wide open and Roland standing alone. Actually, this brought a smile to Roland's face. The chaos of family was refreshing to his structured single life.

Barbara turned the corner and headed for the door. She was wearing a long one-piece dress made of stretch jersey that extended to her ankles. The cloth surface gave the impression of black-purple velvet. Martha Graham often used similar dresses in her choreography. Its form-fitting elasticity showed off Barbara's well-toned body.

She gushed over him. "Oh, Roland. It is so good to see you." She helped him off with his coat, hat, and gloves, placing them in the hallway closet. The warmth of the house embraced the smells of home cooking.

Barbara gave Roland a big long hug. "It's been too long. What has it been?"

"Almost four years," said Roland as he flashed a big smile.

Barbara had to compliment Roland. "Gosh, you're looking good." She gave him another hug and led him by hand down the hall to the dining room. The room was decked out with holiday spirit. It was a mixture of fall decorations and Christmas joy. The table was already set with fine china focused on a fall cornucopia centerpiece surrounded by glass silver balls and bells. I walked in carrying a china serving tray.

Barbara yelled to the kitchen. "Honey, Roland is here." She turned to me and directed me to "get your brother."

Bill responded from the kitchen, "I'll be right there."

Barbara guided Roland to a chair next to hers. "Here, sit here."

"Is there anything I can do to help?" asked Roland.

Barbara brushed his comment aside and said, "Oh, no, everything is ready. We just need everyone to sit down."

Barbara walked back to the kitchen, temporarily leaving Roland awkwardly by himself. He admired the decorations on the table and realized how much he appreciated being invited to the family meal of a lifelong friend. The aroma of so many classic holiday dishes triggered memories of past gatherings—both good and terrifying.

As if on cue, all four of the family burst into the dining room in a choreography of carrying food, placing plates, and sitting down.

Barbara turned to Nick to remind him about manners. "Take the hat off at the table, young man." Barbara was pleased Nick complied without complaint.

Bill shook Roland's hand while he sat down and said, "Very good to see you again."

"Always a pleasure." Roland truly appreciated how well Bill managed Barbara. Having danced with her for a decade gave him a deep understanding of interacting and living with her.

Barbara spoke up and pointed toward me, "and you remember Marie."

I, too, wore a dress, but something more appropriate for my age and less revealing.

"She has grown to be a lovely lady," Roland said while he reached for her hand and kissed it at the same time, saying, "M'lady."

I giggled at the formality.

Nick spoke up. "Kissing the hand of the person you meet or shaking hands is a ritual to check the other person for a weapon." He squirmed in his seat.

"Is that so, young man?" Roland piped up. "I'm sure the only weapon your sister has is her beauty... and that is apparent to all."

Barbara smiled at Roland's use of compliments, a trick he employed to calm her nerves on stage. "Ah, Roland and his compliments. His magic worked for me when we danced together." She directed everyone to pass the food. "We're not formal here. Just dig in."

Nick immediately took a heaping of potatoes and carefully placed peas and corn around the perimeter, simulating an ancient Aztec Calendar Stone.

Bill spoke directly to Nick. "Come on, guy. Just eat your food."

Nick explained, "It's an ancient Aztec Calendar. You may not know this, but the Aztec Calendar was based upon the Maya calendar, and if you calculate the Long Count as 13.0.0.0.0, it corresponds to the August 13, 3114 BC in the Gregorian Calendar. Anthropologists think that corresponds to the Mayan creation myth."

Roland was bemused at the little Sherlock Holmes and said, "That's very interesting, Nick. You have really grown up since I last saw you."

Nick interjected, "I want to be an anthropologist."

"We take him to museum classes on weekends to enrich his schoolwork," Barbara said with pride and amusement.

Roland turned to Nick. "I'm sure your parents are very proud of you, Nick." As usual, Nick was absorbed in what he was doing and oblivious to what was happening around him.

Roland next turned his attention to me. "And Marie, what are you doing now? Are you out of high school? Are you still dancing?" Roland noticed how much I had grown and matured in the past years. With my hair down, I so much reminded him of how Barbara looked when they were dance partners.

I hesitated. I wasn't too keen on talking about my dancing in front of my family. If anything, I was always embarrassed to talk about my ballet goals when my mother was nearby.

Barbara interjected, "My school and dance company is producing the *Nutcracker* again this year. Marie is the understudy to Clara and a dance captain."

Roland was pleased and praised me. "Oh, dance captain. You must be very good. Your mother has taught you well." *Dance captain* was a term Roland had not heard in years, and a rush of memories swept over him as he glanced toward Barbara. "Your mother was an excellent dancer. She was, and always will be, my *best.*"

Barbara melted and began to act a little girlish, behaviors I had never seen in my mother.

"Oh, Roland… Stop," pleaded Barbara.

"Oh, no. I've had many partners in my life, but Barbara was the best. We had good times together."

"Some of the best… even when times were tough," said Barbara.

Roland sat up straight and excitedly said, "Oh, God, remember Madrid? That bizarre company that hired us… and that crazy director."

"… and that flea-speck of a hotel room they put us in… "

"… and the single bed… "

"… and the horrid cockroaches. You were so awkward sharing a bed with a woman." Barbara flashed a knowing smile.

Barbara and Roland laughed together. Bill and I were perplexed by what was obviously an inside story I hadn't heard before.

Barbara was full of memories and continued to tell the story. "We were so poor. We had to stay for the job... regardless of the single bed or cockroaches."

Again, Barbara and Roland laughed. I was surprised and pleased by mother's gaiety. I had not seen her so happy for a long while. Barbara tended to be, well, *efficient*. I couldn't remember the last time mother laughed out loud. Mounting the *Nutcracker* each year took its emotional toll. I knew mother and Roland were dance partners at one time and always spoke of Roland in the highest terms. They must have shared many adventures.

Roland jumped in, "Speaking of being poor. I finally gave up the dance studio."

"No!" exclaimed Barbara.

"I was tired of being poor, so I sold the dance studio right after the last time I saw you. An opportunity came along I couldn't miss. I now work with companies in computer animation and games to help with the movement of their characters. I prepare a lot of the greenscreen work where dancers and athletes are used in motion capture techniques."

Barbara and Bill were impressed and said in unison, "Really?"

"Cool," Nick chimed in. Nick's ears selectively heard anything dealing with technology and science.

Roland became animated while he explained, "I finally own a home in San Jose. I mostly work from home. That's why I am here now. I will be in town a few weeks consulting with a computer firm helping with their next film. We are doing some greenscreen work next week at a nearby warehouse on the *Nutcracker*."

"Well, that's great. Congratulations," said Bill. Bill really didn't know Roland very well, although he had met him many times in the past twenty years. Yes, Roland had been there from the very beginning of Bill and Barbara's relationship, but dance consumed everything. It pleased Bill that Roland had been such a positive person in Barbara's life.

"I really enjoy it. I sometimes miss dancing. It was a large part of my life for so long, but I don't miss being poor, and my body just couldn't take it anymore. Besides, once my nephew completed his training under me, he got an agent and is now working professional jobs. I had no reason to hang onto the school." Roland absent-mindedly shoveled potatoes onto his plate.

"*Nutcracker*! Did you say *Nutcracker*?" It just dawned on Barbara what Roland had said. "Are you part of the filming with Nutcracker Ltd.?" All eyes turned to Barbara. "They're using my studio for their rehearsal space."

"What a coincidence," added Roland. "I'm sure we'll see more of each other."

Barbara had an idea and bounced it off of Roland. "Since you are going to be in town, anyway, how about being in my production of *Nutcracker*?"

Roland was surprised and hesitated. "Dancing? It's been years. I'm way past wearing tights." Roland sat back in his seat, folding his hands behind his head, and grinned from ear to ear.

Barbara reassured him and clarified, "Just the first act as one of the fathers. Bill and Nick are also in it."

Bill liked the idea of Roland participating. Roland's integrity and knowledge would help Bill with the rehearsals; besides, he knew how to work hard yet make it enjoyable. Bill said, "Yes, Roland. Come on. It'll be like the early days of Barbara's studio when you helped then."

Roland was conflicted, yet the idea intrigued him. He hadn't been on stage for years, but as we all know, *once in show business, always in show business.*

Barbara decided to sweeten the deal by twisting his arm. "Better yet, you can be Drosselmeier?" Barbara gave Roland a devilish look and smile. "I don't really have a commitment from any of the fathers."

Roland sighed and said, "Why not? When do I show up?"

Barbara was pleased. "Tomorrow, Sunday. We're working on Act 1 at 9:30 at the studio."

Nick picked up his plate and took it to the kitchen. He was not delicate placing it in the sink and made a considerable racket.

Roland reached into his shirt pocket and pulled out a DVD. He handed it to Barbara and explained, "A gift for you... its animation computer software that I work on. It's pretty technical, but you can program dances on it."

Bill and Barbara found that incredible and said, "Really?"

"I thought you might find it interesting, and maybe Marie could play with it," Roland added.

During dinner, Roland noticed that I ate very little. That concerned him, and he thought it would be good to have some alone time with me. "Do you have a computer at home? Maybe I could show you how the software works."

Bill spoke up. "The best computer in the house is in Marie's room."

Roland asked for permission. "Do you mind? I could show Marie."

"Sure, that would be great," replied Barbara as she handed back the software disk to Roland. "We will clean up."

*

6 — Prima Dances

My room was decorated like a typical girl ballet dancer with posters and dance items strewed about and too much pink. A bookcase contained a few dance figurines and trophies. My one special possession was a pair of old pointe shoes from a famous ballerina hanging on the wall as decoration. Above my desk was the well-known poster of a dancer in *demi-plié* in old ripped over-tights. On my desk was a computer and screen. As we entered, Prima lugged herself away from her puppies and out of her bed basket to greet us. I carefully picked up Prima.

Roland greeted Prima and said, "Oh, how adorable. No one can resist a Yorkie."

"Her name is Prima," I added. "She had puppies recently."

"Prima?"

"Yes, as in *Prima Donna*," I said with a big smile.

We both laughed at the inside joke.

Roland and I walked over to the dog basket and peered at the puppies. Their eyes had recently opened, and they waddled around while making small squeaking noises. Roland petted Prima. You could tell he cared for animals and cherished the sight of newborn puppies. I replaced Prima with her puppies.

Roland handed the DVD to me. "Here, it's a large program, so it will take a while to spin up and load."

I sat at my desk and started the computer. Roland looked around the room, admiring the décor. He spied a photograph of Barbara and himself back when they were young dancers in their prime. It was a spectacular photo where Barbara, in a tutu, was being held overhead in a bird lift. It was a difficult lift, and Roland remembered how well Barbara could nail it, something many other women never achieved. After the loud start-up chime, I inserted the disk, and we both waited.

Roland said, "Thank you. I think you'll really enjoy this... the last time I saw you, you were, what twelve- or thirteen-years-old? I remember that you were a good little dancer... your mother must be proud of you."

47

I smiled and made a few clicks with the mouse. The pause gave me time, and courage, to ask Roland a deeply personal question about my mother that I had always wondered about. "Why did Mom stop dancing?"

Roland was surprised. "Barbara?"

"Many times, she told me that it was because she was pregnant... with me. I always wanted to know."

Roland paused. He wasn't sure if he wanted to talk about Barbara's past and her personal life. "I remember when she met Bill... she was so excited. She so much wanted to meet a man that she could connect with... and, at the deepest level, have a family. I was her dance partner and loved her dearly, but I couldn't provide her with what she needed. He was one of the therapists at the clinic she went to."

"Mom... in therapy?"

"Uh... I thought she told you?" Roland fumbled, realizing that he was sharing too much information about my mother and didn't know if he should continue. Yet, I was so trusting.

There was a long reflective pause.

"She had a love-hate relationship with dance at that point in her life and sought counseling to resolve the issue. I tried to help, but I couldn't get her to break through the, the... self-hate."

"Mom?"

"I think you are old enough to understand. What do all the girls down at the studio complain about?"

I was puzzled. I didn't understand how this was related to my mother.

Roland could see that I was confused. "I noticed how little you ate at dinner."

I looked down. I immediately knew where Roland was going with this. I could get out only one word, "Oh."

Roland saw how vulnerable I had become. "I've seen it many times. Remember, I lived the dance. I know how we all starve ourselves... how we constantly think we are fat and ugly even when everyone else thinks we are emaciated... Well, your mother just couldn't find a balance between the constant starvation, performing, and wanting a family."

"Family?" I said quizzically.

"Very much. Something I couldn't give her," said Roland emphatically. "Remember, I worked... lived with her for years. Once she got pregnant... "

I interrupted, "With me... "

"Yes, with you... she... "

"Quit." I was resolute. "She quit... and I'm to blame... "

My eyes moistened, and my voice trembled. Roland reached out and embraced me.

Roland gave his most caring face. "Marie. No. No. No. You did not cause her to stop dancing. She wanted a way out and in her mind being pregnant was the end of it."

I choked up. "I'm the blame for her giving up ballet."

"I'm sure she never said that."

"No... no, but I felt it," I said meekly.

Roland became more forceful. "I've known many women dancers who took a year out of their careers to have a child and then return... better than before. There is a wonderful change in a woman dancer once she has a child. They seem to get a sensitivity, or maybe it's patience, that comes across on the stage, and they become good, no, great dancers. No, Barbara wanted out and used having a child and getting married as her way out... Please, don't ever blame yourself."

Roland took my hand. "Perhaps it is good that I'm here now. You remind me so much of your mother. I want to be your friend." Roland shook my hand. "Friends?"

I smiled and said, "Friends."

Roland stood up and moved toward the computer. "Here, let me take over."

Roland and I exchanged chairs. Roland took charge of the mouse and clicked on the program icon. "Here, watch this. I programmed it to Act 1 of *Nutcracker*."

Nutcracker music swelled up from the computer speakers. I recognized it immediately. It was the music where Drosselmeier winds up one of the mechanical dolls during the family party in Act 1. It was a favorite dance for the audience. People found it fanciful that a wind-up doll could dance. One year, I danced the role of the mechanical doll, and it was fun. The dancer not only dances but gets to move like a robot. In some ways, it is similar to robot breakdancing, and I could goof around at school doing the dance. It was probably one of the few times I felt like one of the regular kids at school and not such an outcast.

On-screen, an anatomical stick figure danced to the music. It was very lifelike.

Roland explained, "See how natural it moves? It took a long time to get the software engineers to capture that look. That's my job. To make animated figures move naturally."

I was mesmerized. In a soft voice, I said, "It's so perfect. I wish I were perfect."

Roland stopped the computer program and looked intensely at me. "I want to share with you something very profound… something your mother never understood. Although I don't expect you will completely understand what I'm going to tell you, at least I will have planted the concept. There is no such thing as 'perfection.' If you seek it, you will always fail. Your mother was a good dancer, and I really enjoyed her as a partner, but she was far from perfect. She often stressed out and became brittle… you know, can't hold an extension without wobbling or fell out of turns. She wanted to be perfect, and that held her back. These computer figures are perfect, but who wants to watch them? They are sterile. Think about the great dancers… Who do you like?" Roland paused. "Who's your favorite dancer?"

I thought for a moment. "Uh, Alessandra Ferri. She's retired now, but she was so lovely. Those are her shoes up on the wall."

Roland glanced at the pair of old pointe shoes dangling on the wall as art. "Is she perfect?" Roland asked forcefully.

"I guess so," I stuttered.

"What do you think she would say if you asked her if she were perfect?"

I thought a moment. "Yes… no… I don't know."

Roland pressed. "Come on, think about all the dancers you know. How do they think?"

50

I was perplexed. "I guess not."

"Right," Roland leaned back in his chair. "I bet you she could immediately list all the things about her that are not perfect... like her feet or her arms or something. All of us dancers do that. We can all list our shortcomings. But why do you like her?"

I struggled with the question. "I just like watching her."

"Right. There is that indefinable quality that makes us just want to watch her. That is called charisma." Roland made his point. "What do you think makes a dancer charismatic?"

I felt like I was in school and being put on the spot. "Being good."

"Not really," clarified Roland. "That is not enough. There are many good if not excellent dancers out there. Some are near perfect like the computer." Roland pointed at the computer screen. "But who cares. No, you watch the stars because they become the dance. They trust the music, they accept whatever level they have reached, and they dance for the joy of it. I tried to teach that to all my students, and I am proud to say that many of them have gone on to become respected professionals ... but are they perfect? No... but you want to watch. Dance is ultimately about entertainment, and audiences want someone exciting to watch." Roland paused. "I could never get your mother to understand that... and she quit... Well, not really quit since she still has a dance studio and company... Here, do you have a picture of your dog on the computer?"

I was confused by his request. "Prima?"

"Yes, Prima."

"Sure. Sometimes as wallpaper on my computer," I shared.

Roland leaned back in the chair. "Will you get it for me?"

I reached over to the mouse, made a few clicks, and a large picture of Prima appeared on the screen.

PRIMA DANCES IN TUTU ON THE COMPUTER

"Great. Here, watch." Roland copied and cropped the picture, pasted it into his program, and made many clicks and changes. Finally, he mapped the dog's photo onto the anatomical stick figure. With a few more clicks, he created a 3-D model of Prima but in human form. Roland was pleased. "This will be fun." He pressed play.

On the computer screen was Prima dancing to the *Mechanical Doll* dance sequence from the *Nutcracker*. When the music swelled, Prima reached higher. When the music swirled, Prima spun. And when the music staccato, Prima made tiny steps; all the while, her face moved from side to side with her fur flying showing off her beautiful smile.

It was so much fun. I was amazed. Roland and I laughed loudly.

"Here, let's change music and put her in a snowflake costume." Roland showed off his skill and software. Prima was now in a white snowflake tutu. It looked cute and ridiculous at the same time. Roland ran the program. The ever-lovely *Waltz of the Snowflakes* played, and the 3-D model of Prima danced to the music. I rushed to pick up Prima and show her the computer screen.

I gushed. "See Prima. You truly are a prima ballerina."

Roland and I laughed again.

"See, you have to watch." Roland made his point and said, "You can't take your eyes off her. It's fun. It's more fun than watching the stick figures or perfect dancers."

I couldn't take my eyes off the screen and laughed again.

KNOCK, KNOCK. The bedroom door rattled a bit.

"It's Mother," said the voice through the door. The door opened, and Barbara poked her head in. "Hey, what's going on in there?"

I yelled out, "Mom, Mom, come in... You've got to see this."

Barbara walked in and looked over our two shoulders at the computer screen.

I pointed at the screen. "See. Look... Prima is dancing. She IS a prima ballerina." I squeezed Prima tightly and put her down with her puppies.

We all laughed.

"I can also make this play faster." Roland pressed another button to make the program play at three times the speed. Little Prima in tutu spun faster than any dog ever tried to catch its tail and jumped higher than any Doberman. It was hysterical.

This time we roared with laughter.

Barbara jumped in. "That's incredible. Roland, is that what you do?"

Roland laughed again. "Fun isn't it. I can't believe I get paid to do this."

We all laughed and looked down at Prima, who was nursing her pups.

"Prima, we'll have to hire you for next year's *Nutcracker*," concluded Barbara.

We all laughed again.

"Marie, I want to steal Roland back to the living room to socialize." She turned to Roland and said, "Come on. We have so much to catch up on."

Roland stood up to leave and turned to me. "I'm sure I'll see you at the studio."

I was engrossed with the dancing dog on the computer, then turned my head to Roland. My face was beaming. "Thank you. Thank you so much."

Roland added, "You are welcome. Be sure to show your mother how to use the program." He then gave a serious face. "And remember what we discussed."

Roland and Barbara walked out of the room. I was alone, humming with the music. I looked lovingly down at Prima, pointed at the computer screen, and said, "See, that's you."

*

7 — Meeting Stars

For most ballet companies, the *Nutcracker* is a major source of revenue. Small companies are often closely tied to a local dance school. Act 1 of the *Nutcracker* tends to use many children from the dance studio to play the parts of the family and guests. Some productions have been known to pack in as many children as possible, thereby utilizing every child of the school, resulting in filling the audience with mothers, fathers, siblings, uncles, aunts, grandparents, neighbors, and friends of the child. Ticket sales depend on using as many children as possible. During the weeks leading up to the shows, rehearsals that use children are held on weekends to better fit school and family schedules. During the week, small solo parts are practiced at the end of class, but, in general, dance studios are empty for most of the day during weekdays.

Barbara's dance school was no exception and was vacant during the day on weekdays, and that was when Nutcracker Ltd. agreed to use the studios to prepare for their filming. However, actual filming at the mall was scheduled for late at night once the mall closed to the public. Filming was expected to last into the early morning hours.

Once Barbara made the announcement of the collaboration with the production company, many changes took place in the studio. Signs went up saying, "Do Not Approach the Talent," meaning that the studio's children were not to talk to, or annoy, any of the visiting professionals related to the film. Likewise, signs next to the reception desks stated, "Nutcracker Ltd. Personnel—Use Studios C & D." A special sign-in sheet at the front desk helped monitor who came and went, besides issuing badges to all Nutcracker Ltd. personnel. Barbara reinforced these rules in every class. It was a fantastic opportunity for Barbara's school and company to have so many visiting professionals.

One benefit Barbara secured was for her top students' right to attend the practice classes of the visiting professionals. Professional dancers never stop taking class. It is not so much to learn anything new but rather to keep in shape and hone their skills. Each day, at about 11 AM, class was scheduled for the professionals to attend if they wanted.

Paul was hired to conduct the daily class, besides being the choreographer for all the new pieces in this film production of *Nutcracker*. Paul was a sturdy-built retired dancer in his mid-thirties. Although he worked in New York, he came from a small town in Arkansas and still had a southern drawl, which became more pronounced when he was under stress. Paul was never a ballet superstar and had to retire early to have his hips replaced. He was known for being an excellent teacher with phenomenal memory—a memory that made him the perfect dance captain since he could remember everyone's choreography. Paul played an essential role in seeing the filming completed on time. Paul also helped coordinate the requests, needs, and communication between talent, producers, and technicians. Luckily, Paul was even-tempered, not easily fazed, and could be counted on to calm down any situation. Paul was invaluable to the success of the project.

Barbara guided Jasmine, Peter, John, and me into Studio C— the large room used for dance practice. The room was filled with dancers from all over the United States and other countries. The Nutcracker Ltd. production was unique. Not only was it an updated version of the *Nutcracker* using the toys and technology of today, but it was also situated in a mall. It was hoped that the film would attract young viewers and introduce a new generation to ballet. It was also a legacy production. Unlike all previous films of the *Nutcracker* that featured one dance company, this production drew upon stars and choreography from many companies. That way, it would capture, in one film, the ballet stars of today. Finally, the producers wanted to ensure this *Nutcracker* was ethnically and racially diverse. Ballet, like gymnastics, swimming, skiing, skating, and similar sports, is predominately white. The racial divide is not because the activities are racist but because they are activities only the middle and upper class can afford. It was hoped that having a more diverse cast for the *Nutcracker* would encourage a more diverse population to gain an interest in ballet.

The room had dancers from the American Ballet Theater, New York City Ballet, Pennsylvania Ballet, San Francisco Ballet, Atlanta Ballet, Los Angeles Ballet, Dance Theater of Harlem, Cuban Ballet, The Royal Ballet of Britain, and others. Never had so many dancers from so many companies representing so many cultures and ethnic groups been in the same room at the same time. The room bubbled with excitement.

Sandra saw Barbara, Peter, and the students enter the room, looking lost. She quickly walked over to them. "So glad you could make it." She shook each of our hands and glanced around the room with a smile. "Most everyone is here who will be filming this week. You are welcome to attend all the practices. Also, get to know some of the guests. They may help with your future dance plans."

Barbara was pleased. Peter was eager to get going. Jasmine, John, and I were a bit overwhelmed. Although I had attended various ballet summer programs, including some prestigious ones in New York, I had never been in a room with so many professionals. The first thing I noticed was the color. These dancers wore virtually anything. Dance schools and dance camps all have required uniforms. For girls, it is mostly pink tights, black leotards, pink pointe shoes, and hair pulled up tightly in a bun with an optional pink or black overskirt. For boys, it is usually black or grey tights, a white t-shirt, and white socks with white shoes. But here, these were professionals with no dress requirements. It looked like most were wearing old tights and over-tights, many with holes, discarded from old costumes. Some even wore shorts and ripped shirts, and a few of the guys were bare-chested. The room was a rainbow of colors. In many ways, they looked like tights and over-tights tattered from years of use but tools used to create beauty.

In her usual authoritative way, Sandra took the center of the room. "Hello everybody... May I have your attention." The room quieted down. "I want to welcome all of you here today. This is a momentous occasion to have so many stars from so many companies participating in the same dance film. Let's see, over here we have ABT," she pointed right, "and Dance Theater of Harlem," she pointed to the center, "and dancers all the way from Cuba."

The room broke into applause. More than applause, it was a genuine heartfelt recognition of so many nationalities working together.

"You've each been given a schedule for classes and filming over the next few days. It also includes contact information for me and the other production assistants. If you need anything... anything... just contact us. We've also posted the information on the walls in this and the studio next door. If you haven't been to Studio D, we have set up stations for you to try on costumes, put on makeup, many chairs, and light food. There is also a freezer containing bags of ice and compresses for those of you who may need them. Of course, during filming, all this will be at the trailers located next to the sets in the mall. We will provide ballet class each day taught by Paul Shipton." She turned to Paul, "Paul, will you say a few words?"

Paul stepped forward. "Just a few quick words. I'll be teaching a light class, basically to keep you limbered up." He then pointed to a couple of dancers, "Hey Cathy and Chuck, good to see you again... I see I know some of you from New York... Well, if there are any particular steps or routines you would like to work on, just let me know. Once the class is over, we can work on any choreography you want to go over. There'll be a class each day. I hope to see most of you over the next week. I'm also the official choreographer for the production, meaning that I will adjust minor changes to meet the challenges of the filming. Any questions?" He belied his southern upbringing when he drawled out the 'ion' suffix of question.

Many of the dancers stood and stretched. You could see they were getting anxious to work.

"OK then, let's get to the barre."

The dancers randomly placed themselves at the barre. Peter jumped in, whereas Jasmine, John, and I quietly took to one end of the barre.

Paul fiddled with his music player choosing the right music to begin with. Barbara gave a slight wave to the kids and Sandra and proceeded out of the room.

"Let's loosen up the feet first." Paul took hold of the barre to demonstrate the first exercise. "*Tendu,* flex, *tendu,* fifth, *tendu* second, flex, point, fifth, *tendu* back, flex, point close fifth, *demi-plié, relevé sur le cou-de-pied, demi* fifth straighten up. Repeat everything in *demi-plié* then the other side."

The routine was simple and familiar. 'Good,' I thought, nothing I hadn't done thousands of times before.

Paul pressed play. He used piano music composed for the ballet classroom by Michael Roberts. I was very familiar with his work. The songs are very Chopin-like in texture and melody, yet with a consistent beat needed for teaching dance. Michael had been an accompanist for the Royal Ballet in London before working for dance companies in Los Angeles and understood dancers. His unique skill was appreciated worldwide, and the melodies are truly inspirational. The music selection reassured me.

The class was structured just like any ballet class in the world, working first on the feet, then *plié, rond de jambe* both *à terre* and *en l'air, beats, grand battement,* and finally stretching before going to the center. In some ways, I feared that there would be something I did not understand and that would make a fool of myself. Yet, my mother had obviously given me a solid training and an understanding of ballet French terminology. I was relieved. Only when Paul demonstrated the *rond de jambe* was I confused. It was a simple routine, yet I couldn't remember it! How frustrating. I noticed both Jasmine and John also struggled with it. Why was it so hard to remember? I looked closer. It then dawned on me that I was mesmerized by the shape of Paul's shinbone down through his ankle to his feet. I thought to myself, 'They're gorgeous... ha ha ... only another dancer would appreciate what I noticed, and yet how preposterous that sounded. His feet and legs transfixed me so much that I lost my concentration."

During the *grand battement*, Paul walked by and complimented me for my flexibility. I was well aware of how high I could kick. Often, I did a complete split to the front, back, side, and could hold the split if needed. I looked just as good as any of the professionals in the class. But I also noticed that Jasmine wasn't kicking as high as everyone else.

After the stretches, Paul took the classroom center. "OK, now a quick adagio and then some jumps and turns." Paul composed a quick 24-count routine. It was lovely and fit well with the piano music. The second time through, I was confident and flying. Really, when the music is right, and the steps are right, the dancer becomes *beauty*, and this is what I felt. It all seemed so natural. The steps were steps I had done before, not necessarily in this order, but nothing new. But looking in the mirrors and seeing myself in a class of equally talented dancers was amazing.

Men are supposed to excel at jumps. Paul created a jump routine that combined high jumps with low landings. Peter flew. He jumped just as high and far as any other man there. Then some of the dancers started innovating. Most of the men added *battu* or additional twists to each jump. These were probably tricks they used while performing solo work; still, it was exciting. Peter had a trick or two to show the other men. Paul encouraged the deviation from the routine. Unlike a student ballet class where you would be chided for improvising, Paul allowed dancers to work on what they needed in the professional class. He trusted professionals to work on what they needed to practice. I thought how refreshing this was.

Through it all, I noticed that Jasmine struggled. I had never seen *little miss perfect* struggle before. Everything— from her extensions to kicks to jumps— seemed not up to standard. The more she pushed, the more she wobbled. And she looked frustrated. Her face was flushed and on the verge of anger and tears.

Paul ended the class with a series of turns. In my experience, *fouetté* turns were something worked on occasionally and as an individual action. In Swan Lake Act 3, the woman dancing the Black Swan variation is expected to do thirty-two *fouetté* turns. Audiences are known to count them out loud. Ballerinas dread doing them because they are so difficult. Yet, the younger generation of woman dancers is expected to perform *fouetté* turns with a mixture of single and double turns. Here, Paul combined *piqué* and *chaînés* turns along with *fouetté* turns in a quick and dynamic routine. I had never approached such a difficult turn combination and looked over at Peter. He gave a knowing nod assuring me that I could do it. I attacked the combination with gusto. It was thrilling, scary, and fun all at the same time. I nailed it. Jasmine, unfortunately, did not and walked off partway through. She looked thoroughly disgusted.

As with tradition, the class applauded Paul when class ended. The dancers were all flush-faced and happy.

The best image to explain how one should feel at the end of a dance class is to think about a bunch of dogs having a fun day at the dog park. They run, jump after Frisbees, chase after balls, all the while their tongues hang out, breathing hard, and their tails wagging. That happy smile and energetic love at the end of the day is how it feels (and looks) after a good dance class.

I felt compelled to thank Paul for the class. "Thank you. Really, thank you," I said as I extended my hand.

Paul shook my hand but held onto it and said, "You are most welcome. You really kept up with the class."

"Oh, no, they were much better than me."

"Honey, you are good. I hope you get to New York soon," Paul said, drawling out the "soon" that softened his New York directness.

"The teachers must be much better there."

"It's not about the teachers; it's the students. The first rule of dancing is to never, I mean never, be the best in class. If you are, hightail yourself out of there because you have nothing more to learn. No, I'm not a *great* teacher, *good*, yes; very few teachers are *great*. I'm only as great as the students in my class, and this is a remarkable collection of dancers, I must say." He let go of my hand.

I turned away while Peter also thanked Paul for the class. Jasmine was already over at her dance bag packing up. She looked like a drowned rat, soaked in sweat and not happy.

Paul spoke up to the entire room. "Attention! We'll start rehearsals in a few minutes. Tomorrow night we'll be filming the *Spanish Dance, Arabian Dance*, and *Dance of the Reed Flutes*. So, let's start with those first. Please check your schedules. You can either wait here or go next door to Studio D to cool down. I think the costumer will be there to check costumes on you. There's also water and food. OK?"

Many of the dancers picked up their bags and headed out the door. Some stayed behind, drinking water from their own water bottles. Many cell phones came out and were checked for messages.

Paul continued, "OK, *Spanish Dancers*, let's see, that's the group from ABT. Where are you?" Paul surveyed the room and caught sight of the dancers, "OK now, get your people together and be ready in a five."

Jasmine was already out the door. Peter, John, and I retrieved our dance bags and thought we would check out Studio D. We were all pleased with the class.

John spoke up. "I overheard what Paul said to you, Marie... makes a lot of sense... once you are the best, it's time to change schools."

Peter and I turned to face John. He didn't speak up often, so what he said was more important.

"I know that I'm not as good as Peter or like all the men of this professional class. Yet, I'm the best male dancer at your mom's studio. I really need to move on." John looked sad yet resolute. "And you too, Marie. We're both seventeen and at the top of the class. It's time we take the plunge to see if we can really be professional dancers."

All three of us were silent, deep in thought, when they turned the corner and entered Studio D.

*

8 — Whitney Arrives

The warm moist air and loud booming voices virtually pushed Studio D door open into my hand. The room was stuffed with about thirty dancers and their friends, family, and others, all sitting about on folding chairs or the floor. A couple of cots were brought in that were quickly taken over by some of the occupants. Everyone was talking, even those sitting on the floor sewing ribbons on pointe shoes or darning holes in their tights. Although smoking was not allowed inside the building, it was obvious that some, actually more than some, of the people were smokers whose clothes were saturated and stained from the smoke. Some people were talking. Others were on cell phones. A few dancers had bags of ice on their ankles or knees. Peter couldn't wait to mingle. John and I found this to be a bit overwhelming. This was our hometown dance studio, and we had never seen such a crowd in it before.

Peter headed straight to the refrigerator, where bottles of water were offered. John and I tagged along. As soon as Peter opened his bottle and took a swig, he headed over to one of the groups of dancers. Without hesitation, he introduced himself by saying something like, "Hi, I'm Peter Blair, winner of this year's New York Metropolitan Ballet competition, and I've been hired to dance the prince and *Pas de Deux* for this company's *Nutcracker*. And you are... " I admired his directness while at the same time intimidated by his assertiveness.

Soon, Sandra made her way through the crowd to John and me. "Marie... John... I may have forgotten, but you will need to obtain a release form from your school to allow you to miss a couple of days of school to attend the professional class and the filming. Jasmine will need to do the same." Sandra handed John and me a form and then looked around the room. "Jasmine. Where is Jasmine?"

BANG.

The studio door swung wide open, smashing against the wall with a loud BANG. In walked two men in dark clothes and sunglasses playing loud hip-hop music. If I didn't know better, I

63

would have thought they were bodyguards or something. Just behind the men was a small skinny teenage girl with a mop of hair wearing clothing appropriate for a twenty-something sexy model. Behind her were a few more people in street clothing. Hidden behind them was Jasmine.

A few people in the room voiced the name 'Whitney.' The name seemed infectious as it spread around the room, multiplying in intensity each time it was spoken.

Whitney stopped at the door, paused, and surveyed the room. Once all eyes were on her, she walked further into the room. The music accented her entrance. The crowd parted as Whitney, and her entourage, plowed into the room. They headed for the last unused space near one corner. Unfortunately, there were not enough chairs, and her goons intimidated those nearby to give up their seats.

"Whitney," sighed John. He struggled to get his cell phone out quickly to take a photo of the star.

"Who?" I asked over the din of voices and music.

"Whitney. You know, Whitney Smith, the hottest teenage singer on the planet?"

I was always confused about the interest in movie stars and pop singers shown by my peers and self-conscious about my lack of knowledge about pop culture. I lived in the land of classical music and classical art. I did not listen to the radio except for National Public Radio and the classical channel. I didn't read the newspaper and ignored TV when it was on at home. And I did not participate in gossip at school.

There is always a deep divide between average kids and those training for something more. The kids who dedicated hours a day practicing, whether it was dance, musical instrument, swimming, or the brainiacs spending hours alone studying— often did not fit in with the other kids simply because we did not know, or care about, popular culture. And the average kid often teased the dedicated kids for being different and standoffish. I never felt stuck up, although I was often accused of that attitude. Rather, I knew I did not fit in and kept my distance. Perhaps, it was elitism, but I did not see it that way. It was a conflict that I faced daily.

"You know… Whitney… with the cool song *Baby You Make Me*. It's all over the radio. That's what she's playing now." John was in awe and swayed to the music.

Peter looked at me and threw his hands up in the air, meaning, "What?" or, better yet, "Who cares?"

Jasmine made a beeline for the cooler and pulled out a couple of waters. She walked over to Whitney and her group. Whitney took one bottle without even acknowledging Jasmine's existence. With no chairs left, Jasmine stayed standing slightly behind Whitney.

"Oh, there's Jasmine. I need to speak with her and Whitney," Sandra broke the silence.

"Is she part of the show?" John asked hopefully.

Sandra spoke up. "Whitney is the star of the musical. She will have a few scenes shot here, whereas the bulk of the work will be shot back in L.A. on set."

Sandra left the group to walk over to Whitney. As she approached, the bodyguards blocked her path. She pulled out her identification and showed the men. She said a few words, and they let her by. She said a few more words to Jasmine and handed her a form. Sandra leaned down to speak with Whitney. Although the conversation could not be heard on the other side of the room, it was evident that the discussion was not going well. Hands flailed about in the air as voices rose between Sandra and Whitney.

Whitney's raised her voice, "What, you don't need me for two more nights?… You chirping me?… What fool told me to be here tonight?"

Sandra tried to calm her down, speaking low and soft.

Whitney shot off her chair and yelled, "I gotta bounce." She quickly walked out of the room with her bodyguards and Jasmine in tow. The room became hushed without Whitney or her music playing.

A sudden wash of conversations swept the room, mostly about the self-important Whitney. Not all dancers cared about what transpired with Whitney. They had all seen unruly behavior before and only cared if it affected their performance.

Peter spoke up. "Well, I'm outta here... Going back to my hotel. They won't need me until tomorrow."

"I'm tired too. It's been a day," I said with relief.

"Me too," John piped in.

Peter summed up the day, "It was good."

*

9 — School Permission

RINNNNNNGGGGGGG

Period 2 Pre-Calculus class finished, and students bolted from their desks. I gathered up my stuff and placed it in my backpack. I pulled out the release form I had received from Sandra the night before. I needed each of my high school teachers to allow me to miss a few days of class yet turn in assignments by their scheduled due dates. Being a good student, I expected no resistance from my teachers.

I walked up to Mr. Silver. I handed him the form and quickly summarized the situation, "I'm deeply involved in the filming of the *Nutcracker* the next two weeks. I'll be missing a few classes, but I can still turn in everything on time. I just need your signature on this form."

Mr. Silver took the form and glanced at it. There was still considerable commotion with students filing out for morning break, and he was momentarily distracted. Mr. Silver was a well-respected teacher of 40-years' experience. He was demanding but always fair, characteristics I appreciated.

"Oh, a film, how exciting."

"They're using my mom's dance studio space and filming at the mall late at night. I've been allowed to attend the ballet classes for the professionals besides be in bit parts in the film."

Mr. Silver looked over the form through his bifocals. He sometimes came across as being stogy. "You know, I was in a couple of films when I was younger."

"Really," I exclaimed. There was very little gossip about Mr. Silver, and I had never heard about him being in films.

"Yes, a long time ago… in a galaxy far far away… that's a joke… I played saxophone in a band, and we were cast in a couple of those teenage surf movies of the '60s and '70s… Those were the days."

"Saxophone? But you teach math."

"We were performing all over the country… but then it died out. We were a one-hit-wonder… couldn't make a living anymore. Changed to math," said with an oomph.

"Must have been hard to give up. Ever miss it?" I inquired.

"Miss it, sure. It was a highlight of my life. But I always loved math. It's a different kind of love, a different kind of high. Glad I had it."

I was confused. In a culture that emphasized "best," everything was rated, including life experiences. I couldn't comprehend how being in a band and movies could compare to teaching math.

Mr. Silver looked carefully at my face. The cogs and wheels of his mind turned until he found the right words. "You will have many highs... and lows in your life. Never compare them. I don't compare music with math. They are very different experiences yet satisfying in their own way. And, when I retire, I may take up writing. I've thought about writing novels... Whatever it is, I will make the most of it. For you, today, dance is the center of your life. Live it to its fullest. But be prepared to find another interest or another job that fulfills you in a different way, a satisfying way. Life as a dancer is very short, even shorter than that of a musician... That's all. Sorry for rambling on. Just trying to be of help."

He signed the form and handed it to me with a slight smile.

I was surprised. I never suspected an artistic side to Mr. Silver. I rushed out of the classroom and walked to my locker to change books for Period 3 U.S. Government. As usual, the hallways were jammed with kids walking and talking, many on their cell phones, sometimes loosely grouped around a locker. My locker was located almost next to John's and half a hallway away from Jasmine's locker. An expletive was spray-painted on John's locker. It had been over a week since it was discovered, and it was still not cleaned up. I was somewhat complacent about the epithet since it often happened to John. I wondered why it was taking the school janitor so long to clean it up.

John was the identified openly gay kid in the school. Not that there was anything obvious about John, but dancing ballet didn't help his reputation. It didn't matter that sexual orientation is not related to ballet and that most male ballet dancers are straight. All boys going into ballet report being harassed by peers. It is a challenge they all face. This small northeastern town wasn't known for its acceptance of "alternative lifestyles."

I had known John since kindergarten. We had often played together. John was artistic and was called a 'sissy' or 'twinkle toes' or worse by the other boys from the earliest days of elementary school. I enjoyed his company; he was a good dancer and an adequate partner. I was confident he would mature into a great partner once he bulked up.

"Marie, Marie, did you hear?" Bonita slid up next to me. "Did you hear Whitney is in town?"

I glanced down the hall and saw Jasmine surrounded by a gaggle of excited girls giggling loudly.

"I hear you met her too." Bonita gave me a large smile and asked, "What's she like?"

I really didn't want to talk about Whitney. "She was at the studio last night, but Jasmine... "

A loud SQUEAL came from the girls surrounding Jasmine. Bonita bolted from me and rushed down to the commotion.

Jasmine spoke loudly, "... and then we got into Whitney's limo and... "

The girls SQUEALED even louder when Jasmine mentioned *limousine*.

Jasmine took a side-long glance at me and continued with her story.

"Tonight, she is holding a private gathering at the hotel, and I'm invited."

More SQUEALS.

I had had it with idol worship and closed my locker. John came up and unlocked his locker. He just ignored the slur painted on his locker.

I smiled slyly. "She's milking it for everything its worth," cocking my head toward Jasmine.

John wasn't talkative. He seemed preoccupied and anxious.

John spoke up. "You don't need your books for Period 3. Remember, today is the Senior Talent show. The entire class will be at the auditorium."

I looked down at my book. "Oh, yeah, now I remember. Hey, can I put it in yours for right now, so I don't have to carry it?"

"Sure," answered John. I placed my book in John's locker, noticing the pictures of shirtless male dancers taped to the inside door. We often shared lockers.

"Do we go directly to the auditorium or check-in at class first?" I forgot the procedure.

"Class first, then the auditorium. We can get our release forms signed first."

I did not want to attend the talent show. In the past, I danced, but the students were rude when anything classical was performed. I just didn't see the point. It was like physical education. I didn't know why I had to attend PE throwing a ball around since I exercised more than any girl in the school. I felt PE was redundant, and it was in PE that I was surrounded by girls who didn't understand me and were rude.

"Maybe we can get the teacher to allow us to study in the classroom while everyone else goes to the show?" I suggested.

John showed a moment of panic. "Marie. I need you there... I'm going to dance a solo... don't you remember?" John's eyes widened.

"Really?" I asked. I didn't remember John mentioning this.

"I thought, 'what do I have to lose?' I'm the school's gay boy anyway... always have been. Why not give us something to remember me by?"

"Wow!"

"I'm using a short opera piece from *La Traviata* but without words... wearing white tights and the most *flouncy* satin costume shirt I have. That'll show them." John looked resolute as he forcefully put books into the locker.

"Well, of course, I'll be there."

RINNNNNNGGGGGGG

70

The passing bell rang, and all the kids immediately walked to their third-period class. Jasmine and her entourage walked by John and me. Jasmine looked over and said in an extra loud voice, "... and I'll be with my REAL friend Whitney... "

I didn't know how to respond to the changes in Jasmine. I had not done anything to her.

John could see that I was disturbed by Jasmine's insolence and said, "Come on, she's not worth it." John grabbed my hand to pull me down the hallway.

John and I had no problems getting the teacher to sign the release form. Although Jasmine was in the same class, she was nowhere to be found.

The twelfth graders filed to the auditorium. They were loud and rambunctious, often throwing things across the room. Most did not want to go to the assembly, but at least it got them out of class. The auditorium filled up with about 800 kids and a few teachers acting as monitors. Although cell phones were not allowed at school, it seemed as though half the kids were on one. Since the high school was built in the '40s, the seats were wood, and the stage was larger than most, with full velvet curtains. The wood seats creaked, encouraging some students to tweak the seats at every opportunity.

Norman, the twelfth-grade class president, walked onto the stage and took the microphone. He quieted the audience, and the lights dimmed but were not completely black. The lights were low in the audience, so teachers could monitor student behavior.

The first act involved identical Wilkey twins singing a current pop song. The girls were well-liked at school and reasonably talented. Their upbeat song was a good opening. For the next thirty minutes, there was a succession of acts; some good, most not. One girl played a classical piece on a French horn; the audience was rude and talkative. One group of guys sang rap to a hip-hop song. The crowd became unruly and really enjoyed the song even though the singers were not good. It didn't matter because the act encouraged loud audience participation, which overruled any consideration of talent.

Then the strains of *La Traviata* filled the room. John had chosen a piece that was fast and perfect for jumps. John flew onto stage. The spotlights made his white tights and satin shirt glow. The audience burst into laughter. The steps John performed were typical audition steps; *tombé, pas de bourrée, glissade, assemblé, pirouette.* He turned at least four times in the *pirouette,* which showed how good he was. The kids laughed even more. There were boos and catcalls and whistles. Some objects were thrown toward the stage. I became embarrassed for John and actually felt fearful sitting in the crowd. I looked around to see what the teacher monitors would do, but they only looked bored and took no action. The room became more and more unruly. I had never been this uncomfortable at a dance performance before and felt like I, too, was being bullied.

Just then, a remarkable thing happened. About fifteen girls in the front row of the audience stood up, turned to face the crowd, made a fist with one hand, and started pounding it into the open palm of their other hand. They yelled out, "SHUT UP... OR WE'LL POUND YA!" The room quieted a bit. The girls kept repeating the hitting motion and yelling, "SHUT UP." Soon the room became quiet.

John could glimpse what was happening since the auditorium lights were not turned all the way down. Like with all the harassment he experienced in his life, he ignored the threat. He was going to show them. He ended the routine with *grand coupé jeté en tournant ménage,* his favorite series of big jumps in a circle. The audience applauded, not a standing ovation kind of applause but still a significant turnaround from the harassment. For many, it was probably the first... and last... time to see a male ballet dancer live. John bowed and left the stage.

I was angry and fearful at the same time. My sight blurred from the tears in my eyes. The experience was very difficult for me, and I sought a friend. I looked around the audience to see if there was anyone I knew from my ballet world, anyone to give me solace. There was not. Suddenly I felt very alone and anxious. I had never before been surrounded by so much hate and anger aimed at something I thought was the highest and, therefore, an uncontested art form. I had to get out of there.

I stood up, scooted through the aisle, and walked out the front double doors. One of the teacher monitors tried to stop me but to no avail. I had to escape. I pushed right past into the outdoors. The natural light was blinding, and I gasped for air. I was shaking and did not know what to do next. To calm myself down, I took deep breaths. A sense of duty came over me that I must find John. I felt a responsibility to stick with a kindred soul. I turned and headed for the stage door. I walked around the side of the brick walls to the metal stage door at the back of the auditorium. It was locked. I knocked loudly. I felt frustrated. The door opened, and there was John. I threw myself into his arms.

"Oh John, oh John," I repeated.

John held me. He felt me crying.

"I never realized," I said with a haunted voice.

John was confused. What transpired seemed usual to him. With a quizzical face, he asked, "Did you like it?"

"Of course, of course. Excellent choice of steps and music... and you were marvelous."

"Not as good as those guys last night, though."

I looked John's face over. Only then did I realize he was more concerned about the quality of his dancing than the ugly hate thrown his way. "Better."

John beamed. "Come, I need to change. Come sit with me." John beckoned me backstage to the dressing rooms. John's dance bag and clothing were piled in one corner of the room. His makeup kit was open with the perimeter lights on. John was glad to have a dressing room. Too often, male dancers are treated as an afterthought and have to change in hotel bathrooms or closets while the women dancers get the only official dressing room. Unfortunately, the dressing room that day was also shared with the boy rap group and boy hip-hop dance group. Those eight boys wore mostly black hoodies and baggy pants that contrasted with the elegance of John's costume.

John took off his blouse and tights down to his dance belt while I sat beside him. The other boys in the room seemed to watch too closely. Perhaps having a girl in the men's dressing room was the problem. Maybe it was because John was too open for them. Maybe it was simply seeing a boy casually undress next to a girl. Three of the boys broke rank from their friends and walked directly up to John and me. John and I feared for the worse.

"Hey man, I just want to say that it took some guts to do what you did," said one of the boys.

"Yeah, you showed them. You're right with me," added the second boy.

John and, in particular, I were unsure how to respond. The boys indicated they expected a hand bump. John reached out and gave the obligatory hand slap and knuckle bump. The boys walked away and joined their friends while waving a peace hand signal. Through the door, the MC could be heard announcing bows. The boys quickly left the room.

John was dressed and ready to go. He checked himself in the mirror and said, "What is it that Belle says in *Beauty and the Beast*? There 'must be more than this provincial life?'" as he sang the last couple of words. "Can't wait to move away."

"Aren't you going to take bows?" I asked.

"You want to? Sure, I've got nothing to lose... come with me?" John's eyes pleaded to me. We joined hands and walked to the wings.

Norman announced, "Let's give a big round of applause for our talented performers today... Please come on stage."

The various groups walked on stage to polite applause. John was called last and grabbed my hand, pulling me on stage with him. The room broke into thunderous applause. John took a step forward, and I clapped with pride.

I piped over to John, "I'm not so naïve to think they are applauding because they liked your ballet routine."

John spoke through his clenched teeth in a fake stage smile, "No, it's courage."

*

10 — *Chocolate Dance*

Even on weeknights, the mall was bustling with shoppers in the last week of November. The cold did not deter even the most casual of shoppers. Perhaps the after-Thanksgiving sales were too good to pass up. Word was out about the filming in the mall, which brought many curious people to see what a professional film production looked like. The arrival of the first of many large trucks and trailers into the mall brought a level of excitement not seen in years for the otherwise average mall. A few stores advertised 'Filming Special' sales to capitalize on the increased traffic.

A confluence of factors made this mall the choice location for filming the updated *Nutcracker*. Although it was recently constructed, its décor was the 19th century in design, with most stores located outdoors. Being in the northeastern part of the United States, it captured the crisp, clean air of fall in each shot. At the same time, it was known to receive very little rain or snow before January, thereby facilitating an undisturbed filming schedule. It was also located in a quieter suburban area away from a major city and all its distracting sounds— like airplanes, ambulances, helicopters, and such. The background noise would be easier to control. Most importantly, the mall was widely known to be the most decorated, if not over-decorated, mall around. The use of so many lights and decorations helped with the festive ambiance of the mall in supplanting the Land of the Sweets described in the traditional *Nutcracker* story.

A few days earlier, technicians prepared the first three stores for filming. Scaffolding was erected around storefronts for lighting and sound. Special vinyl covering was laid over the leveled plywood to provide a good dance surface for the artists. Cameras and cranes were in place. Many trailers surrounded the area for artists, editing, technical equipment, makeup, and catering. Besides the mall security, police were brought in to set up a perimeter defining where the public could stand and watch. Many chairs lined the edge for film crew personnel, and a special area with tables and chairs was provided for special guests and media. There was probably more movie equipment and technicians here for this one shoot than found in the rest of the small city. Town folks were excited at being chosen by 'Hollywood' for this film, so much so that the local TV and radio stations sent reporters to cover the event.

Filming had to wait until the mall closed at 9 PM. The goal was to shoot the first number by 10 PM and wrap up all three numbers by midnight. It would be cold but not so cold that breaths would appear on the film. The schedule seemed doable, given each number was only one to two minutes long.

Sandra arrived at the dance studio at 9 PM and met the group in the reception area. She was there to escort non-performing personnel to the set to allow us to watch. Sandra gave security badges to Barbara, John, Peter, Jasmine, Tom, and me. She hung lanyards over our necks. "The badges will get you in, but you can't roam around. There is an area for special guests to watch. Please stay there and stay together. You are welcome to the craft service area too. Are there any questions?"

I wanted to ask a million questions but was too excited to say anything.

"Good, just follow me."

Sandra led the way out the front door and into the walkway. Everyone was used to the weather and dressed appropriately except for Peter. He had on a coat that was way too large, including a hood edged with fake fur. He looked like an arctic explorer.

Barbara reached out to Peter's hood and pushed it back off his head, revealing that he had on a knit cap. "Oh, Peter, you look like you are on an expedition to the North Pole!"

The group gave a small giggle.

"I'm from California. What do you expect?" said Peter innocently.

"You'll die from heat exhaustion if you wear it too long. Here…" Barbara unbuttoned the front buttons giving a bit more air. "Maybe after we are sitting in the cold for a couple of hours, you could button up."

John jumped in and said, "We'll call him *polar bear* from now on."

The kids began chanting, "polar bear, polar bear, polar bear... " Peter cracked a crooked smile when he realized he was being accepted by the group as a friend and not just as a hired 'star.'

Sandra stopped the group at the edge of the security perimeter. "Let's quiet down."

The mall was ablaze with lights. The mall administration covered every tree, light post, walkway, and even the permanent kiosks, with small white lights. The mall center decorated the cluster of pine trees with a flurry of white and colored lights besides bright balls, ornaments, and ribbons from the base to the star-tipped top. Stores tended to use colored twinkling lights in their display window and around the outside entrance. Lights were everywhere. Large arc lights were used in the area of the three stores being filmed that night. Some of the arc lights were situated directly on the ground. Heat shimmered about the light fixtures showing how hot they were. The extra lighting allowed workers to work at night. It was almost as bright as daylight.

The group looked in awe at all the equipment, people, and lights. This pleased Barbara immensely. She was glad, no, tickled that she could land such a special and expensive deal for her dance school. This truly was a once-in-a-lifetime opportunity for the people of the community to appreciate the quality of her school and connections. She flirted with the thought, ever so briefly, that this might facilitate her dance company to jump to the next level of being more than a regional dance company but something more professional. The expansiveness of the filming project gave her hope for something more.

"Just show them your badge and follow me to the guests' area." Sandra led the group through security to the guest area. Nearby tables had containers of coffee, tea, and hot chocolate. "Help yourselves to a hot drink."

Peter jumped in, "Here, let me help." Tom also walked over to help.

Sandra, Jasmine, John, and I sat next to some other guests. The guest area accommodated about twenty people and was near the Director's chair, located centrally to the stage.

Barbara walked back and handed Sandra and Jasmine a cup.

Tom returned and gave John his hot chocolate saying, "with mini-marshmallows."

Not to be outdone, Peter handed me a cup of chocolate and said, "with whipped cream... for M'lady."

Jasmine scoffed at the added attention Peter gave me, whereas I gave a small smile.

"ACTORS IN POSITION," yelled the Assistant Director, often called the 'AD', on a bullhorn. The command was echoed by workers at the back of the set.

The first number to be filmed that night was the *Chocolate Dance*. Although Tchaikovsky's original name for the short variation, most productions have renamed it *Spanish*, a name most people know it by. The chocolate candy store was all lit up and ready to go. It was only then that Barbara and the kids noticed that people in heavy trench coats were hovering around the hot arc lights on the ground with their hands extended over the lights, like warming their hands over a fire. The people pulled off their coats, revealing Spanish-style costumes and tutus underneath; aha, the dancers were trying to stay warm before coming on stage to perform. In walked a boy about fifteen years of age dressed in a *Nutcracker* soldier costume. Next to him was a bit smaller girl dressed in a flowing chiffon knee-long dress. The dress was white with tastefully added silver trim around the neck area. Her hair was loose and shoulder-length with small flowers woven in. The dress looked more appropriate for summer than the cold of the night. The two kids seemed vaguely familiar, but I couldn't quite place where I had seen them before. And finally, a very short man in a mouse costume was carrying his headpiece walking with their Second Assistant Director.

I leaned over to Sandra and asked, "Who are the boy and girl?" The rest of the group leaned in to hear what she had to say.

"They are the brother-sister twins acting team you've seen on TV. That's Jim and Bonnie Stewart. They're the current hot teen stars of 'Meet the Murphys.'" Sandra paused to see if any of us showed any recognition. We didn't. "As you can see, he's playing the part of the *Nutcracker*, and she's playing the part of Clara. In our version of the *Nutcracker*, a Mouse will be leading the Nutcracker Prince and Clara through the mall from store to store for Act 2."

Tom spoke up, "Oh... so the mall is filling in for the Land of the Sweets."

"Precisely," Sandra responded. "We figured the kids of today would better relate to a fantasy about mall stores than they would with a mythical land of candy. Also, it allows us to update the toys, costumes, and other things. It should be fun and exciting."

The actors went to position, and the Mouse put on his head.

"OK, THIS WILL BE A TAKE. QUIET ON THE SET." The dancers also moved to position.

"LIGHTS." Most of the arc lights were turned off, leaving just the background and spotlights in position, lighting the store and dance area to sparkle with magic.

"SPEED" was called by Sound. The clapperboard was snapped in front of the central camera.

"ACTION" yelled the Director.

Music filled the outside space. The Mouse entered, making some flips and summersaults, then beckoned the Nutcracker Prince and Clara forward. The Mouse took their hands and pulled them to the entry of the candy store. Four sets of dancers burst forward through the door entry to the space in front of the store as the strings swelled up for the familiar melody. The Nutcracker Prince, Clara, and Mouse stood off to the side to watch.

CHOCOLATE DANCE

The dancers were excellent. They were world-class professionals from the Cuban Ballet Company. Everyone watched closely. Even the technicians and catering stopped what they were doing to watch. Near the end of the number, pieces of chocolate that looked like chocolate kisses wrapped in foil danced out from the store to interact with the ballet dancers. Barbara and the kids were not expecting the addition of dancing candy, although we were familiar with other dance companies using outlandish costumes for these numbers.

The music ended, and the dancers held their poses. The Mouse jumped up and pulled the Nutcracker Prince and Clara to their feet. The three of them ran through center stage, then off to the right.

"CUT," called the Director. "BACK TO NUMBER 1."

Arc lights were brought up. The actors drooped their shoulders and walked back to their offstage position. All the dancers rushed to the arc lights to stand over them for warmth.

Both John and I spoke up, "What was wrong? They were perfect."

No one answered, but soon, we saw the Director and Assistant Director walk out onto the dance floor and look up at the overhead lights. It seemed something was wrong with the lighting. The Director asked a couple of the dancers to come over and run one more section. The Director walked back to his monitor and called Paul and the Assistant Director over to consult. Paul called out for the dancers to move, which they did in silence. The Directors and Paul could be seen talking, pointing at the monitor, and then pointing to the overhead lights. The Assistant Director got on his headset and barked out some orders. Workers scrambled to adjust some of the overhead lighting. After the lighting was corrected, Paul walked back to the dancers to give them some subtle changes to work the lights better.

Sandra spoke up. "This will take a few more minutes to adjust lighting and rerun the scene. So much of shooting a film is waiting for technical to make adjustments."

John spoke up, "So how many times will they run this?"

"I've worked with this Director and crew before. My guess he will not run it more than three times unless there is a major problem. It costs a lot of money to keep rerunning scenes, and we have two more scenes to do tonight."

Sandra was correct. The Director was able to get what he wanted on the second take. That showed the technical team's professionalism in setting up the lights and stage to specification.

"OK. THAT WAS GOOD. THANK YOU, DANCERS. ONTO TO SET 2," yelled the Director over the bullhorn.

*

11 — *Arabian Dance*

Finishing touches were made on Set 2 in front of the Arabian Bazaar store, giving John and Barbara time to speak with Sandra.

John spoke up, "I guess that means the dancers from the Cuban Ballet Company will be leaving since the Spanish dance is done. Those guys were spectacular in class. Their skill truly inspired me."

Barbara was impressed. "I can see why this is such an expensive undertaking. You have the world's best dancers flying into this small city just to shoot one short number."

"We wanted, what is termed, a *heritage recording*, a recording with the best dancers of today all in the same movie. It's been decades since the last time this was attempted. And, yes, it is expensive," explained Sandra.

"I think you will find this adaptation of the *Arabian Dance* very entertaining. We hired a magician to help with the special effect. We felt that, with this being the 21st Century, the *Nutcracker* should have lots of action, special effects, and magic. We are not limited to what Tchaikovsky could imagine in the 19th Century. I don't want to spoil it, so just watch," Sandra continued.

Technicians were able to transfer the equipment to the nearby set surprisingly fast. The store had a single main entrance with two very large show windows on both sides. The lobby had a larger-than-life black-and-white poster of a beautiful young woman with flowing hair and a half-unbuttoned shirt. The side windows also had large black-and-white posters of extremely good-looking shirtless young men showing off their finely toned bodies wearing only button jeans. This time, the dancers were nowhere to be seen and definitely not hovering over the arc lights for heat.

"POSITIONS EVERYONE," yelled the Assistant Director.

Last-minute adjustments were made. The Disney actors, Mouse, and Second Assistant Director came out of their staging tent still in full costume. They walked to the side of the stage.

The Mouse put on his head, the Nutcracker Prince adjusted his jacket, and Clara straightened her dress.

The Assistant Director yelled, "LIGHTS." Most of the arc lights were turned off, leaving only the stage light and spotlights.

"WE'RE ROLLING." The clapperboard was snapped in front of the central camera. "SPEED."

"ACTION," called the Director.

As before, the Mouse ran and performed a summersault, grabbed the Nutcracker Prince and Clara's hands, and pulled them to the store entrance. Magically, the black-and-white center poster changed to color, and a young woman appeared to come to life. The Nutcracker Prince extended his hand to help her step out of the poster and onto the ground. It was a wonderful effect. As she danced to the center, the Nutcracker Prince, Clara, and Mouse moved off to the side. The dancer was exquisite in her sensuality. Her costume was a unique blend of a contemporary dress shirt with traditional Arabian pantaloons that were open along the side, exposing the skin on her legs. About a minute into the number, horns played prominently in the music. On the first flourish, one of the side black-and-white posters changed to color, revealing a live male model. He catapulted out of the frame onto the ground. All the spectators gasped at the effective special effect. On the second horn flourish, the other black-and-white poster changed to color, revealing a different live male model. He, too, catapulted out of the frame onto the ground.

Barbara and the kids couldn't contain themselves and whispered to each other about how "cool" it was.

The two shirtless men and a beautiful young woman performed a flawless, very athletic rendition of the Arabian Dance. She barely touched the ground, constantly being lifted by one man, then the next, and back again in a combination of one-handed and two-handed lifts. It was spectacular. On the fading bars of the three-minute routine, the two men and woman were magically pulled back into their posters, which drained of color into their original black-and-white contrast.

ARABIAN DANCE

The Mouse jumped to his feet and pulled the Nutcracker Prince, and Clara offset.

"CUT. THAT WAS GREAT. EVERYONE HOLD POSITION UNTIL WE CHECK THE MONITORS." Arc lights were turned up.

"What did I tell you?" smiled Sandra.

All of us were finally able to breathe. We didn't realize that we were holding our breath through much of the dance.

"Wow," exclaimed John and Tom.

"Cool, they were sexy," added Jasmine.

"Breathtaking, just breathtaking," Peter and I jumped in.

"I've seen many productions of that dance, even similar ones with two guys and one woman," Barbara exclaimed, "but they were so good, and the idea of them coming out of the posters was inspired... truly inspired... how did you do that... special effects?"

The group couldn't contain their excitement, and all talked at once.

Sandra clarified, "Actually, we used some standard magic illusions that even live stage productions could use. We used only practical effects. The dancers came from the Los Angeles company."

"Wow," said the group.

The Assistant Director got on his bullhorn, "THAT WAS GOOD. JUST ONE MORE TAKE TO GET SOME OTHER CAMERA ANGLES. WE'LL START IN FIFTEEN."

Sandra excused herself from the guests. "I'll be back in a bit. I need to thank the Cuban dancers for their hard work and meet up with the next group of dancers from Pennsylvania."

It had been a while since there was a break, and everyone stood up to stretch, find a restroom, and get more coffee or hot chocolate. Jasmine jumped to her feet and walked over to the Bazaar set, where the two shirtless men stood over the arc lights for heat. The lighting angle accentuated their musculature. Soon, Jasmine could be seen taking selfies with each of the guys and sometimes sandwiched between the shirtless men. She was making a fool of herself, considering that she had already seen the men in the professional dance class and didn't pay them any attention when fully clothed.

Peter and I wandered around the various trailers and trucks to better understand the setup. It was approaching midnight and cold. Peter buttoned up his coat and put on the hood.

"I'm famished," exclaimed Peter. "I hear there's always delicious food at these shoots. Let's find catering."

The two of us did not have far to walk and found a tent that was wall-to-wall food— all kinds of food, not just light snacks for approaching midnight but full, heavy main courses. Signs were placed on each dish so people with dietary restrictions or allergies would know what they were eating.

"Wow," exclaimed Peter. "Gotta be choosy to keep this body."

"Ha, ha, *polar bear*," I laughed. "Can't see anything under that heavy coat."

Peter laughed.

"You know, I've danced the Arabian number with a different ballet company just last year."

"Really... like theirs?" I asked.

"Sorta, but they did have us two guys wearing a vest that was open exposing our bare chest."

I saw a dish labeled *gỏi cuốn* and just had to try it. They were simple uncooked Thai rolls wrapped in rice paper and filled with glass noodles, mung beans, tofu, and Asian basil. Dipped in peanut sauce, they were light and heavenly. "Here, try one." I held one of the rolls to Peter's mouth for him to try. He took a bite.

"Hmm, I've always enjoyed Spring Rolls... and these are great."

It struck me how much I enjoyed spending time with Peter. Unlike the guys at school, he had depth. "Did you see the way Jasmine was shining up to the two shirtless guys? I'm sure those selfies are all over the internet by now."

"I wouldn't put it past her," Peter snickered. "I never understood when people would make comments about a ballet dancer being 'hot' or 'sexy.' When I danced on stage without a shirt or almost nude in dance belt, sometimes friends would later say I was 'hot' or 'sexy.' I didn't get it. I've never heard professional ballet dancers use those terms to describe each other. And dancing on stage is not sexy. I mean, we spend a life training and are in better shape than most... I understand that we have beautiful bodies, but to make a sexual suggestion about it just didn't make sense to me."

Peter took another bite of the Spring Roll. "I have a tough time relating to regular people. I tried dating a girl who was not a dancer once while in college... "

Peter could see that I was confused by his reference to college and had to explain.

"... after high school, I still danced daily but went to junior college for some classes in psychology and philosophy... I've always had an interest in human interactions... and it just didn't work out. I think this is true for all of us dedicated to art, whether or not it is ballet, playing a classical instrument, or graphic art. We just can't have regular friends... or girlfriends. That's not a put down of regular people, but we just are not like them. And I think it is more than just that we devote so many hours to perfecting our skill. People who bicycle, or engage in long-distance running, or swim for hours are not like us... although they spend an exorbitant amount of time practicing as we do, our activity has the added dimension of being an 'art'... a romantic art on top of that."

Peter thought he was losing me, yet I seemed interested. "Do you know what romantic art is?"

"I know that you mean more than 'romance,' but I'm not sure."

"Romantic art is an art that explores and demands the highest moral values. Art explores the human condition. Romantic art looks at what humans can be and what they can achieve. That's what classical ballet is for me. It is the attempt to reach the highest human ideal. And regular people just don't get it. I'm not interested in gossip or TV or sports or personal drama... and unfortunately, most people place sex as the highest emotional state. How sad. I think the sublime transcendental state we can achieve in a ballet class is much more intense and satisfying."

I was transfixed by what Peter was saying. He was able to put into words what I had felt for so long. I didn't hear these words at school, and most of the girls at the dance studio were so young they had no awareness of being able to verbalize their feelings.

"I'm sorry. I sound like a lecture. I didn't mean to. Just girls like Jasmine are… annoying. She thinks that by landing a guy, she gains whatever esteem he has when, in fact, it just reinforced her own lack of self-esteem."

"WE START IN FIVE. REPORT TO FIRST POSITION," boomed over the set and through the canvas walls of the catering tent.

"Here, let's take a little 'care' package of food to the guest area," Peter said as he placed some food in a small box. The other people and workers in the tent wandered out to their respective areas.

Peter and I walked out of the tent to the guest area. Barbara was already seated, sipping more coffee. Tom and Jasmine were on their cell phones. John was chatting up some other guest sitting next to him. Sandra had not returned.

"Here's some nibbles if you need any." Peter extended the box toward the group.

"Oh, great." John took a couple of cookies while Peter and I sat down.

"TAKE POSITION. QUIET ON THE SET." Everything was in position for a second take of the Arabian Dance.

"LIGHTS." Most of the arc lights went off.

"WE'RE ROLLING… SPEED… ACTION."

*

12 — *Dance of the Reed Flutes*

The second take of the Arabian Dance was just as exciting as the first. Even though the trick of the dancers coming out of the black-and-white posters was anticipated, it was still magical. The guests and technicians applauded wholeheartedly at the end of the dance. The Director declared the take good and ordered everyone to the next set.

During the second dance, Jasmine tried to snuggle up to Peter. Each time she pressed her body against his, he scooted away. After the third try, Peter forcibly pushed her back. Jasmine was both confused and angry. This brought out the worse in her as she pouted, a technique she was sure would win his acquiescence. It did not.

Jasmine pulled out her cell phone and messaged someone. Moments later, she rose and declared to the group, "I'm going. Whitney needs me... my real friend." The group sat silently and did not beg her to stay, which angered her more.

Barbara spoke up, "OK, Jasmine. We'll see you tomorrow at class and rehearsal."

Jasmine did not speak but quickly left her seat for the exit.

John felt he needed to say something about Jasmine's behavior, considering how she berated him at rehearsal. "I don't know if this Whitney is a good influence on Jasmine. She seems more... more selfish than usual." The group chuckled at the use of the word *selfish* to describe Jasmine's behavior; how appropriate.

The technicians moved the camera and monitor equipment to the next set, which would be the last filming of the night. The *Dance of the Reed Flutes* was being shot in front of a music store with dancers and choreography provided by a Pennsylvania ballet company with an added twist of including a marching band.

Sandra returned to the guest area and sat next to Barbara. It was fast approaching midnight, and breaths were starting to show in the intense light. "Hope you are all having a fun time."

"Oh yes, very much," everyone chimed in.

"Bet you are glad you wore that extra heavy jacket, Peter?"

Peter gave a smile, "It's better to be a warm polar bear than a cold seal."

The group gave a quizzical look.

Sandra interjected, "If you look out onto the set, you will see Paul helping to block out the dance. The dance company has choreographed a very nice all-girl routine for this number. If you remember, the *Dance of the Reed Flutes* music has a theme that is repeated twice at the beginning and again twice at the end. In the middle is a loud horn section. It was thought to have a marching band come out of the store during the middle section with trumpets, trombones, saxophone, and tuba and line up behind the dancers. Paul is helping to block that right now. One of the things we are trying with this *Nutcracker* is to make it more accessible to boys. Too often, ballet is seen as simply a girl art. So, we are bringing in more things we think boys will like."

Paul was on set talking with the dancers and band members. Sometimes he placed tape on the floor to guide the performers to their spots. The Director walked over to Paul, and they held a brief discussion. The Assistant Director raised his bullhorn, "WE'RE GOING TO HAVE A RUN-THROUGH WITH CAMERAS AND LIGHTS. EVERYONE TAKE POSITION."

The band members walked back into the store. The band uniforms were very striking, using red and gold. Behind them followed the eight girls from the dance company. Their costume was very much in contrast, looking more like summer pastel chiffons with ribbons braided into their hair.

"QUIET ON THE SET... LIGHTS... SPEED... ACTION."

Beautiful music came booming over the set with some feedback screech. Barbara and the kids clenched their shoulders in response to the grating noise. Sandra spoke up and explained, "Don't worry about the music. That's for the performers. There is actually a direct feed to the cameras from the recording so that we don't pick up any outside sound."

The girls and choreography really captured images seen in 18th Century paintings of girls frolicking in the countryside with flowers in their hair and ribbons waving in the breeze. Everyone enjoyed the dancing. Then came the middle section, and the brass band marched out of the storefront. Their overall red uniforms with gold accents, gold helmets, and white bib fronts made an imposing sight and helped frame the back of the set.

John spoke up, "I think it works... it really does."

"The girls can hold their own. Of course, it will depend on how it is edited," Barbara chimed in.

"CUT. STAY IN POSITION."

The dancers stopped in place, and the marching band members dropped their arms, waiting to see what happened. The Director left the monitors and walked to the set. Paul met him there. Although they could not be heard, from the way they waved their arms, it seemed that some of the action was extending too far out of camera range. More tape was brought out and placed down on the ground defining a smaller space. Paul first worked with the dancers and then with the marching band to learn their new spots.

"THIS IS A TAKE. EVERYONE IN POSITION," yelled the Assistant Director.

The Stewart twins, Mouse, and Second Assistant Director left the tent and walked to the stage. The dancers and marching band members warming themselves over the large arc lights, returned inside the store entrance. The Mouse put on his head.

"LIGHTS... SPEED... ACTION."

The Mouse did some gymnastics on the edge of the stage and pulled the Nutcracker Prince and Clara to the storefront door. They pulled at the door handle, and the music swelled as dancers glided out. The Nutcracker Prince, Clara, and Mouse retired to a nearby bench to watch the dancing.

This take seemed to be going flawlessly. A crew of maintenance workers was off to the side at the adjoining store.

Treble-Clef

WORKER LOSES CONTROL OF BUCKET AT *DANCE OF THE REED FLUTES*

The three men wore overalls and caps and carried brooms and mops. They were pushing a very large bucket of cleaning water on wheels. Obviously, they were the nighttime cleaning crew for the other store. The men were captivated by the dancing and stopped what they were doing to watch. They started playing around, dancing with their mops. One of the workers lifted his mop toward his mouth, imitating playing the trumpet.

John spoke up, "Hey, everyone, look." He pointed in the direction of the workers. "See, everyone wants to dance ballet." We all turned our eyes to watch the workers.

One of the workers dancing with the mop tilted it back and acted like he was kissing it.

"I really don't think it's the dance, but rather the pretty girls," chuckled Peter.

The juxtaposition of the ballet girls, band, and dancing workers was captivating. Just then, one of the workers kicked the bucket very hard. Being on wheels, it coasted toward the set. The man ran after the bucket but was unsure if he should stop the bucket or stop running at the edge of the set and let it continue rolling. He grabbed at it with his broom. He was too late, and his indecision let the bucket roll onto the set directly into the middle of the floor. Just then, the girls were running into *grand jeté* from each corner.

I gasped at the impending crash and yelled out, "OH NO! They don't see the bucket... she's going to be hurt."

The first dancer noticed the bucket too late and couldn't stop. She decided to jump over it. With skirt fluttering and a full *grand jeté*, she easily jumped over the bucket. Seeing that the take was ruined, a few other girls made the most of it and made spectacular jumps in full splits over the bucket. My group couldn't restrain from laughing at the absurdity of the situation.

"CUT. CUT. GET THAT BUCKET OFF THE SET. NOW!"

The worker who kicked the bucket ran over and grabbed it. As he pushed it back, he couldn't resist and took multiple bows with an occasional jump. It was very funny.

"Whoa, that's great. Now the guy is taking bows." John and the rest of the group laughed.

Barbara looked at her watch and noticed how late it was. "Marie, honey. It's after midnight, and I think we should go."

Sandra added in, "Yes, it looks like this number will require multiple takes… considering all the problems. You don't need to stay to the end." Sandra turned her attention to everyone. "You kids get some sleep. I'll see you at the professional class tomorrow."

All of a sudden, I was struck by how tired I was. All the excitement masked my weariness. And it was getting very cold.

Barbara said, "C'mon Marie… and we'll drop off Peter and John on the way." Barbara stood up. Actually, it was more like she unfolded since she stiffened up sitting in the cold for so many hours. "It's so cold."

Peter had to get in one more jab. "And you all laughed at my coat."

John and I joined in with a chorus of, "polar bear, polar bear, polar bear… "

*

13 — Being Used as a Barbell

I was very tired, but it was a good kind of tired. The filming the night before, John's act of bravery at school, the challenging steps in the professional dance class, Jasmine's cattiness, Peter's insight and kindness, and preparing for my own *Nutcracker* performance pulled my emotions all over the place. Each day was exciting and filled with unexpected surprises and knowledge.

By the middle of the week, many of the professional dancers who were there for the first night of filming had left, and a new batch of dancers arrived who would be in the second night of filming. The professional dance class was different yet the same. Paul truly knew how to structure a dance class that benefited the needs of professionals.

The professional class completed the *barre* warm-up and moved to the center. Peter, John, and I were feeling good. The morning exercises eradicated the bite of the early morning cold. Although the classes were not mandatory, it was surprising that Jasmine failed to show up or call to let anyone know.

Paul called out to some dancers, "Our friends here from San Francisco would like to review a segment from their *Waltz of the Flowers*. Let's all join in. The floor is all yours." Paul stepped back, relinquishing the floor.

A tall woman dancer came to the center and called out, "It's just a 24-count section that is a bit tricky… I think you all will enjoy it."

It was an intricate series of steps. The choreographer attempted to capture flowers waving in the wind. That required many weight shifts, often moving in opposite directions to the center of weight. At first, the dancers felt awkward, and a few complained under their breath. After a few trials, the music was put on. Music made all the difference in the world. The music helped prepare the dancer's weight so that quick direction changes were possible. Small groups of four dancers at a time performed the routine, crossing from one end of the room to the other end until all dancers had the opportunity to run the routine. Some dancers struggled, but most, once they let the music flow into their bodies, just flew. They really looked like long-stemmed flowers bending in the wind.

I whispered to Peter and John, "That was difficult... but you know, once I listened to the music, it made sense." We both nodded in agreement.

After the routine, Paul ended the class with a series of jumps. As before, many of the dancers added additional *batterie*, twists, and kicks to the jumps. It was very exciting, and John began trying the more difficult variations. I understood that John could benefit from being in a class with male dancers who were better than him.

One of the other male dancers walked up to Paul and had a conversation. The dancer turned to call for everyone's attention. "We would like to form a lifting line. First, we will perform our variations, and then we ask the other four male dancers to replace us." The four male dancers from San Francisco formed a diagonal line across the floor. In stepped one of their women and demonstrated. "The first lift is a simple in-place *grand jeté*. Just up and down in a gentle arch. The second lift is a *grand jeté* but taken overhead with a full layback for one full revolution and gently down." The woman dancer stepped to the second male dancer and demonstrated. The woman jumped into the man's hand with her back leg bent in attitude position while the man took her completely overhead until his arms locked. In that position, the woman lay on her back, and the man supported her along her lower back. It was a classic lift used extensively in *Swan Lake*. "From there, the woman will run toward the third man for an over the head leg throw ending in a fish position."

I had never seen or heard of a woman throwing her leg over a male dancer's head. The fish catch is one of the earliest lifts a beginning dancer learns. But the throw over the head made it an advanced lift.

The woman ran toward the third male dancer, where he placed one hand on her waist and the other under one of her thighs. From there, he could throw her leg over his head, and it naturally ended in a fish. Really, all the woman had to do was hold position, leaving it up to the man to catch, throw, and hold. Actually, it was easy but visually spectacular; what is called a 'high-return' movement—easy but looks hard.

"Finally, we will end with a classic bird. We will have a spotter just in case." The woman ran toward the fourth male dancer, who bent down and placed the palms of his two hands on the woman's hipbone. If it is timed correctly, the woman flies over his head until his arms are locked. She is expected to arch her back with one leg bent looking like a bird in flight. A second man stood nearby to quickly catch the woman if she pushed too far and, basically, jumped over her partner's head.

I was excited and fearful at the same time. Dancing with Peter was my first experience dancing with a professional male dancer who was better trained and stronger than John. Now, to be partnered by so many more professional male dancers, and at the same time, was overwhelming. I vowed to myself not to hesitate and trust the men implicitly. I would throw myself into each lift with exuberant abandon.

The fifteen or so women lined up in one corner. Speaking to no one in particular, one of the women said, "I hate when they use us as barbells."

I didn't understand and turned to her to ask, "What?"

The woman could see that I was just a student, and with a fairly snide comment, said, "When we travel for gigs, the men often don't have a gym to continue working out arms, so they set up these 'lift lines' where they lift one girl after another in rapid succession. Sometimes we feel like we are just pieces of meat to be manhandled. You know it takes time to fully trust a man to do some of these harder lifts."

I hadn't thought of that. All I could do was think about how exciting it was to have powerful male dancers make me fly.

Some music was put on, not so much to dance to, but to help keep the tempo. One by one, the women ran from one man to the next. I could tell that all the women were trained in all four lifts. There was a fumble or two, mostly from the approach. But it looked easy once the man lifted the woman in the air.

Peter came up next to me to point out some subtleties. "Notice how some of the women put their hands on the wrists of the men? Ideally, the men should be able to lift you without their hands sliding up, but so much depends on how strong or tired the man is and the shape of the woman's waist, and more. So, if you find the man's hands sliding up away from your waist, you may want to put your hands on his wrists and hold yourself up, kinda like you were holding yourself up on parallel bars."

I had experienced that before. The only man who had partnered with me was John at the studio. He had not bulked up enough to lift the girls with ease. I usually placed my hands on his wrists when taking a *jeté* lift or a *bird*.

It was finally my turn; I was the last girl through the line.

Peter spoke up, "Don't worry, I'll spot you on each lift."

I ran to the first man who easily lifted me up and down in a *grand jeté*. In a way, it was a warm-up for the bigger lifts. The man placed me gently down on one foot in an *arabesque*. It really helped that the men were much stronger than John.

I turned to the next man. I knew the approach was the same but that I had to have a much higher trust level with him to allow myself to arch back fully and that his hands would slide from my waist to my lower back. Peter was there as a spotter— just in case there was a problem. I ran, and once I felt his hands on my waist, I leaped into a *grand jeté* being lifted way over his head. I arched back and closed my eyes— probably not my best decision. I just couldn't imagine looking at the ceiling in that position.

I heard Peter yell out, "That's the way, Marie. Looks great." I was rotated once around and then brought down. I was to land on one foot in *arabesque*, just like the previous lift, but I was overwhelmed by the height, the strength of the men, and the power of the lift; plus, I still had my eyes closed. The man controlled my descent, but I didn't see the floor. Although my left foot was extended to land on, I had no idea where the floor was. A woman should sense when her toe touches the ground to flex her foot and knee to absorb the landing. I didn't. Regardless

102

of the man's strength, my left leg was out of position for a soft landing.

PLOP.

My left foot brushed the floor and swept up under the man. There was nothing to support me, so I fell to the floor. The man tried to hold me up but to no avail. He did what he could, but he risked injuring himself. John and Peter ran over, as did a couple of the women dancers. I lay there, not knowing if I was hurt, but more than anything, I was frustrated and embarrassed. The male partner tried to help me up. I brushed him away while on my hands and knees.

I said with exasperation, "I'm sorry. I'm sorry."

John bent down to me and asked, "Do you want me to help you up, or?"

In my mind, I surveyed my body. Nothing seemed to hurt. So, I lifted my hands off the floor, grabbed John's arm, and stepped up on one foot and then on the other.

SHOOTING PAIN.

Ah, the pain! My left ankle had burning pain. The foot I was supposed to land on, which slipped under the man, must have twisted while I fell to the floor. "Aww," I cried out. "It's my ankle."

John slipped his shoulder under my arm and helped me hobble off the floor. Peter had already left the room, went next door to Studio D for ice, and returned ready to place ice packs on my injury. Once I was seated, Peter applied the ice, and John put a sweater over my shoulders.

Paul also came over. "Honey, are you alright?" His southern accent made the question ever so sweet.

"Please, please. I'm all right. Just... go dance."

"Let us know what you need. We're here for you, dear," Paul reassured.

I gestured my hand at them with a waving motion and said, "Really. It was my fault. I should have had my eyes open." The small group of dancers and Paul slowly dispersed.

Paul took control of the room and resumed the music and the lifting line in the other direction.

John spoke up, "Is there anything we can get you?"

"Yeah, anything," added Peter.

"No, no. I'm sure it's not bad. I'll probably be good as new in two to three days."

"Are you sure?" John gave his saddest eyes and pushed out his lower lip.

The music stopped.

"Sure," I answered while giving John a kind hug.

Peter stepped in and said, "OK, we'll be right back, but John and I need to finish out the lifting line." Peter and John turned and walked to the center of the room, taking up their position in the lifting line.

I was glad to be left alone. I hated when people fussed over me— especially when I was injured or sick. I was a very independent and strong young lady who did not want to burden anyone. Instead of worrying about the injury, I sat there and watched the twenty women dancers be lifted by the four men in the lifting line one by one. Peter was indeed a professional and clearly up to the task. John was definitely still a student. Although he was given the easiest first lift to do, he did not have the strength to keep his hands from sliding up the girl's side. As such, most women grabbed his wrists to help support his hands on their waist. Still, I knew John and knew he had a ball dancing with professional women dancers, unlike the girl dancers in the studio.

Barbara rushed into the studio, spotted me, and slid to my side.

"Marie, Marie... honey. I just heard. What happened... are you OK?"

"Don't worry, Mom, it's a small strain. I'm sure I'll be all right in a few days."

Barbara sat beside me, removed the ice pack, and inspected my ankle. "There's no external bruising. That's good. Can you flex it?"

I rotated my ankle with no difficulty except at one point.

"Only right there. A slight pain."

Barbara looked closer and saw nothing.

"You're probably right." She put the ice pack back on the ankle.

"It was my fault. I didn't have my eyes open and missed the floor coming down."

Barbara was never very 'motherly' and not good at consoling me in my pain. "I understand. Being partnered by strong men takes getting used to. OK, I'll have you sit out the next couple of rehearsals but still be there to observe."

I didn't expect much sympathy from her. "Of course, Mom. Don't worry; our *Nutcracker* will still go on."

Yes, mom was a caring person, just not very emotional. And she was under a lot of pressure being responsible for the annual production of the *Nutcracker*.

Barbara stood and looked around the room.

"I don't see Jasmine. Do you know where she is?"

"She didn't show for class today. I think someone said that she's next door in Studio D."

Barbara turned to the door to leave. "OK, but if you see her, let her know that I'm looking for her… Keep the ice on. See you later tonight."

Barbara walked out of the room, leaving me by myself. The lifting line would last another fifteen minutes, and I felt cold sitting in wet clothes. I decided I might as well go to the dressing room and change into drier, warmer clothes. I carefully removed the ice pack, placed it on the bench next to me, and stood up. *Ouch.* My ankle really did hurt. I took a few steps. It was painful but bearable. I tried to convince myself that it was only a minor sprain. Dancers are used to pain.

I hobbled out the door and down the hall. There were no younger students crowding the hallways since this was a midday class on a weekday. Entering the dressing room, I was struck by my image in the large mirror. In my eyes, the injury made me look so much older. I wondered how that could happen so fast. I turned the corner around the divider to the open dressing area. Benches lined all three sides with the odd sweater or shoes strewed about. It was only then that I noticed someone crying. The small body was curled up in a fetal position in the darkened corner of the room. The cries were muffled but mournful. The young woman obviously wanted to be alone, but her cries pulled at my heart. I walked up to the woman and touched her shoulder.

"Are you OK?" I asked.

The woman did not respond.

"Do you need help?"

The woman slowly turned and unfolded from her fetal position. I was surprised, actually shocked, that it was Whitney. Mascara smudged her eyelashes, which ran down her cheek.

"Oh... Whitney. Is there something I can do?" although I had no idea what I could do to help an international pop singing star.

"Awww." A very guttural cry emanated from Whitney. I had never heard such a primal moan. "I hate my life. I'm such a failure... Awww... why, why." Tears flowed down Whitney's face. Her eyes were bloodshot and swollen. She continued to use the palm of her hand to wipe the tears from her cheek and eyes. "I hate him... hate him, hate him, hate him. Gads, I want it to all go away... "

I sat next to Whitney and held her hand. Whitney responded by leaning into my shoulder.

"That girl... she's the one who did this... Everything was fine until she showed up... oh, Bobby, why did you have to do this?"

I was completely perplexed by all this. I had no idea why Whitney was so sad or who "that girl" was, or who Bobby was. All I knew was that Whitney needed someone to listen to her.

"You know Bobby Jones?" Whitney asked me.

I nodded my head with a mixture of *no* and being confused.

"You know... the greatest rap singer in the world!!"

My face showed no recognition, which frustrated Whitney to no end.

"He's my boyfriend, awwwww... He was caught with that skank last night at the Raptor Club." Whitney held up an article ripped from a tabloid exposé showing Bobby embracing a woman other than Whitney. It was crumpled and wet from being clasped tightly in her tear-soaked hand.

I tried to cheer her up, "You know you can't believe everything you read in those rags... I would imagine they have printed things about you that you knew not to be true."

"... but look at how his arms are around her!!! Awww..." Whitney let out another round of deep, deep sobs.

"You must really love him," I consoled.

It took a moment for Whitney to compose herself. She wiped more tears away and smoothed her hair.

"Actually... not really. He's a self-centered boy always hanging with his buds and rarely spends time with me. And when he's with me, he's mostly looking in the mirror or his phone, or spotting a paparazzi to take our picture... no, the agency thought we would make a good match... you know, hot teenage girl singer with young rising rap star... Awww... I'm worthless." Whitney went into another crying spell. All that I could do was hold her and let her sob.

"I hate the industry. I hate it all... all the phony people, the ones who want to know you because you are famous—like your friend Jasmine. She's a phony. And they keep forcing me to sing songs I don't even like... all that sex, sex, sex... that's not really me." Whitney looked into my eyes, pleading for understanding. "Really. I started singing in my mother's church when I was a young girl. I loved those gospels and the harmonies. I loved how the songs were about a better world and devotion—something worthwhile. But this commercial stuff I have to sing, and the worthless boyfriends, and the paparazzi, and the money, and the pressures... augh." Whitney calmed down with short whimpers.

I became aware that the hip teenage talk Whitney originally used was gone. She actually talked like a real person.

"You don't really know what I'm talking about, do you, Marie... it is Marie, isn't it?"

I hesitated. I only knew what I read and was never interested in pop culture or celebrity worship.

"Only what I read. Sorry, but I don't know any of your songs, I don't know who Bobby is, and classical dancers are always poor; we dance ballet for the love of it and feel lucky if we can support ourselves."

Whitney straightened up and reached for her purse. She pulled out her wallet and driver's license. "I hope I didn't offend you. You are the first sincere person I've met... in a very long time. Here, look at my driver's license."

The license had Whitney's face on it from a few years back. I wasn't sure what she was looking for.

"Look at the name," chimed in Whitney.

I saw that the name was 'Annabel Smith.'

"Annabel. That's your real first name?" I asked.

Whitney gave one short sniffle.

"That's my name, Annabel. I wanted you to know the real me... not this product that I've become."

I didn't know what to make of all this. It was so quick, almost rehearsed, but it did feel genuine. I gave her a hug and said, "Annabel is a lovely name."

"Often, I wish I could be that little girl again and find the joy of singing. I really do like to sing. But with these big concerts where I lip-synch and now that they process my voice through Auto-Tune every time, I have no idea what is real any longer."

"I just didn't know."

"... and the money, the money... the money. So much pressure when there is so much money involved. Can't I just be a young girl once in a while?"

I had an idea. I thought it could help in a small way.

"How about if you were a mouse?" I asked.

"What??" Whitney was taken entirely by surprise.

"A mouse... in my mother's production of *Nutcracker*. You would be completely covered by costume, and no one would know who you are."

"A mouse... really?" The idea intrigued Whitney. "And people wouldn't know?"

"You would be covered from head to toe, you could change into costume in a different room, and my brother could guide you through the battle. No one would know the difference... and you would have fun again... show's in two weeks, and we do six shows."

Whitney was intrigued. "Here, let me give you my personal cell number. Give me your cell phone." I reached into my bag, retrieved my phone, and handed it to Whitney. Whitney punched in her number. "Only a handful of people know this number. Call me next week after filming, and I'll let you know."

I was happy. Whitney seemed calmer and actually perked up. "OK... Annabel."

The two girls smiled and hugged.

Just then, Jasmine walked in and saw the embrace. "What! What's going on here!" demanded Jasmine.

"Girl, we're just chillin'... being authentic," Whitney said in her coolest voice.

"They need you back in Studio D about something," said Jasmine, who took an aggressive stance with me, trying to establish ownership over Whitney.

I stood up to move to another place in the room. I limped a step or two before sitting back down.

"You a'right girl?" Whitney asked.

"I hurt it in class. Some ice, and it will be better in a day or so." Marie could see genuine care in Whitney's eyes. "Thanks for asking."

Jasmine butted in and said, "Come on, Whitney. They need you... and your friends." The icy glance from Whitney just seemed over-the-top drama.

Whitney stood and walked out of the dressing room. When she reached the door, she turned her head to me and made a 'phone me' action with her hand.

I smiled. I did not know what to make of all this. I was uncertain if I wanted to become involved in the drama surrounding Whitney. But she seemed like a good girl, just pulled by many forces that she couldn't control. Why not? Whitney as a mouse! Who would have guessed?

*

14 — *Chinese Dance*

Luckily, the weather was holding for the second night of filming at the mall. Although cold, breaths would not be seen on film, and there were no clouds in the sky. It would be a perfect night for filming. The schedule for the night was to film the *Chinese Dance, Dance of the Clowns,* and *Waltz of the Flowers.* The mall sparkled with holiday lighting. Equipment had been set up so that filming would take place in a Chinese-style restaurant for the *Chinese Dance,* then switch over to a department store for the *Dance of the Clowns,* and end the night at a flower shop for the *Waltz of the Flowers.*

Being a non-school night, many more families turned out for the filming than had on the first night. Bill brought Nick and Sheila to sit with Barbara, John, Peter, and me. My ankle was still a bit swollen, but I gave it a day's rest from class and rehearsal. The whole family was there, but, as usual, Jasmine was nowhere to be seen. Sandra gave everyone stage passes that allowed us to sit near the cameras in the guests' area. Mall security and one police officer kept the rest of the crowds behind a security line. The crowds were much larger than before, so security had their hands full, keeping the noise down.

Dance floors were placed at the entrance and front of the stores for the first night of filming. For some reason, there was none in front of the Chinese restaurant this time. There were large arc lights shining through the windows, and people could be seen entering and exiting the restaurant's front door, but there was no dance floor. We could see Paul through the large plate windows working with many different people. I was curious about what was different. Sandra walked up and joined the family.

"Sandra," I asked, "there isn't a dance floor in front of the restaurant. Are they dancing?"

Sandra looked over her shoulder toward the restaurant. "Oh, that. We're filming the number inside the restaurant. You've been inside, I would guess?"

I nodded my head, 'yes.'

"They have a very large entry waiting area surrounded by large private eating booths that are spaced apart like the spokes of a wheel. It will work perfectly for the dancers to look like they are performing for the diners. I'm sure it will look great."

Barbara added, "That's inventive and never been done before."

Paul rushed out of the restaurant and walked directly to Sandra. He looked very irritated and flustered.

"Sandra, Sandra, we have a problem."

Sandra got up and walked a few feet away so they could speak in private. Paul's hands flailed about as he spoke—must be some of that Southern expressiveness he so held onto. Sandra pulled out her cell phone and made a quick phone call. She, too, became very agitated. While on the phone, Paul paced quickly back and forth in front of Sandra. The only words that could be heard were, "we're out of time" and "find someone fast." At that point, the Assistant Director walked over, and the three of them discussed whatever the problem was. She put away her phone and walked directly to Bill and Barbara.

"Barbara, Bill, kids, we have a crisis. The actors we hired to act like a family eating in the restaurant... are delayed. We can't wait. Will you... I mean, will your family want to play that part? It's straightforward. Paul will show you what to do. We need eight people, so that means... " Sandra looked around the group and pointed when she said their names, "... we need Bill, Barbara, Marie, John, Peter, Nick, and Sheila."

Nick spoke up, "that's only seven." He was always an observant scientist.

"Ah... " Sandra hesitated.

Paul stepped up and said, "I'll sit with you. I guess it'll be my un-credited cameo. Come on; you can do it."

Barbara and Bill looked at each other and around at the kids, who were all excited by the prospect of being in the film.

"Good, good. Well, no waiting. Have fun. We'll take care of the legal details later."

'Wow,' I thought, how fast that decision was made. The previous night seemed like everything was thoroughly planned and ran smoothly. Decisions can happen quickly when there's so much money on the line.

"Come follow me. When we get inside, you will want to take off your coats." Paul gave directions quickly and confidently.

We had to step over heavy power cables running everywhere when we walked into the restaurant. It was very warm from all the additional lights. Paul took us to a large dining booth with even more lights and cameras.

"Ah, I need to get you in the booth by height, tallest in the back. So, let's have Bill, Peter, then Barbara and Marie, John, and Nick, then Sheila. Slide back a bit because we need to leave space for the Nutcracker Prince, Clara, and Mouse to sit at the edge of the table when they come in. I'll squeeze into the back just before filming."

Paul extended his arm. "Hand me your coats. I'll place them behind the lights; out of the way." When Peter gave him his very heavy coat, the one everyone made fun of, Paul commented, "My, that is some coat. Planning a trip to the Arctic?"

"Come on; it has never snowed in Los Angeles. I didn't know what to expect on this trip."

John and I couldn't resist and began chanting, "polar bear, polar bear... "

The chant confused everyone but relieved some of the anxiety we felt being thrown into this situation so quickly. Makeup artists rushed over and began putting base powder on everyone just to reduce the shine. Nick was not too keen on that.

"OK, you are all in position. Let me explain what will happen. Just like in the ballet, the Nutcracker Prince, Clara, and Mouse will enter, sit down at your table, and when the music begins, there will be two dancers entering stage right. They will dance the *Chinese Dance* that you are familiar with. The only difference is that about halfway through, four waiters will come rushing out with large trays of food. They will swirl a couple of times and place the tray down in the middle of the table between all of us. You just need to look happy and excited. The camera will catch your expressions. Most likely, your faces will only get a few seconds total of screen time, plus they will cut back and forth between you enjoying the food and the dancing. Simple? Yeah. Plus, I'll be here with you. Just follow my lead. We're going to have a couple of run-throughs before the actual filming."

Nick squealed, "Ugh, makeup."

Barbara gave Nick a stern parental look to make him behave.

Nick pushed the hand of the makeup artist away. "It's not my shade." Everyone was surprised by his comment. We thought he was complaining as a 'boy' hating to wear makeup. He never cared how he looked. "Hey, I can goof around sometimes too! Besides, Pancake Base #ME2 was my color last year." That made everyone at the table chuckle.

The room became crowded, very crowded. The lighting technicians made their final adjustments. The two-camera operators took up position. There were several grips, and, almost as an afterthought, the two dancers were off to the side along with the Nutcracker Prince, Clara, and Mouse.

Paul yelled out, "I need the waiters. Come forward. We're going to mark through this."

In came four waiters in traditional black long-tailed tuxedo-style uniforms. They looked like penguins, which matched the décor of panda bears. The men were of all racial groups. In their right hand, they balanced a large circular platter. Over their left arm hung a small white towel.

"Good, now when you get closer, make two spins and place the platter on the table." The waiters hit their mark. "And make one spin away and walk off stage... Good." Paul was pleased with how smoothly it was going.

Paul took the center of the room with the Assistant Director. The Assistant Director spoke, "OK, we're going to run and film the dance sequence first. Then we'll reshoot with the waiters. This is a take. Everyone take position."

*

114

15 — Honored by the Mouse

CHINESE DANCE

The center of the room cleared. Paul joined the family at the table.

"LIGHTS... " Some of the arc lights turned off, replaced with more targeted spotlights.

"SPEED... ACTION."

The Stewart twins playing the Nutcracker Prince and Clara, along with the Mouse, entered from the side, looked around, and sat down with my family. The glorious Tchaikovsky music filled the room. The stage area, which was the entry and waiting room of the restaurant, looked like ancient China. In came the dancing couple. They both wore typical flowing silk pants with blousy long-sleeved shirts under vest tops. The most significant difference between them was that the woman dancer had her hair elaborately arranged with many rhinestones and carried a fan. In contrast, the man wore a traditional Chinese hat. The costumes were very formal and festive, with added decorations and trim. Their dancing was fun and infectious. They often used the style of their index finger to point to the sky. Many variations of this dance have used the stylized finger motion. The dancers were great, and the steps unusual and interesting.

Paul leaned over to the group and whispered, "The two dancers are a married couple from China and are also trained in Chinese folk dancing. We went back to the roots of Chinese dance to try and make this as authentic as possible... I find this refreshing."

Peter spoke up, "But the finger gesture is offensive!"

"What?" said Paul. He was confused by Peter's comment.

"The finger movement was created by a white choreographer to stigmatize the Chinese," reinforced Peter.

The group did not know how to react and went silent.

Peter continued, "We went through this discussion last year with the other ballet company I danced the *Nutcracker*. It turns out that hand style was never used in traditional Chinese dance or theater and was, in fact, a style created by a white choreographer way back in the 1900s to stigmatize the Chinese... so we decided to drop it from the dance."

I knew exactly what he was talking about. I had seen it used often and always wondered about it. It didn't make any sense to me, yet I blithely accepted its use. Mother's production of the *Nutcracker* used two girls dancing with parasols and not the finger gestures. I wondered if mother did that on purpose or even knew that Asians took offense to how the *Tea Dance* is usually portrayed in the *Nutcracker*.

The final bars of the music ended, and my family prepared to clap when, to our surprise, the music continued, and

116

some dancers in giant panda bear costumes ran out to perform a tumbling routine.

We all looked around the table at each other for reassurance.

The music lasted for another thirty seconds. Basically, it was a repeat of the second half of the music, but during that time, two large panda bears and two cubs came out. Obviously, the bears were people in panda costumes performing gymnastics. It was fun. The two Chinese dancers also danced with the bears. For the final musical count, the Chinese dancers used *chaîné* turns to reach the edge of the table where we were seated, and the bears were right behind, forming a nice pyramid tableau. What an ending! Very exciting.

We couldn't contain ourselves and applauded wildly.

"CUT," yelled the Director.

The Assistant Director spoke up, "BACK TO POSITION ONE. WE'LL START IN FIVE... WITH WAITERS."

Bill also couldn't contain himself. "That was wonderful, Paul, really wonderful. Very up to date, and we love the bears." Even Nick and Shelia gave a 'thumbs up' for the number.

Paul was still thinking about what Peter said about the choreography. "Are you sure?"

Peter whipped out his phone. "Here, I'll show you the website where we learned about the gesture... Here... Here, take a look." Peter handed his phone to Paul, who looked it over.

"Why, I never knew... It has its origins from the look of peasant farmers hauling buckets with a pole across their shoulders and their hands on the pole." Paul poked around the phone some more. He handed the phone off to the Chinese dancers. "Here, I want you to see this," Paul said while handing the phone to the two dancers. "Did you know about this?"

After a moment, the Chinese woman dancer spoke to Paul. "We thought American audiences wanted it."

"We hired you because you are experts in Chinese folk dancing besides ballet. Would you ever use that finger motion?"

"No... "

Paul asserted himself, "Then we need to remove the gesture. Just use regular ballet arms."

The two Chinese dancers nodded in agreement and walked away to practice the changes.

The Mouse squirmed in his seat, took off his headpiece, and placed it on the table. "God, it's hot with that on," he commented.

Jim and Bonnie, who played the Nutcracker Prince and Clara, relaxed. "I didn't realize how uncomfortable it is to wear tights for hours," Jim complained.

Peter spoke up, "Actually if you are wearing them correctly with a good fitting dance belt, it would feel like you are wearing nothing."

Jim and Bonnie looked at Peter with disdain, like, 'who is this person to tell us what to do?'

Peter extended his hand, "Hi, I'm Peter. I'm hired by this woman," he glanced toward Barbara, "to dance your role in her *Nutcracker*. I wear tights every day for hours without problems."

Bonnie spoke with great insolence, "Do you know who we are?"

Silence. No one at the table spoke up. Finally, Shelia, in her small squeaky voice, said, *Meet the Murphys* on TV.

Jim spoke up, "That's right, we're the Stewart twins, and we are in every teen magazine on the planet. Millions of kids and fans know who we are."

"Sorry, I didn't imply anything, but I could help you with your tights if you want," Peter suggested.

Everyone sat through the awkward silence.

The Mouse finally spoke up. He was a little person, about thirty years of age, who did gymnastics. He was a straight shooter and said, "Give it a rest, twins... These people probably know nothing about you two. I would guess they are all classical ballet dancers and only know classical arts, and they probably don't watch TV. If it's any consolation, they will probably be poor their entire lives while the two of you already have millions, and you're not even twenty years old yet." Surprisingly, that did perk up Jim and Bonnie. Stroking the ego of self-centered people can be so easy.

The Mouse continued, "But in my book, they are blessed people. Only a few thousand humans, out of all the humans who have ever lived, have experienced the classical ballet dream. Their art is divine, and I honor them." The Mouse stood up and bowed to everyone seated at the table.

However, before the Mouse could complete his speech, both Jim and Bonnie walked away on their cell phones, totally disinterested in the conversation.

"I know it was wasted on them, but I wanted you guys to know how I feel. As a young boy, I wanted to dance ballet, but who's ever heard of a Prince Charming who was a little person? I'm glad I got this gig. There aren't many opportunities for little people in show business. If there is an acting job, we are always jesters and clowns. That's why I can tumble... while wearing a mouse headpiece."

Bill spoke up. "Well, we... Barbara and the kids... appreciate your sentiments and insights and wish you the best."

"FIRST POSITION, EVERYONE," yelled the Assistant Director.

The Mouse picked up his head, "Gotta go. Keep dancing."

"Wow," sighed Barbara.

"Yes, wow," added the rest of us.

"It takes all kinds," chipped in Nick with the worn cliché.

Everyone laughed.

Paul stood up. "Time for the second shoot."

The Assistant Director took the bullhorn this time and yelled, "EVERYONE, TO FIRST POSITION. THIS TIME WITH WAITERS."

"LIGHTS... SPEED... ACTION."

As choreographed, the Stewart twins entered with the Mouse and came to sit at the end of the table. The music started, and the dancers were as lovely as the first time, but this time without the offensive finger gesture. About halfway through the song, pairs of waiters from both sides walked in and then twirled twice before putting down their platters on the table. In some ways, it reminded everyone of the Chinese dancing mushrooms in Disney's original *Fantasia*. One of the cameras was on a boom and zoomed over the table as the platters were placed down, showing everyone grabbing a plate.

"CUT," called the Director.

Everyone relaxed.

Paul leaned in and explained to the group, "OK, they are now going to shoot a few short seconds after you are served food. Just act like you are eating, laughing, and having a fun time."

Nick checked out the bowl of wonton soup. He picked up the bowl and turned it upside down. Nothing fell out. "Hey, this is fake," he sighed while pounding the transparent plastic in the bowl that was made to look like soup, "and now I'm hungry."

"It's all fake. Plastic made to look like food. I'm sure you've seen that before in the display case of some Asian restaurants. That way, it can't be spilled while they are spinning. So, use your spoons or chopsticks and act like you are eating. Remember, <u>act</u>."

"FROM SECOND POSITION. THIS IS A TAKE... LIGHTS... SPEED... ACTION."

Again, the camera zoomed over the table while everyone faked eating fake food, all the while acting with a fake laugh and looking outward toward the Chinese dancers. The only thing not fake was the excellent dancing.

"CUT... AND HOLD POSITION."

The Director and Paul reviewed the tape on the monitors. After a bit of discussion, the Assistant Director took the bullhorn.

"WE'RE GOING TO RUN THIS PROBABLY TWO MORE TIMES AS WE ADJUST LIGHTING. TAKE 10."

Paul sat down at the table. He was very 'up' and, at the same time, very tired. He had been on set most of the day, taking care of last-minute details. And then the last-minute snag of the actors needed for the restaurant not showing up just added stress. It was lucky that Barbara and our family and friends were willing to jump in quickly.

Having ten minutes with nothing to do seemed an eternity for Paul. He was impatient and became talkative. "I once filmed the *Nutcracker Pas de Deux* for a TV station in Los Angeles. It is the pinnacle dance piece in the *Nutcracker* but lasts only nine minutes, yet the filming took five hours. They kept adjusting the lighting and tweaking this and that. Very exhausting. Never once did they ask us dancers which take we preferred and... oh God, now I remember... " Paul had a look of amused astonishment on his face, "what happened during that filming. It was a quick pick-up job. I was brought in to teach the choreography and dance the Cavalier part. I taught it to three ballerinas one Sunday and the next Sunday we filmed it with the ballerina of their choice. She was a good dancer but my same height. Immediately I took out all the one-hand lifts. There was no way I could do those with a stranger in just one take and with someone my same size. Well, during the filming, there was a guy running around in the empty sound studio taking photos of the woman and me. My partner informed me that it was her husband. I thought nothing of it. You get very used to people taking your photo at all times. Anyway, we're halfway through the filming, taking a break, standing over the arc lights for warmth, when she threw her arms over my shoulders and started sobbing. She whispered into my ear that she was getting 'a divorce.' I wasn't sure what to do. She sobbed even harder and began shaking. I mean, I only met this woman once before a week earlier, and here we are in the middle of filming the *Pas de Deux*, she's in a full tutu, and I'm in silk and gold lamé, and she dumps on me that she's getting a divorce. Gads, I just wanted her to hold up to the end of the shoot and the dancing to be good. So, I patted her on the shoulder and said something lame like, 'relationships can be difficult' or something equally true but inane. During the rest of the shoot, I kept telling her how good she was. I mean, what would you have done? Anyway, we pulled it off, and I never heard from her again."

Everyone expected a punch line or conclusion, but Paul was silent in reflective thought.

"I guess it prepared me for much of what I do now. I run around the set, solving problems, and putting out fires, so the filming seems smooth."

Barbara spoke up and said, "My partner and I had a few of those crisis situations, sometimes right before a show. You do learn how to roll with it. The audience is never the wiser to what transpires behind the scenes."

Nick, who had pulled out a hand-held video game through the break, spoke without looking up from the game, "*Que será, será.*"

Paul was taken back by the rich bon mot. He reached out and rubbed Nick's head and said, "Hey little buddy, you have a saying for every occasion."

While still concentrating on his game, Nick said, "To every thing there is a season... A time for every purpose."

That made everyone laugh. Nick raised his head to acknowledge their snickers yet never averted his eyes from the video screen.

Paul was correct. It took another hour for the additional takes. I was surprised at how tired I was. Maybe it was the heat from the lamps, or the being on edge the entire time, or the excitement, but regardless I was glad when it was done.

*

16 — *Dance of the Clowns*

With the filming of the *Tea Dance* completed, all the technicians, cameras, and other equipment were moved outdoors to the front of the department store for the *Dance of the Clowns*. My family walked into the brisk night air to the guest seating area. I welcomed the chilly air on my face. John helped me walk since I still had a slight limp from the ankle injury. Bill, Nick, and Barbara made a detour through catering to bring back a couple boxes of snacks. Eventually, we all had cups of coffee or hot chocolate and were seated in the guest area munching through the boxes of goodies.

The crowds outside the security perimeter had almost dissipated. Not only could we not see what had transpired the past two hours in the restaurant, but it was also clear that Whitney was not going to be there, although the word was out that she was going to be there the next night for the flash mob scene of Act 1. So, it was pretty quiet except for the bustle of workers and dancers in costumes in front of the store. There were twelve dancers dressed as clowns or upscale porcelain dolls. Sandra was talking with some of the dancers when Paul finally joined in. It looked like they were discussing some of the lighting with the Director. A brief time later, Sandra walked over and sat next to Barbara in the guest area.

"We're almost ready. We got most of the details out of the way while they were filming the *Tea Dance*."

Everyone turned to Sandra to hear what was going on.

"This is the *Dance of the Clowns*. That is what Tchaikovsky originally named this piece of music. It has been adapted by many ballet companies into what is commonly known as *Mother Ginger*. With the more upbeat, fun version of the *Nutcracker*, we decided to use the original concept of dancing clowns and dolls."

"ACTORS ON SET. WE WILL BEGIN IN FIVE."

124

DANCE OF THE CLOWNS

The Stewart twins and Mouse walked out of their tent waiting area. The Mouse was holding his head and gave a wave to Barbara and our family as he walked by. A real connection had formed there. Although the twins were in their Nutcracker Prince and Clara costumes, they were still texting on their phones and not in the least bit friendly to anyone. They walked to stage right for their entrance. The dancers disappeared through the front door of the store.

"ALL QUIET ON THE SET," called out the Assistant Director, which was echoed around the set.

"LIGHTS." Most of the arc lights were dimmed, and a new set of colored lights was shown on the department storefront. The additional lights were not expected, and the crowd made an "ooh" sound at how pretty they were. Considering how over-decorated this mall was, these new lights really put the store way over the top. Even my family caught our breath at the glorious sight.

"I bet those could be seen from space," quipped Nick.

"Shush," Barbara whispered, although everyone found it funny.

"SPEED... ACTION."

The Nutcracker Prince, Clara, and Mouse came onto set. The Mouse did his dance and tumble, pulling the two other actors to center stage. The music began, and the dancers in clown costumes poured out the front doors of the store. There were many unique styles of clown costumes; some were famous and related to the circus. The Nutcracker Prince, Clara, and Mouse moved to the side of the stage.

The dancing was excellent. Considering that the clowns were to act like soft Raggedy Ann and Raggedy Andy dolls with loose limbs and lanky movements, the dancing was impressive since it is usually hard for classically trained dancers to perform difficult steps on pointe while also being 'loose.' The moves reminded me of Twyla Tharp's unique style of choreography. I could identify many of the dancers from the professional class. I also recognized the man who dropped me; well, actually, I fell because I closed my eyes. It was entirely my fault for not having my foot in the right place to support my landing. My ankle still ached from the mishap but had gotten better. All the dancers were excellent, far above my mother's dance studio's quality and what I experienced each day.

"AIN'T NOTHIN' BUT A HOUND DOG," played on someone's cell phone in the crowd.

"AIN'T NOTHIN' BUT A HOUND DOG," rang a second time.

Unfortunately, this was within earshot of the Director, who threw his chair crashing back to the ground, grabbed the bullhorn, and yelled, "CUT." He charged in the direction from where the sound emanated.

"SECURITY. FIND THAT PERSON AND THROW HIM OUT."

Filming came to a stop. Dancers stopped and stood fast. All eyes turned in the direction of the escalating confrontation. Security moved in on the small crowd. There was lots of confusion. One person after another denied they were the offender and held up phones to show they were off. After a few moments, security uplifted their hands to indicate they found nothing.

It took the Director a few minutes to calm down. He paced back and forth. He put the bullhorn to his lips, "I KNOW THE OFFENDER IS NOT FROM MY CREW. THEY KNOW THAT IF A CELL PHONE GOES OFF WHILE WE ARE FILMING, THEY WILL BE FIRED. YOU, OTHER PEOPLE, WILL BE BANNED IF YOU CAN'T BE QUIET. NOW, TURN OFF YOUR CELL PHONES."

There was a very awkward silence.

"FROM THE BEGINNING." The Director swiveled around and faced the crowd, "JUST SO YOU PEOPLE UNDERSTAND, EACH TIME WE STOP FILMING, IT COSTS US THOUSANDS OF DOLLARS." He turned his attention back to the set.

"LIGHTS." Arc lights were dimmed, and store lights were brought up.

"SPEED... ACTION."

The next take went smoothly with no interruptions, and it looked grand. By the end, Paul and the Director reviewed the monitors. Lighting technicians were sent to the set to make some adjustments.

During this downtime, Peter received a phone call on his cell. It was on vibrate mode, so no one heard it. He pulled it from his pocket, looked at the number, excused himself from the group, and walked over toward the catering tent, which was a safe distance away from the action so as not to be a nuisance.

The Assistant Director took to the bullhorn, "OK, TWO MORE TIMES. IT WAS A GOOD RUN, JUST MAKING A FEW ADJUSTMENTS."

Peter walked back and announced to Barbara and the group, "I've got to go. It was a strange text from Jasmine... something about Whitney. She's crying. Not sure why she's calling me, but I'll see you all tomorrow at practice."

Barbara asked, "she's crying... what for?"

"I really don't' know. I'll see you tomorrow." Peter shook hands with Bill and John and walked out past security to the rental car in the lot.

"You know," Bill jumped in, "from what you have told me, she seems to have become unstable since Whitney came to town." As a psychotherapist, Bill often saw people seeking passive ways of getting out of doing something by finding a way to blame it on someone else. He added, "Maybe Jasmine really wants to get out of classical ballet, and Whitney will be her excuse."

My father's comments struck me. Wasn't that what Roland had said about my mother, that she used her pregnancy with me as an excuse to retire from dancing? I wondered if my father was aware of Barbara's passive-aggressive behavior when they met. I wondered how much everyone knew and was not sharing.

Barbara was concerned and said, "I'm watching... closely... I can't have her impact our *Nutcracker*."

They completed two full takes over the next half hour.

"STRIKE THE SET. MOVE OVER TO SET 3," the Assistant Director called on the bullhorn. "IS ROLAND HERE?"

*

128

17 — *Waltz of the Flowers*

Barbara was surprised to hear Roland's name called. She looked around and only then noticed that he was sitting just a few feet away from her, talking with Sandra. Roland jumped to his feet and walked to the Director. He was too far away for Barbara to hear what they were saying, but Roland pulled from his pocket a computer disk and handed it to the technicians at the monitor and recording computer tables.

The set in front of the flower shop was already prepared, just waiting for the camera and crane to take the position. Sandra leaned in to tell Barbara and everyone what was happening. "We're using the shop for the *Waltz of the Flowers*. Makes sense, right?" We all nodded our heads. "But as an added bonus, for the opening bars of music, there will be long stem flowers jumping out of the vases inside the store, and, as they fly through the front door, they will transform into full-size full-life ballerinas. Roland is here providing the special effect section for the opening. That way, the Director can see how it works, although the final effect will be laid over later at the studio to make it photo-realistic."

"Oh, umm," murmured everyone.

"OK. OPENING POSITIONS. REPORT."

The Stewart Twins and Mouse walked over to their starting position. A Second Assistant Director, on a walkie-talkie, strode along with the three of them and reported back to the Director. A handheld camera took up position in front of the three of them.

"LIGHTS," the arc lights went down, showing off the beautiful glow of the mall. "SPEED... ACTION."

The Director wanted a different camera angle on this number, something he had not done on the other numbers. He wanted to capture entering the store from the point-of-view of the Mouse, Clara, and the Nutcracker Prince. A handheld camera was held waist level and followed the actors into the store.

WALTZ OF THE FLOWERS

The music began, and the three of them backed out of the store. Nothing happened for a few short moments— and then, when the music swelled, twelve ballerinas rushed through the doorway to the floor placed in front of the store. Their costumes were lovely.

Actually, they were the best costumes Barbara and I had ever seen for the *Waltz of the Flowers*. We had seen a company dress the girls into sunflowers with bonnets that, unfortunately, made them look like the Jersey Maid maidens. Here was a combination of short tutu and long summer chiffon ending at the knee. The different length skirts reflected diverse kinds of flowers.

Sandra spoke softly to the group, "We went to great effort to assure that all racial and ethnic girls were used for this number. We blended dancers from many companies to get this mix. I think it really works and how each skin tone is accented in the different costume style."

That's what caught my eye. Most companies put the girls in the same costume— as a flower or a girl dressed for summer with flowers all over. Here, each girl represented a different flower with different coloring and detail. I had never thought about that before, and it worked. This really will be an updated and more inclusive *Nutcracker*.

For the final bars of the music, the flowers danced back through the entrance, and the Nutcracker Prince, Clara, and the Mouse waved them goodbye.

"CUT. THAT WAS GREAT. JUST HOLD POSITION."

Roland and Director walked over to the monitor and reviewed the dance. A monitor faced the guest area so my family could watch. Sure enough, the special effects had long stem flowers jumping out of their vases that transformed into the dancing ballerinas. It looked pretty good. The Director seemed satisfied. Roland returned to the guest area and sat next to Barbara and me.

"Could you see the monitor? That is a rough idea of the special effects for this number. We didn't need a full

131

greenscreen. We'll be doing that early next week for a couple of numbers. What do you think?"

Bill, Barbara, and my family agreed and said, "Wow."

Barbara added, "That gives me an idea for my own production."

The Director called over the handheld camera technician and held a closed conversation.

Barbara told Roland, "I didn't see you come in."

"Oh, I only got in a few minutes ago. I was hung up at security a bit longer than I anticipated." Barbara looked perplexed. "Yeah, ever since I got these metal hips, I set off the metal detectors, and it always takes more time."

"Really, you replaced your hips… you didn't tell me," Barbara looked concerned.

"Had to… about three years ago. I was in a walker. Once the hip joint goes bone on bone, the pain is unrelenting. Really glad I did it. I shouldn't have waited so long."

"Did it hurt?" I asked.

"No, the moment they cut out the old hip, the pain went away. The technology is so advanced and routine now, I highly recommend it to anyone who needs it. Don't wait."

"Cool, bet they're titanium," interjected Nick.

"You bet little, guy— titanium and plastic. They'll may have to be redone in about fifteen years or later."

Bill added in, "I hear it's common nowadays. Didn't Paul say he also had his hips replaced?"

"I would guess almost one-third of the dancers from Barbara's and my day have had the operation. People often think dancers ruin their feet, ankles, or knees; well, the deep dark secret of the ballet world is that it destroys hips. There are websites devoted to nothing more than dancers discussing hip replacement."

"Would you do it all over, you know, the classical ballet… knowing what you've gone through," asked Bill?

"In a heartbeat. Ballet was an extraordinary experience. It has made my life fuller than anything else I can imagine. It is a transcendental experience where we, the dancers, become beauty. We are the art. What other activity gives you that? I know most people have no idea what we mean when we say these things, but I'm sure Barbara, Marie... and John understand."

The three of us had a connection that transcended words at that moment.

Barbara looked at her watch and saw that it was almost midnight. "Oh, we've got to be going. I promised to get Sheila home by midnight, and Nick and the rest of us are exhausted." Even before she finished, Nick was standing, ready to go. Obviously, he was prepared to go a while back. Barbara leaned over and gave Roland a big hug. Bill shook his hand. "Remember, Saturday we need you for our rehearsal of Act 1. Thanks for being Drosselmeier." John also shook his hand, but I leaned in to hug him.

"I'm so glad you are here. You are really helping my mom, and I so enjoy hearing what you have to say. Thanks." I gave one more hug before my family moved out. John helped me limp out with my ankle still aching.

"OK. ONE MORE TIME. TAKE POSITION ONE."

Roland waived the family goodnight. He was really glad this assignment brought him back in touch with his ballet memories and cherished friends.

*

18 — The Manicure

The next day the dance studio was a whirlwind of activity. Tom had a very difficult time managing the reception desk and waiting area. Not only was there the usual flow of students for a Saturday morning in four different classes, but there was also the flow of professional dancers, technicians, agents, support staff, makeup artists, costume designers, and the like related to the *Nutcracker* movie. Luckily, Sandra was responsible for staffing a separate table to handle all the movie stuff, including keeping the general public out. There were lots of *lookie-loos,* especially since it was known that the world-famous singer Whitney Smith, and the TV personalities Stewart Twins, were to be there. A security guard was posted at the front door to handle the throngs of kids trying to sneak a look. Of course, there was the occasional conflict between dance studio students and security. Sometimes, Tom had to intercede to calm students and parents down.

The biggest studio, Studio A, was reserved the entire day in preparation for filming Act 1 of the *Nutcracker* that night at the mall. Act 1 not only included hired professional dancers but also sixty other people to perform a flash mob. The flash mob routine was very simple yet an interesting interpretation of some of Tchaikovsky's music.

Barbara and I found ourselves being pulled in all directions. Most dance classes were combined or canceled to free up studio space. Likewise, rehearsals for Barbara's *Nutcracker* could not overlap the *Nutcracker* movie schedule since many parents and families were involved in both the ballet and flash mob sequence. Tight scheduling made it all work out. By 4 PM, everything was wrapped up, and the studio was vacated except for some of the movie personnel in Studio C & D. Jasmine was on her best behavior that day, and the *Pas de Deux* with Peter was perfect. Jasmine had been upset because Whitney asked her to stop pushing into her life. Peter seemed to talk some sense into Jasmine. I walked through her parts as an understudy to give my ankle one more day of rest. I could tell the sprain was minor and wouldn't affect my upcoming performance.

I was sitting in the reception area chatting with Tom when I received a text. I looked at my phone and smiled. Barbara arrived a moment later, and I quickly put my phone away, almost as though I was hiding a secret.

"Come on, Mom. It's time to go," I implored.

Bill and Nick arrived from down the hall. Nick buried his face in his hand-held video game.

"Bill, honey, please take Nick home and try to take a nap. We're all due back here at 9 PM for the filming," Barbara spoke to Bill. "And Tom, you can close up. The school is closed for the day... Security will keep an eye on everything else."

Tom nodded and stood up, putting on his coat. "I'll be back at 8:30 to help with the filming. Until then... " Tom walked out the door. The wind caught the door and blew it open. It had surprisingly become blustery, with leaves blowing around, reminding us that winter was on hand.

Bill walked up to Barbara and kissed her goodbye. Barbara gave Nick a hug. "Mommy will be home soon. Get some rest for tonight." Nick ignored her. Bill put his hand around Nick's neck and ushered him out the door.

"OK, young lady. Where are we off to?" asked Barbara. "You're keeping a secret."

"It'll be fun... and just what you need." I slipped my arm through my mother's and escorted her out the front door. We walked a bit through the mall, admiring the decorations. The overabundance of holiday lights truly justified the mall's reputation as the most festive mall in America. I bought two large salted pretzels for both of us.

"Wow, that's been a while... really good," Barbara said while biting her way through the distinctive brown crust and salt.

I took her arm and, after a few more feet, was at the door of the brand-new nail salon. The salon had opened the week before in time for the holidays. Although the lights were on, the place looked vacant, and the door was locked. I knocked on the door. A woman in her thirties unlocked the door and let us in, guiding us to the back of the store. Decorative freestanding screens were used to define specific workstations. The store was very light, clean, and bright.

Whitney jumped out from behind the screen as we approached the last workstation,. She gave Barbara a big and unexpected hug.

"Weeeee, so glad you could make it... just the two of you... I made them hold the store just for us." Whitney was so happy.

Barbara looked around, seeing that it was just the three of us with six workers. "Only us?"

"I bought it out. I wanted this to be special."

Barbara was impressed and self-conscious at the attention as the workers guided each of us to sit down at a station of soaking baths, products, mirrors, and perfumes.

I piped in, "This is great... and a well-kept secret."

"I'll say it was a secret. I had no idea," said Barbara, who looked around and realized that it had been years since the last time she was in a hair or nail salon.

"I've also ordered champagne and some special cookies," said Whitney pointing at the chilled bottles for the workers to open. "And here is some chilled sparkling peach juice for you, Marie, and me." Barbara was given a glass of champagne, whereas Whitney and I sipped our peach juice.

The ladies sat back and allowed the women workers to place our feet in a soaking tub and our hands in smaller bowls.

I yanked my feet out of the tub of water and spoke up. "Oh, I can't have my feet worked on."

Whitney seemed miffed. "Why?"

"Non-dancers wouldn't know this, but a pedicure makes feet swell for a few days, and I won't be able to dance on pointe."

Whitney made a frowny face.

"Maybe sometime when I'm not performing, I could have a pedicure." I gave my best caring face. "I'll love the manicure."

The containers were filled with warm soapy water that steamed with the scent of fresh roses.

Whitney chimed in, "I'm really glad you are here. Having a manicure and pedicure twice a year was something special my mom and I would do. We were so poor, and Mom was a single parent. She saved a little bit each month so we could have our 'girls' day out, just the two of us. I'm so happy that I could do this for you two."

"Oh... you really didn't need to. I mean, your production company has taken care of everything, and you have your own trailer." Barbara was embarrassed by the expense of renting the store out for the three of them. "I bet you have a staff that would give you a manicure every day."

"But then I couldn't have spent this alone time with you two." Whitney lifted her glass to the other two. "And Marie has become a dear friend. You've seen how it is. People constantly surround me, and they all want something. They want my picture, they want my autograph, they want money, they want... want... want... Being here, in this small town and your dance studio, has been refreshing. I mean, you two didn't even know who I am, yet you were always gracious and thoughtful. I feel that I can really talk with you, and you'll give me truth."

Barbara spoke up, "You know, I had a ritual and special time with my mother... I don't think I've told this one to you, Marie. But for a couple of years in elementary school, I was in speech therapy class. I had difficulty hearing and saying words that contained the 'ct' sound such as found in *structure*. So, once a month, my mother, your grand-mom, would pick me up at the school and take me to a special speech center for an hour one-on-one meeting with a speech pathologist. On the way back, there was a taco stand... it's not there anymore... and we would buy some taquitos with guacamole sauce. It was the only Mexican restaurant in the city and fairly exotic for our area. We'd each get one for a dollar and dip it in the savory green sauce. It was all homemade—not like today's fast-food chains. Anyway, it was the only special time I had with Mom that wasn't shared with anyone else in the family. I really miss that special time with her. We could talk about anything, and I was, for that moment, the only one in her life." Barbara choked up when she

138

said, 'only one in her life.' Barbara really missed her mother, who died a few years earlier from cancer.

"I love my mother too," Whitney added in. "She plays the organ at our local church. I was always there with her. When she was learning a new piece, it would often be just her and me on the bench learning the piece together. Then we would teach it to the choir. I admired that she actually wasn't very religious yet played for the church every week. She often mentioned how she didn't agree with the excessiveness of the church and how it seemed to exclude and discriminate against people. She saw Jesus as a great teacher espousing love and acceptance. That's why she loved the music. It was inspiring and preached love... and that music can transcend petty life troubles and hate... I miss my special times with her. I miss singing inspirational songs... not the pop I have to sing to my 'adoring' public. I've had to stop singing at the church when I visit home because of my notoriety. I miss that. It's a shame. But Mom and I do get our manicures; together. The public doesn't bother us there. I get to sing at home with Mom on our small piano. The church time should be about church, and the beautiful music my mother provides, not her famous daughter who overshadows the message of peace and love."

The story piqued my interest. "So, if you hate being a pop star so much, why do you do it?"

"What can I say," said Whitney with a shrug. "I'm rich, famous, and most people envy my life. I guess... guess the perks are enticing. I mean, who wouldn't want to be rich and famous?"

Barbara's eyes were closed. Neither of us said a word. I had no idea what to say, considering Whitney was a roller coaster of emotions.

"I know I can be a bitch sometimes... but I have to be strong when I'm in the public's eye and with my employees... but it can be too much." Whitney became very introspective.

By now, the workers had massaged Barbara's and Whitney's feet, trimmed the nails, cleaned the cuticles, and applied lotion. Barbara and Whitney took another sip of their drinks. This was a special moment for us all. The workers shifted to each of our hands.

Music could be heard through the shop windows, emanating from the mall speakers. Sure enough, it was melodies from the *Nutcracker*. That made me reflect. I realized that I wasn't aware of any 'special' time with my mother. Dance, in itself, was very special, and I spent a lifetime in the beauty of my mother's dance studio and productions of the *Nutcracker*. But special, one-on-one time with my mother, alone, I did not remember. Maybe I was missing something? In the dance studio, there was never alone time with my mother since students, parents, employees, and others always surrounded her. Even when I was alone with my mother, she ignored me to work in the office on something... but, no, no real special time between us. I thought that that was odd and sad.

"What about you, Marie. Any special time with your mother?" Whitney asked.

Barbara's head was tilted back with her eyes closed, luxuriating in the hand massage given her at that moment, but I knew she was listening attentively. I had to be careful how I constructed her answer. Better yet, perhaps I could find a way to divert the question.

"Ballet has always been special and special between my mother and me." I carefully balanced the question without directly answering it. I really didn't want to be put on the spot about my relationship with my mother.

Whitney pried some more. "Isn't there some special time for just the two of you... you know, when you can share intimate details?"

I didn't want to go there. Although my mother was beautiful, a famous ballerina in her day, and very respected, she was not especially warm. Not that she was mean or uncaring, just not someone you would share life issues with. Barbara was one of those people who would give you solutions if you shared a feeling or thought, and often that felt more like a lecture than genuine emotion. I felt trapped and hesitated to speak.

"Mother is always there if you need advice." I knew I didn't share much and didn't answer Whitney directly.

"Don't you have a special friend or two at school?" pushed Whitney.

I squirmed. "I've always hated that question. Answering it makes me seem lame. If you are serious about your art, it's really impossible to have regular friends. They just don't understand. It takes so many hours each day of practice that we just can't 'hang,' and we don't fit in at parties, and then we seem standoffish. Sometimes I wish I could be like the other girls, but I'm not. And I have no interest in 'girl' things like shopping, or gossip, or the like. Only other ballet dancers or classical musicians, or nerds understand what I'm going through. Jasmine is more normal than I am and is popular at school." Whitney scrunched up her nose at the mention of Jasmine's name. "I'm not sure how she does it, but we are not close friends. John is probably my closest friend... I've known him since elementary school, and we both love ballet. But he's more like a close sister than a friend."

Whitney laughed at the idea of John being a 'close sister.' "I think we have all had a best gay male friend. They're about the only ones who allow us to be who we are yet won't take dirt from us and are supportive at the same time." The three ladies laughed. "But, of course, we can't ever be completely close since they are not interested in us that way."

Barbara lifted her champagne glass and sarcastically said, "Amen to that sister." She was a bit tipsy. I was surprised at my mother's attitude.

I explained to Whitney, "Mom's long-time ballet partner and very best friend is Roland. You've seen him around here this week. He is responsible for some of the special effects and greenscreen work. He would never have completely satisfied my mother, not like dad."

Barbara reflected on the conversation and added, "I pined over him for the longest time. Finally had to face the fact that I would never be his wife. I would not be able to change him from being gay. But he is a great friend... don't you think, Marie."

"Yes, Mom, Roland is the best."

"Glad I met your Father. Bill is great, too." Barbara looked a bit forlorn.

"Yes, Mom, Dad is great too," I echoed.

The workers put the finishing touches on our nails. Whitney spoke up, "Ah, don't put any polish on. They're going to be fixing it up very soon for tonight."

"Tonight?" I repeated.

"Yeah, tonight. I'm filming one of the songs tonight during the crowd scene."

"Oh, wow."

"I'm due at the trailer soon so the makeup team can do their thing... it's a new song for the movie. I won't actually be singing but rather lip-syncing while I move through the flash mob."

"We're going to be there. We're part of the flash mob." I became very excited. "We'll be there together!"

For the past hour, the three ladies totally forgot about their busy lives: the rehearsals, the show, the filming, everything. It was relaxing. Maybe Whitney was onto something to share a manicure and pedicure with her mother ever so often.

"Where'd the time fly," Barbara spoke up. "We need to get home, Marie, and pick up your dad and Nick for the flash mob later tonight."

"Wasn't that fun?" Whitney joined in.

"Thank you. Thank you." I gave Whitney a big hug.

I beamed at mother, who seemed relaxed and in good spirits. I placed my arm through mother's arm and guided her out the door. "Maybe we should make this a tradition between the two of us?"

Barbara smiled.

Whitney gave me a 'call me later' signal with her hands and then waved. Whitney seemed happy, too.

*

19 — Flash Mob

The crowd near the center of the mall was crushing. Although the mall had closed at 9 PM, it was a well-known secret that Whitney would be there that night to film her new single for *Nutcracker the Musical* coming out next year. The Stewart twins were also going to be on stage for an extended time. There was media everywhere and TV station vans with large satellite dishes. It was a circus.

Luckily, the weather was still holding out. It was cold, and having everyone bundled up in heavy jackets reinforced the impression that it was winter, which was important for the film's style. And the mall's bright and colorful Christmas lights on every building, tree, lamppost, and bush, exaggerated the festive spirit exemplified in the *Nutcracker*.

A computer store anchored at one end of the mall's central courtyard. The main walkway passed in front of the computer store and emptied into a circular center with a pond and water fountain display. An outdoor ice-skating rink was installed for the season, allowing skaters to be encircled by holiday displays and lights as they glided on the ice.

The families and children hired to dance the flash mob assembled a bit away from the computer store on the main street. Lights for filming were arranged around the computer store entrance leaving the space in front of the store open for dancing and more. In the instructions given to the flash mob dancers, it was explained that the traditional music for the *Nutcracker* was being rearranged to accommodate the story better as it unfolded in the mall setting. Now, the first number was going to be the March using a marching band coming down the main walkway. The camera would follow the band as it passed by the computer store. Then Clara and her family and friends would be introduced to the film while Godfather Drosselmeier bought computer tablets and other electronic devices for each child and adult. This would lead to a dance between parents and children using computer tablets in very inventive ways.

Bill, Barbara, Nick, Peter, Sheila, and I, along with Sheila's parents, stood in the walkway with the other flash mob dancers. John was a distance off with his family, also participating in the crowd flash mob.

Paul climbed a stepladder and faced the crowd using his bullhorn. "MAY I HAVE YOUR ATTENTION... PLEASE QUIET DOWN... WE WILL BE STARTING THE STREET SCENE IN A FEW MINUTES. AS WE PRACTICED IN THE STUDIO, YOU ARE TO MILL AROUND, AND ONCE THE MARCH MUSIC BEGINS, MOVE BACK ALONG THE SIDEWALK TO LET THE MARCHING BAND THROUGH."

The marching band took up position at the end of the walkway. The crowd mingled about. There were cameras on trailers, overhead beams, and a handheld in the center. The Director took over the bullhorn, "POSITION ONE... LIGHTS... " many of the floods were turned off, and spots came up on the crowd, "SPEED... ACTION."

My family milled around with the other crowd members trying not to look at the camera as we were instructed in practice. The *Miniature Overture* from the *Nutcracker* played over the speakers. I knew that the crowd scenes and opening music would be used for the movie titles and opening credits. Different cameras zoomed in on different sets of people walking, looking in windows, and more. All this would be edited into an exciting opening sequence.

"CUT," called out the Director. He walked over to the monitor table and reviewed the shots with Paul. Surprisingly, the shots and lighting were well done.

Paul climbed the ladder again and used the bullhorn, "THAT WAS GREAT. WE ARE MOVING ONTO THE MARCH. EVERYONE PLEASE BACK UP TO THE SIDEWALK AND ACT LIKE YOU ARE WATCHING A PASSING PARADE."

My family and Peter moved to the sidewalk, putting Nick and Sheila in front so we could see. The street opened up, revealing the marching band at one end. The marching band had truly colorful uniforms, mostly a rich red fabric with white fronts and gold edging.

The Director spoke on the bullhorn, "POSITIONS... LIGHTS... SPEED... ACTION."

A handheld camera and best boy ran down the center of the street toward the band holding the camera inches off the ground to capture the marching feet and legs. The crane-mounted camera also swooped in. The Drum Major gave a four-beat countdown and stepped off as the band began to play Tchaikovsky's March.

I was surprised at how loud it was. Being that close to brass instruments was an eye-opening experience. The March had never sounded so full or strong and bright before. I wondered why no one had ever used a marching band for the *Nutcracker March*. It seemed such a perfect fit.

Nick and Sheila really enjoyed all the action and bounced around and clapped their hands in joy. Most of the crowd really got into it, with lots of laughing and clapping.

The drum major stepped off to the side when he came to the central camera and held his place. Obviously, he had been instructed to take that position to better frame the marching band in the camera as it went by.

The band marched in perfect step with the music. At the musical transition that occurs about halfway through the music, the cheerleaders and flag twirlers burst through the center of the band. I hadn't noticed they were in the crowd, but they brought an exciting change to the repetitive marching. I imagined how good this would look when edited together.

When the band passed the central camera and played its last notes, the crowd flowed into the street, filling in from side to side.

"CUT. HOLD POSITION," yelled the Director.

The musicians lowered their arms, and everyone relaxed while staying in place. Paul and the Director reviewed the monitors. The sound technician was also actively discussing the take.

MARCH WITH MARCHING BAND, FLASH MOB, AND SKATEBOARDERS

The Director took the bullhorn and climbed the ladder. "IT WAS A GOOD TAKE, BUT THERE IS TOO MUCH BACKGROUND NOISE. THIS IS LIVE MUSIC PLAYED BY A LIVE BAND. WE MUST BE ABLE TO PICK IT UP WITH NO ADDITIONAL NOISE. SO, PLEASE, THE CROWD, NO TALKING DURING THE SHOOT. TURN OFF ALL PHONES. YOU MAY CLAP BUT WITHOUT MAKING NOISE. <u>ACT</u> LIKE YOU ARE HAVING FUN, BUT DON'T MAKE ANY SOUND. LET'S DO IT ONE MORE TIME. BACK TO POSITION ONE."

The Director turned to the very large crowd outside the perimeter. "WE ALSO NEED ALL OF YOU TO BE QUIET. IF YOU ARE NOISY, YOU WILL BE ESCORTED FROM THE GROUNDS."

With so many people, band members, and cheerleaders, besides camera and film technicians, it took a while for everyone to get back to the opening position. I hoped it would be a good take since many people were involved.

The second take went just as well as the first take. The band sparkled, and the music was clear. I found it odd seeing people in the crowd clapping hands and laughing without making a sound. But the strategy helped, and the scene did not need to be reshot.

Paul climbed the ladder and spoke, "GREAT WORK EVERYONE. THE BAND IS RELEASED. THANK YOU FOR ALL YOUR SUPPORT. PLEASE LEAVE THE SET... "

Paul spoke with the Director standing next to the ladder and resumed talking on the bullhorn. "WE ARE NEXT GOING TO FILM THE FLASH MOB SEQUENCE. PLEASE GET INTO POSITIONS THAT WE SET IN THE STUDIO. I WILL BE AROUND TO HELP SET THIS UP."

Paul climbed down the ladder and entered the mob in the center of the main walkway in front of the computer store. He grabbed certain people and guided them into better positions in relation to the camera. Just then, Whitney appeared at the door entrance to the computer store. A makeup artist was still touching up her face and spraying her hair. A lighting technician checked light levels around her, noting them down on a chart while speaking into a headphone. Sandra initially stood next to her. Although Whitney was known to be at the dance studio, very few people had seen her. People whispered her name in a chain reaction that reached the outside crowd. A roar of gasps and sounds of bodies squeezing by each other escaped from the crowd. A rush of cell phones lifted overhead and tried to take pictures of Whitney on the set.

The Director was an old pro with similar situations. He knew it was best to let the crowd do its thing for about ten minutes before enforcing quiet on the set. That would allow all the neck-craning and picture-taking to die down since Whitney would simply be standing still. He was prepared to make multiple takes of the sequence, considering the crowd would surely be noisy the first time through. The Director knew it was important to balance optimal filming conditions and public access to stars.

It really had not sunk into me what was happening during the flash mob scene. I knew it was simple, big steps and that a stand-in walked to various parts of the set while the music was playing. It just hadn't occurred to me that it was going to be Whitney. Of course, that was a reasonable assumption, just that I hadn't thought that far through the number since a stand-in actor was used during rehearsal.

Paul yelled over the bullhorn, "WE'RE GOING TO WALK THROUGH THE NUMBER. PLEASE FOLLOW MY COUNT... FIVE, SIX, SEVEN EIGHT... ONE, TWO, THREE, FOUR, AND ONE... " Paul counted the number out, and the crowd marked the steps they had learned in the studio. Whitney and the stand-in walked down from the front door into the crowd facing a handheld camera the entire time. In the crowd, she did some of the steps and other times interacted with members of the crowd. At one point, she spotted Barbara, Peter, and me and gave us a nod. The number was about three minutes long, with many repeats in the simple choreography.

"... FIVE, SIX, SEVEN, AND STOP. HOLD POSITION." Paul turned to the crowd. "ARE THERE ANY QUESTIONS?" he yelled over the bullhorn. "OK, NO QUESTIONS. BACK TO POSITION ONE. THIS WILL BE A TAKE." Paul turned to the crowd behind

149

the perimeter tape, "AND WE MUST HAVE IT QUIET OUT THERE. YOU WILL BE REMOVED IF YOU MAKE NOISE OR FLASH CAMERAS."

Nick spoke up to Barbara, "Mom, this isn't fun anymore."

It had been about two hours of standing in the mall walkway in the cold. It was getting very late for young children.

"Honey, we probably will do this just two more times, and then we can go. We'll get some fast food on the way home!! You'll like that."

Sheila's parents leaned into Barbara and added, "Sheila's tired too. After this take, we'll leave regardless. We could take Nick if you want."

Barbara was relieved, "Oh, thank you. We'll talk after the next take. Thanks." Barbara was also feeling tired but felt it was important to be there supporting our family in this once-in-a-lifetime opportunity.

The Director climbed the ladder and used the bullhorn to announce, "TAKE POSITION... LIGHTS... SPEED... ACTION."

The music coming over the speakers was the same as used during rehearsal. It was bland and a generic simplified version of one of the melodies in the *Nutcracker*. It sounded like Karaoke background music that one would sing over. Whitney came out of the computer store singing, but her voice was almost inaudible. She was just one small person in a large crowd, and her voice was impossible to hear. I was surprised and confused. I thought that I would have heard Whitney's voice over the loudspeakers. Everyone kept dancing, and Whitney wound herself through the crowd. When Whitney came near my family, she made a direct path to me. For a short while, she embraced me and looked like she was singing to me. The handheld camera caught the girl's happy and playful expressions. Then Whitney worked her way down the walkway toward the mall fountains ending in front of the display of colored lights spraying high. It was a nice, strong ending.

"CUT," called out the Director. "RETURN TO POSITION ONE."

Paul came up to me. "Marie, it looks like Whitney will be directly relating to you, so let me give you some pointers for the next take... "

Sheila's parents spoke with Bill and Barbara. I could see that they were discussing leaving the set to get Nick and Sheila home. Peter was also in the conversation. Barbara cut into Paul's instructions to speak with me.

"Honey, we're taking the kids home. Peter has agreed to bring you home once filming is done... OK?" Barbara gave me a sad and tired look.

"Uh, OK... sorry, Paul."

Paul continued, "When Whitney comes up, look her in the eyes at first, then look off in the same direction that she looks. If you stare at her, it is a bit creepy. If she pulls you in a direction, stop dancing and go with it. Only when she moves on do you pick up and continue dancing."

Peter came up and stood next to me and listened in.

"Oh, good, Peter. If Whitney continues on for, say, ten seconds with Marie, please come up alongside Marie and play along. We can't control everything Whitney does, but we can give her a small audience here and there. People like the personal touch on these songs."

I felt that I needed to ask. "We couldn't hear her sing last time. Is there something wrong?"

Paul laughed. "Oh, no, no. She's hearing something completely different on her earpiece." Paul touched his ear. "We really don't want people to hear the real song until it comes out next year. So, she is singing the correct song so her lips match the visuals, but the full song will be laid in later during processing... Last thing we need is all these cell phones recording her new song and spreading it before it is officially released next year."

"Oh, makes sense. Now I understand," I concluded.

The second take was very similar to the first. Whitney was a pro who could hit her marks repeatedly and accurately. She lingered to sing to me, allowing Peter to enter the scene. Whitney genuinely looked happy while singing. I had a lot of fun.

After the take, cameras needed to be repositioned, and the Director called for a half-hour break. Whitney came over, placed her arm through my and Peter's, and walked together to the TV crews and crowd. I didn't know what to make of it. Cameras constantly flashed like a swarm of fireflies. Whitney took us directly to one of the news reporters set up to conduct a quick interview.

Whitney spoke to Peter and me, "Just go along with it. I need to say a few words to the local media. It's part of my job."

The news reporter shook Whitney's hand and directed her to a folding director's chair. The camera came in close to Whitney's face. The lights were blinding.

The reporter shoved a microphone toward Whitney. "I'm speaking here with Whitney Smith, one of the biggest pop singers in the world today. It is an honor that you are in our small town. Tell us, what are you doing here?"

"Bless up. I'm here filming some cool songs for *Nutcracker the Musical* dat will be released next year. Swerve turnt. I'm hanging with Marie and Peter, my mains while I'm here. Hey guys, come over." Whitney sure could turn on that teen street slang when needed.

Whitney waved Peter and me over to her side.

"Marie and Peter are the stars of the *Nutcracker Ballet* playing here next week. You should all come. Yaaasssss."

I was caught off guard by Whitney's proclamation. I was well aware that I was the understudy and Jasmine the star, but Whitney wouldn't let me clarify. I felt very awkward. Cameras flashed in my eyes, which made me blink.

"Well, thank you, Whitney Smith. Anything more to add?"

"It's been cool. Nice peeps here. Good place to moss. Gotta dip." Whitney got up from the chair, walked down the security border, signed autographs, and stood for selfies with the crowd. Unnoticed were Whitney's security guards. They were never far off. After twenty minutes, the Assistant Director pulled Whitney from the crowd. Peter and I walked back with Whitney to the catering tent. We were famished from the hours on the set and needed something to tide us over.

Paul spoke into the bullhorn, "READY FOR SCENE 12. WE NEED THE CROWD MILLING AROUND READY FOR THE FLASH MOB ROUTINE."

"Uh, we need to go," Peter said to Whitney and me. "We're in the flash mob again."

"OK, I'll catch you tomorrow. I'm done with my one song tonight. I sing again on greenscreen in a couple of days." Whitney made the 'phone me' hand signal to me.

Peter and I rushed over to the main walkway.

I spoke up, "You know, for all the complexity in Whitney's life, she is basically a good girl, just caught up in what everyone wants her to be."

Paul continued over the bullhorn, "TO REVIEW THE SEQUENCE. DROSSELMEIER, FAMILY AND KIDS COME OUT OF THE COMPUTER STORE, THEN THE TABLET DANCE SEQUENCE ENDING WITH THE FLASH MOB."

Peter and I took up position along the walkway near the Apple store. John and some of the girls from the dance studio were at the other end of the walkway.

"POSITION... LIGHTS... SPEED... ACTION," called the Director.

Music that typically is used for the arrival of Drosselmeier to the family home came over the speakers. In this case, Roland playing Drosselmeier, arrived with great fanfare in front of the computer store, greeting other actors playing the family. Bonnie, of the famous Stewart Twins, was there playing the part of Clara as she had in the previous nights. The camera followed them into the store, where they emerged carrying packages. The children ripped open the packages revealing that they all had brand-new computer tablets. Drosselmeier gathered the children around and showed them a camera that he was carrying. He demonstrated that what he aimed the camera at showed up on all the computer tablets through Bluetooth. The kids then danced a sequence holding their tablets. Sometimes the tablets showed different pictures; other times, they showed what Drosselmeier was aiming his camera.

COMPUTER TABLET DANCE DURING *ACT 1 DROSSELMEIER GIVING GIFTS*

One time, he aimed his camera at a small dog one of the family members carried. This was spread over the ten tablets to expand the image many feet high. Everyone laughed. Seeing a dog's face over ten feet tall was so cute. It was so immense, and the tablets moved around that it felt like *Clifford the Big Red Dog* from the TV show, ready to lick your face. Near the end of the dance, a group of skateboarders skated in formation and included a quick dance routine.

I was impressed by how computer tablets were incorporated into the children's dance of the *Nutcracker*. Although the traditional dance was appropriate for the 1800s, it does not resonate with today's kids. Really, how many kids today relate to a 'hobby horse' toy? I appreciated the effort to make a dance sequence kids of today would relate to without it becoming street dancing, hip-hop, or break dancing. Too often, attempting to make something *cool* makes it dated and trite.

At the end of the computer tablet dance, the family, Clara, and the children actors walked into the crowd toward the mall center fountain and ice-skating rink. It was at that moment the flash mob sequence began. Peter and I had a grand time. There was no pressure for us to relate to Whitney, and we blended into the back of the crowd. It was a relaxing way to end the long day.

Although Peter and I were in the crowd, we were alone; no parents or students were around. Many times we held hands and waists. Peter came in very close to me; so close I thought he would kiss me. I was both ecstatic and confused. I was uncertain how I felt about liking Peter.

"CUT... THAT WAS GREAT EVERYONE... IT'S A WRAP," called out the Director.

I felt exhausted. "Whew!! Am I tired... from everything."

"Same here," added Peter.

Bonnie, as Clara, walked over to the crowd to give autographs to the adoring fans.

"I guess the scene where the Nutcracker doll is broken by the bratty brother and Clara falling asleep will be filmed next week on the greenscreen?" I asked.

"Not sure. I didn't see that on our instructions."

"We can ask Paul or Roland later."

"I'm sure Paul will know. Who's Roland?" asked Peter.

"Oh, you haven't met Roland, yet? You will. He's in charge of the special effects on the greenscreen next week."

"That should be fun. Never did that kind of work before."

Most of the lights were turned off, and the crowd dissipated after Bonnie finished giving autographs and being interviewed by the local press. Peter and I picked up a few cookies in the catering tent to eat on the way home. It was an exhausting yet very fun day. So many new activities, new sights, new information, and growing friendships filled my head; not with images of dancing sugar plums, but of the marching band, Whitney singing and becoming a closer friend to Peter, and dancing incognito in the flash mob— and all in the setting of Christmas lights, decorations, and splendor. Life couldn't be better.

*

20 — Jasmine Goes Too Far

"You lying skank! You two-time lying cow. You're not the star, I am... and Whitney... Whitney is my friend, not yours," Jasmine screamed at me.

"But, but... it wasn't me," I pleaded.

"And on TV yet... you low... " Jasmine stammered as she ran out of breath and was filled with rage, "I can't even!"

Jasmine yelled directly in my face and paced back and forth like a caged animal. Sunday morning rehearsal at the studio should have been routine. With only a week left before opening night for the *Nutcracker Ballet*, everyone's nerves were on edge.

Barbara stepped in to reduce the tension. "Girls, girls, calm down. Marie couldn't control what Whitney said on TV."

"But, I'm the star... not her," whined Jasmine.

"Yes, you are. And today, we will be taking more publicity shots of you and Peter showing the world that you are the star." Barbara brushed the tears from Jasmine's cheek, "now, we don't want your face puffy, do we?"

Jasmine calmed down but gave dagger eyes toward me.

"Come on. This is our last studio rehearsal before the show next week." Barbara looked around Studio A at all the children, parents, and other dancers there to work on Act 1. Although it was early morning, the room was stuffy. "And we're still fitting some costumes."

The room was very full. Act 1 tends to have a large cast with six to eight sets of parents, six to eight sets of young boys and girls, and six to eight sets of teenage girls and boys, Drosselmeier and Clara. Because the Nutcracker does not come to life until Act 2, Peter was not at the early rehearsal but would be there later that day to take photos with Jasmine.

"Let's take it from when Drosselmeier hands the Nutcracker doll to Clara." Barbara pointed to one side of the room— "Roland, over there"— and pointed to the other side of the room— "Jasmine, over here"—following up with directions— "Marie, be sure to shadow Jasmine. OK, positions."

The parents and other children were spread around the room, mostly standing bored. Some leaned against the ballet *barre*. A very large mechanical device lay on the ground from corner to corner along one wall. This was the Christmas tree prop designed to unroll like a window shade but in an upward direction. It would pull up from the ground to the roof. On the fabric was painted a Christmas tree that got larger and larger the taller it got. When fully extended, the bottom branches are very large to imply the actors on stage are small. This would be used at the end of Act 1 when Clara fell asleep. It would be pulled up, giving the impression that Clara has shrunk to the size of a mouse or doll.

Roland carried the Nutcracker doll and handed it to Jasmine. She clutched the doll and rocked side to side like she was dancing with it.

"That's the way, Jasmine. Look happy. Now," Barbara pointed to the other children, "the rest of you come in and make a ring about Jasmine and skip to the music." Barbara was pleased with the direction. "Now reach for the doll... now, Jasmine run from the group clutching the doll." Jasmine followed the direction. "Now, Josh, run over and grab the doll and smash it to the ground."

Josh was one of the boys recruited to be in the ballet. He really didn't want to be there, but he got to play Clara's bratty brother. The part played particularly well to his natural inclination. Josh grabbed the doll harshly, took it from Jasmine's hands, and aggressively threw it down to the ground, breaking its head off.

Jasmine looked at Roland, took his hand, and then ran over to pick up the doll pieces. She handed the broken doll to Roland and pleaded with him to repair the doll. He placed his hand on her shoulders to console her.

"Good, good, Jasmine. Good acting." Barbara looked around the room for the man playing Clara's father. "Father, Father, where are you. You should be reprimanding the boy."

"Oh, oh, yes. I'm here," spoke up one of the bored men. He quickly walked over and grabbed the boy by his ear lobe.

A cell phone in the back of the room was heard playing Beyoncé *Single Ladies (Put a Ring on It)*. It was very loud.

"ALL THE SINGLE LADIES. ALL THE SINGLE LADIES."

Everyone turned to see who it was. The bearded plaid-shirt father fumbled the phone out of his pocket to turn it off. The song didn't match his gruff persona. It was ironic and funny at the same time. He dropped the phone.

CLATTER.

Of course, as he picked it up, he had to check the message to see if it was 'important' before putting it back in his pocket.

Barbara gave an icy stare to the father. "PLEASE, keep all cell phones off during rehearsal." The man gave a sheepish thumbs-up sign to Barbara.

During the cell phone break, another father was goofing around on the ballet *barre*, trying to put his leg up on the top rail, drawing attention to his antics.

"You, you... what are you doing back there?" inquired Barbara.

"We weren't told what to do. We're just standing here," said the man.

Barbara looked around the room, trying to spot Bill. "I thought Bill directed you."

Bill was over in the corner. He stepped forward and raised his hands with palms turned upward in defeat. Obviously, he had taught the routine, but the father was confused.

"It's just like last year. It's always the same... OK, OK, change in plans. Marie, Roland, Jasmine, take a break. Uh, Jasmine, try on your costume. All the fathers, mothers, and children stay. We're going to walk through the opening scene and dance again."

Jasmine looked disgusted and took the Nutcracker over to the piano for safekeeping before walking out the side door. Roland and I followed behind, exiting into the hallway.

Barbara yelled out, "don't go too far. We'll be ready in a few minutes."

She turned to the parents and children, "Remember, this is a Christmas Party. You are the parents. The children will dance, and Godfather Drosselmeier comes in with a magical Nutcracker... "

Outside in the hallway, Roland and I sat on one of the long benches lining the wall. No one else was around since Jasmine was down in costuming trying on her nightgown used at the end of Act 1.

"I don't know how your mother can do this year after year. She's such a trooper," Roland said with a sigh.

"She loves it."

"I mean, I loved to dance, but the grueling rehearsal with so many non-dancers. I was fortunate enough to dance with some of the best."

I did not respond or add to his comment. Roland was just thinking out loud.

Roland asked me, "Do you plan on auditioning for one of the big companies?"

"I think so... actually, I don't know. After seeing Peter and Jasmine this year, I just don't think I have what it takes. Then again, I had so much fun in the professional classes. That was an eye-opening experience... and when I dance with Peter, I'm much stronger."

The *Gallop* and the *Dance of the Parents* music streamed through Studio A doors.

"Peter?"

"Mom hired Peter this year to be our Nutcracker. He won the New York Metropolitan ballet competition. Jasmine is so lucky. He's so good."

A sly smile came over Roland's face. He knew something that he was not sharing with me.

"You enjoy dancing with him?"

"He's really good and, dare I say, dreamy... a real prince. I find myself thinking about him a lot. But I'm no match. I'm sure Jasmine has him wrapped around her finger. She gets any guy she wants."

"Peter? What's his last name?"

"Blair. I think it's Blair."

A very large smile came over Roland's face.

Just then, Jasmine stormed down the hallway screaming at the top of her lungs. Beatrice followed a few feet behind. Jasmine grabbed the top of her costume and yelled, "LOOK AT IT! LOOK AT IT!!! We'll see. Barbara will tell you."

Jasmine was wearing the nightgown costume for the end of Act 1 and used it in the rest of the ballet. It was extremely tight across her breasts. The tightness pulled the fabric, thereby shortening its length, making it look like a Baby Doll nightgown. It was not flattering and made her look fat.

Jasmine and Beatrice swooshed by Roland and me and burst through Rehearsal Hall A doors.

Roland took my hand and chuckled, "Oh, I don't think you have anything to worry about."

Roland and I stood up and followed them into Studio A.

Jasmine rushed up to Barbara, "Look at it... I look like a *slut*."

John and a few other dancers in the room smirked with their faces agreeing with her assessment.

Beatrice tried to save the situation and said, "I could let it out some, but then it won't fit Marie."

Jasmine demanded, "Make another. I'm the star. Just make another."

Barbara reached out and pulled at the fabric. "I don't know if we have enough time." Barbara waved me to come over. Every eye in the room was focused on the drama. "It fits Marie just fine."

Jasmine was infuriated. "She has no breasts. She's flat as a board. It's no wonder she can't get a boyfriend." Jasmine was on a roll and taking potshots at anyone nearby.

I felt deeply humiliated. Although it was commonly known that many women ballet dancers or, for that fact, long-distance runners, and other very athletic women, have small breasts, it was a different thing to have a peer yell it to a room of strangers. Jasmine went too far.

Barbara spoke up, "Jasmine, that's enough... control yourself."

Beatrice still fiddled with the costume, pulling fabric here and there. "She is a little more... uh... full up there."

"I'm a woman, not a little girl. I'm the star. Make me another costume," demanded Jasmine.

Beatrice looked confused. She was perplexed about how to make one costume fit two girls with very different body dimensions.

Barbara deduced that two different costumes would be needed. She called Beatrice and asked, "Is it possible to make another?"

Beatrice's shoulders slumped, and she looked at the clock on the wall. All of a sudden, she looked very tired and worn. "Uh, OK... I'll fit it in."

Jasmine was triumphant. She gloated at her victory.

"OK, Jasmine, take it off. Give it to Marie," Barbara directed.

Jasmine gleefully pulled the costume off and gave, actually threw, it to me like a worn dish towel. Barbara looked around the room, then up at the clock, and then back to the room full of people trying to decide what to do.

*

21 — Christmas Trees and Mice Don't Mix

Barbara spoke to the room, "Let's call it a day for the parents and children dancers of Act 1. You may go. We're going to go onto Clara sleeping and Act 2 Battle of the Mouse King... All the boys and girls who are mice, go put on your costumes and take up position. Boys and girls who are soldiers, please put on your costumes and come right back. Will someone find Peter?"

For a good twenty minutes, there was a flurry of dancers coming and going carrying pieces of costumes and being in various stages of dress. Beatrice was everywhere at once, helping many dancers with their costumes. This was the first time everyone was together wearing his or her costumes for a run-through. Sheila and Nick were off to one side, putting on their mouse costumes.

Peter entered the studio dressed in the Nutcracker costume. The red military-style jacket with gold epaulets and trim really showed off against his white tights. His musculature and good looks made him the perfect Nutcracker Prince. He was carrying his Nutcracker headpiece under his right arm. After the battle, the Nutcracker's headpiece magically comes off in a cloud of smoke, revealing his handsome human self. Most male dancers complain about how uncomfortable the Nutcracker headpiece is and how difficult it is to see out of it.

Roland walked over to Peter, grabbed the headpiece, and placed it over Peter's head. Peter moved around a bit to see how well it stayed on. Peter pulled off the headpiece, and Roland reached in to adjust one of the chinstraps. Once adjusted, Roland helped Peter put the headpiece back on. Peter ran out to the dance floor and did a series of jumps and turns—all needed for his battle scene with the Mouse King. The headpiece held fast. Peter was pleased, walked over to Roland, and took the headpiece off until it was needed. Both Roland and Peter talked some more and laughed some more. Needless to say, Roland was sharing stories about the days when he danced the Nutcracker Prince role.

At one point, Roland placed his arm over Peter's shoulders for a private conversation. While we were talking and laughing, Peter looked over the room to notice me looking at them. He gave me a thumbs-up OK sign. At that moment, Jasmine butted in between the two men and gave Peter a hug and kiss on his cheek. Peter did not hug her back and just stood with his arms at his side. Roland stepped back with a look of disdain while she walked to the center of the room. I didn't know quite what to make of all this.

"Come on, everybody. We need to get into position to run the end of Act 1 and the battle. Where's Marie?" asked Barbara.

In the large room with about ten mice and twenty soldiers plus the Christmas tree mechanism and assorted parents and friends, the room was very cluttered and easy to miss spotting someone.

Jasmine stood in the center of the room. She was in her usual tights, leotard, and small skirt and looked insolent. I took up position behind her as the understudy. I wore the nightgown over my black leotard with spaghetti straps with pink tights. Wearing a black leotard under the costume did not compliment the look. I couldn't have looked any less attractive than I did at that moment.

"Oh, good. You are both here in position. Roland, I need you to take the broken Nutcracker from Jasmine, make a quick magical repair, and hand it back to her."

While the dancers were blocking out the scene where Clara lay down to sleep, Nick and Sheila conversed near the back of the room next to the Christmas tree mechanism. They were both in their mouse costume but holding their headpieces. They'd put on their heads only when needed since they were so confining and hot.

"I hate this," Sheila spoke up.

"It's amusing and brings pleasure to the tiny children," Nick replied.

"I want to be one of the ballerinas."

"And become a self-absorbed, histrionic drama queen like Jasmine?... Besides, when else can you be a mouse and observe the reactions in humans to anthropomorphize animals."

Sheila adjusted her glasses when Nick spoke.

"We also get to be Christmas trees during the Russian Dance. What could be more educational to impress young minds with the sanctity of nature?" Nick truly could not be nerdier.

"You're smart," added Sheila.

"I want to be an anthropologist."

Sheila did not understand what Nick said and looked blankly.

"An anthropologist... I want to study peoples and cultures and their interactions," Nick said matter-of-factly like an encyclopedia.

"Cool. I like you."

There was that awkward social moment when two young nerds stared at each other, not knowing what more to say.

Barbara spoke up. "We'll take it from the lights dimming down, and Clara goes to bed. Are the workers ready with the Christmas tree mechanism?" The man who operated the equipment gave thumbs up.

One advantage of such a large studio with soaring ceilings and support beams is that the space could be completely outfitted with lights, pulleys, and mechanisms used on stage. That allowed for rehearsals to include all the technical needs of the show. The Christmas tree mechanism was powered by an electric winch that pulled the large backdrop up from the ground to the top of the ceiling, unfurling the cloth and revealing a painting of a large Christmas tree. The lower branches were the thickness of a person and extended from one side of the stage to the other, thereby giving the impression that Clara had shrunk to the size of a mouse or toy. One person pushing a start switch controlled the equipment.

"Everyone, please take position," Barbara yelled to the room.

Jasmine picked up the Nutcracker doll from the piano and walked to her position next to the bed.

Barbara started the music.

Jasmine hugged the Nutcracker doll and danced a slow waltz holding him out like a partner. She was very good at acting, and she truly loved the doll. As the music continued, she crawled into bed, clutching the doll. I, as the understudy, stood a few feet behind Jasmine and mimicked her the entire scene.

Jasmine squirmed a bit on the bed. Her feet got tangled up in the quilt. Unbeknownst to her, the Nutcracker doll dropped to the floor.

Barbara spoke up, "Good. Now dim the lights."

That was the clue for all the mice, including Nick and Sheila, to put on their mouse headpiece and for the worker to start the Christmas tree mechanism.

The music swelled as the tree began to unfurl.

The mouse headpiece and dimmed lights made it very difficult for Nick and Sheila to see what was happening.

Sheila spoke up to Nick, "I can't see!" The headpiece had knocked Sheila's glasses such that they were at an angle and hanging from her nose. With the headpiece on, Sheila couldn't reach her glasses to adjust them.

Nick agreed, "I can't either."

The cross-support rod of the Christmas tree mechanism caught the edge of Nick's costume. He squirmed but was not able to free himself. As the mechanism rose off the ground, so did Nick. Musical note by musical note, Nick was lifted foot-by-foot into the air, ending up fifteen feet above the floor.

Nick yelled for help, but no one could hear his muffled cries through the mouse headpiece. "Help! Help!" he shouted to no avail.

The tree fully extended as the music hit its full crescendo.

Barbara directed.

Jasmine rose from the bed. She hadn't noticed that she accidentally kicked the Nutcracker doll toward the middle of the floor.

Nick continued to squirm. "Help! I'm stuck. I'm up here," Nick yelled.

166

This time the music was soft enough that Nick could be heard.

"Nick is stuck," Sheila yelled out across the room.

Jasmine turned around and looked at the Christmas tree mechanism toward the source of the yell for help. "What? What's going on?"

Barbara hadn't become fully aware of what was happening and turned off the music. "Someone, turn on the lights."

Once the lights came up, everyone could see Nick hanging precariously in the air. Some children laughed at the odd situation, seeing a mouse flaying away in the air on the edge of a giant Christmas tree. Nick pulled off his headpiece and let it drop to the floor with a loud CRASH.

Barbara yelled, "Nick... what are you doing up there?" Too many years of being Nick's mother made Barbara skeptical of his feigned innocence.

"Help. I can't get down."

It was funny. Even Barbara stifled a laugh. "Honey stop moving around. We don't want you falling." Barbara looked toward the Christmas tree mechanism technician and gave him quick directions to lower the boom. "Lower the tree... carefully." Nick was brought safely down to the floor, where he retrieved his mouse headpiece. Many of the people in the room laughed.

Jasmine was distraught by the mishap. "This isn't funny... this isn't funny. What am I doing here with this amateurish company?" She stomped around, angry that her moments on stage were interrupted.

Barbara took the snafu in stride, staring at the ceiling and then looking over to her husband, Bill, and Roland for assurance.

NICK IN A PRECARIOUS SITUATION

She rushed for the door and pushed me out of the way, saying, "Cow!"

Barbara had no choice but to go after Jasmine and try to calm her down. Although she shouldn't have had to tolerate Jasmine's behavior, the show must go on at this point, and she would do anything to keep it all together. Barbara sighed and walked after her. While walking out the door, she gave directions to Roland and me, "I need the two of you to keep the rehearsal going. Run the Battle of the Mouse King."

Peter walked over to me and put his arm over my shoulders.

Barbara asked loudly, "What more could go wrong today?"

Peter laughed, "She could start eating."

I gave a muffled laugh.

Roland heard the comment and shook his head with a smirk. "OK, let's begin. We need to finish this rehearsal."

*

22 — Tossing and Turning

After weeks of stable but chilly weather, a storm front moved into the area, with heavy rains projected to last a day or two. Luckily, the temperature had not dropped, and snow was not in the immediate forecast. The outdoor filming at the mall was completed except for the *Waltz of the Snowflakes,* scheduled in a few days. The weather would break by then. The only other filming for *Nutcracker the Musical* was scheduled indoors at a nearby green-screen facility downtown.

The rain and wind blew fall leaves around yards and against building sides and windows. Small gusts of wind had a life of their own, making windowpanes rattle in anticipation of the coming winter snow. Winter was definitely coming to the Northeast.

Barbara and I sat in my bedroom reviewing photos for the program and advertising. Pictures were strewn across the bed and desktop. Rain pelted the bedroom windows. The room was warm, cozy, and bright, offering a refuge from the coming storm.

In the background, I played Chopin's *Nocturne in D flat* on my music system. Probably no other composer speaks to the heart of ballet dancers more than Chopin. And most melodies, like the Nocturne in D flat, have an underlying melancholy that is always so expressive. A collection of Chopin pieces was assembled into what is known as *Les Sylphides* and choreographed by Michael Fokine in the late 1800s and performed at the Mariinsky Theater in Saint Petersburg in 1907. His melodic tunes are so danceable and allow for deep expression, accents, and counterpoint. I often played Chopin when alone.

I was comfortable in my pajamas with Prima asleep in my lap. The puppies had grown so much in the past weeks and were fast asleep in a pile of adorable cuteness against my thigh and close to Prima.

Barbara picked up one of the photos. "This is an excellent shot of Peter and Jasmine. If we crop here and here… " she used a marker to indicate the crop points, "that could be used for our ads and program. What do you think?" She handed the photo to me.

"It really is the best one. The red jacket and hat really show off Peter's smile."

Prima lifted her head and poked her nose to look at the photo.

A strong wind came up and rattled the windows. It was getting blustery outside.

Barbara glanced at the window and said, "Good. I'll get this to the publicist tomorrow if I can get through this weather."

I gingerly handed back the photo. I found Peter attractive but did not want to say so. Barbara scooped up all the materials and placed them into a large envelope. Barbara leaned over and kissed me on my forehead.

I was hesitant to broach the subject but felt I needed to. "Do you think Jasmine is going to make it to the performance? She was... out of control today."

Barbara brushed some hair off my forehead. "You know Jasmine. She always gets tense just before the show. She was well... let's say she... was not in a good mood today. I know she'll calm down by opening night. She's proven herself to be a trouper before. Besides, she has a really great understudy." Barbara poked me in the side and gave me a heartfelt smile.

"I... I don't know if I'm up for it," I confided.

Barbara did not respond but, instead, gave an exaggerated sad face as she left the room.

I turned my computer off and looked down at Prima and the sleeping puppies. "Come on, babies, time for bed." One by one, I picked up the puppies and Prima and placed them in the large dog bed. Their soft fur was a delight to touch. I turned off the lights and slipped into bed.

The rain continued to pelt the window. A streetlamp could be seen through my window across the back alley to the adjoining property. Sometimes I found myself staring at the lamp. Nights like this, with raindrops obscuring the lamp, made me melancholy. Something about the darkness, rivulets of water on the window, and drops diffracting the light from the streetlamp brought the mind to focus. I found it difficult to fall asleep.

After a while, the rhythmic tap of raindrops quieted my mind. Soon, images of Christmas lights and crowds of people filled my dreams.

Whitney, always an enigma, emerged from the crowd to put her arm through my arm and sang a song. Peter stood next to her and played along, wearing his heavy winter coat. Walking down the mall's sidewalk, a group of chocolate kisses wrapped in foil danced around us. Just then, the little man who played the Mouse appeared and took our hands. He was different this time. Although he was not in costume, he had long whiskers, pointed ears, and a mouse-like black nose. He pulled the three of us ever faster toward the mall center. A mop bucket came rolling past us, followed by flute dancers taking large jumps over the bucket, their dresses flying in rainbow colors. I struggled to keep up as the Mouse pulled us ever faster. Two men in jeans but no shirts appeared and proceeded to lift Whitney and me over their heads. I couldn't tell if these were the men from the Arabian dance or the ones from the lifting line of the professional class. Regardless, I flew as if I would never land.

Flowers floated out of the flower shop and transformed into twirling girls on pointe, circling me in an ever-tightening circle. I flew up onto the shoulders of the dancing panda bears from the Tea Dance. They bucked around with me on their backs. Even in my dreams, I thought it was very odd to be riding on the back of panda bears. I looked around and saw both Peter and Whitney riding on the backs of their panda bears, galloping toward the ice rink in the middle of the mall. I guided my bear to follow suit. Colored lights and Christmas decorations flew by in a canvas of holiday spirit. I felt good and laughed in my sleep. At the rink, the bears disappeared, and the three of us floated on ice skates—the feeling of floating lifted my spirits.

CRASH, BOOM.

A strike of lightning and a crash of thunder happened outside my window. The storm was worsening. The light and sound disturbed me, and I tossed in bed. My dream took a turn for the worse.

A dark and menacing figure loomed at one end of the rink and skated toward us. It was Drosselmeier, not Roland but the traditional mysterious character from the original Nutcracker. He wore a patch over one eye and a stovetop hat covering his shoulder-length white hair. He looked fierce. He took a spin when he reached me and the others, making his knee-length black coat fly out. John appeared from nowhere and stepped between Drosselmeier, Peter, Whitney, and me. He made a fist and pounded his other fist, yelling, "Stop, or I'll pound ya." I was confused and disturbed by Drosselmeier's appearance. Peter stood off to the side and encouraged me, "run, I'll catch you."

I ran toward Peter, anticipating a bird lift. When he put his hands on my hipbone, his strength flew me up into the branches of the surrounding pine tree decorated with Christmas ornaments and lights. Nick appeared next to me in the branches, dressed in his mouse costume. Nick laughed in a mocking mouse squeak. Down on the ground, I saw Jasmine embrace Peter and give him a big kiss. He did not push her away but rather encouraged the affection. Whitney sang a love song while a group of twenty squirrels ran across the tree branches and over my back. I covered my eyes. Their tiny feet felt creepy on my bare skin. But when I looked a second time, it was Prima and all her puppies crawling around her. Prima clenched my nightgown and pulled me to the ground. Somehow, they didn't fall but floated with ease. Jasmine kept her arm around Peter while she pointed at my breasts. "See, she has no breasts. She's flat as a board. It's no wonder she can't get a boyfriend."

I was mortified. Why does Jasmine have to ruin everything? A mirror appeared next to me, and I looked at my silhouette. I stuck out my stomach and slouched. I couldn't believe how ugly I was; no wonder Peter had not shown me any interest. Jasmine continued with her mocking, "I'm the star... not you... and I've got Peter."

CRASH, BOOM.

A second lightning flash filled my bedroom with a bluish-white light making it feel otherworldly. The thunder's boom did not wake me but made me toss and turn even more.

Everyone disappeared from my dream. It became a white space with a fog of very tiny white snowflakes falling. The little man who played the Mouse appeared from the mist, but his costume was white and not grey this time. He took both of my hands and said, "Only a few thousand humans, out of all the humans who have ever lived, have experienced the classical ballet dream. Your art is divine, and I honor you." Peter materialized from the mist, also dressed in white. He extended his hand, and I took an arabesque on pointe. He added, "Ballet is the attempt to reach the highest human ideal." John also arrived in white, took my other hand, and encouraged me with, "... it takes courage."

In the soft white mist, I could make out the silhouette of a ballerina in a white tutu and her cavalier, also dressed in white tights and a white satin jacket. As they came closer, I saw that it was mother and Roland. Barbara was radiant and looked every part of the world-class ballerina she once was. Roland exuded the confidence of a premier danseur. I ran to my mother and embraced her. Barbara uncharacteristically hugged me back and kissed my forehead. Roland took both of our hands and said, "Ballet is a transcendental experience where we, the dancer, become beauty." I basked in the warmth of belonging.

CRASH, BOOM.

A third and final crash of lightning was closer than before and extended from the sky to the ground right outside my window. There was no time delay from the flash of light and thunder being one and the same. Its proximity shook the house.

A horde of people dressed in heavy winter coats descended upon me, chasing the purity of white away with drab browns and grays. The mob began dancing the flash mob routine, and I was buffeted about from group to group. I couldn't find my mother or Roland, nor were Peter, John, or Whitney around. I was alone with the crowd pressing in on me. They kept bumping into me as I spun around out of control. Jasmine appeared directly behind me and began repeating, "I'm the star, not you... I'm the star, not you... I'm the star, not you…" I tried to push her off. Peter showed up dressed in the Nutcracker costume. The red military-style jacket with gold epaulets and trim really showed off his muscular legs covered in white tights. He tried to push his way to me, but Jasmine stepped in between us. She said, "He's mine… you will never be good enough… you cow… you cow." As she repeated the word 'cow,' a large cow appeared next to me that began to lick my face. The crowd turned, pointed at me, and laughed while the cow continued to slobber on my face. I tried to cover my face and slink away.

"No, no… no," I said while flailing my arms. I woke up to find Prima on my chest, licking my face. "Ah, Prima… it was horrible." I trembled. I took short rapid breaths. The nightmare was deep and disturbing. I could not let go of all the emotions. I embraced Prima as I never had before. "I love you… I love you."

*

23 — Teaching Children

The dance studio was still bustling. Daily dance classes for children were held each afternoon. Some of the evening classes with the older students briefly rehearsed their respective numbers for the upcoming *Nutcracker Ballet* opening in a week. Although the professional dancers involved with the first two nights of filming had left, a new set of professional dancers and actors arrived over the weekend for the upcoming snow scene and the greenscreen filming. They still had use of Studio C for practice and rehearsal and Studio D for relaxation.

John and I attended some classes at high school but mostly completed assignments at home and were at the dance studio the rest of the time. My ankle healed nicely, and I was able to dance full out. I attended the professional dance class, careful not to injure myself so near the performance. I was learning, like all professionals, when to push and when to be careful. Whitney and I stayed connected by texting. I wanted to stay away from the craziness surrounding Whitney's world yet be her friend, and Whitney seemed to understand.

Jasmine did not attend the professional classes but opted to take a minimal schedule of classes. She claimed that she was 'saving' herself for her star performance. Besides, her 'friend' Whitney needed her; when, in fact, Whitney's bodyguards often kept Jasmine away.

That afternoon, I helped Beatrice with the last of the costume fittings and a final rehearsal. I walked down the hallway toward the front studios and was surprised to hear the *Waltz of the Flowers* coming from Studio B door. I knew it was a children's class with six- to eight-year-olds, not a rehearsal. I cracked open the door and saw Peter teaching the class.

"That's the way. Let the music come through you. Become the dance," Peter encouraged the very young children.

At this class level, much of the dancing is not technique but rather skipping and running to the music to build rhythmic skills. To many adults, it looks like child's play when it actually is very important to maintain the fun of dance while introducing ballet terms in French. It takes a unique skill set to teach ballet to the very young, something I did not enjoy.

Peter stopped the music. "Excellent. That was fun... and now for our bows."

The group of little girls and one boy formed one line, with Peter standing in front. Peter wore his usual light grey tights and tank top. He put on some music and led the class in bows. "First, we step to the side and then back, take our arm up in a high third, now sweep down our leg... that's good." Very few of the students were together, but they tried. "Now come up and step to the other side and do the same thing." I snickered a bit because many of the students were on the wrong foot or facing the wrong wall, and a few of the girls who wore slip-on pink tutus to class were tugging at the fabric.

"Very good, everyone. Now let's clap." Some children clapped while others rushed to their mothers, who were sitting at the front of the classroom. The children seemed happy, and their faces were flushed from the exercise. Peter noticed me at the door and gave me a smile. Many mothers came to Peter to thank him for his wonderful class. The children were anxious to go and tugged at their mothers to drag them out the door. I walked all the way in passing mothers who also thanked me for having such an 'excellent' teacher for the day.

"I didn't know you taught," I said to Peter.

"Every chance I can."

"I would think that you would teach the advance classes."

Peter picked up a towel and wiped the sweat off his brow. He slowly gathered up his stuff and dance bag. "The advanced classes are challenging, and I like demonstrating in them, but I find I really like the younger children. They still know the meaning of dance."

I was impressed by his kindness and genuineness. "Mother wants us to meet in Rehearsal Hall A for a final run-through of the *Pas de Deux*."

"OK... be there in a few."

I walked out of the studio to the dressing room to change. Many young girls ran around me, and that made me feel uncomfortable. Not that I was stuck up, but I felt most at ease with the seriousness and serenity I found being around professional dancers. Once I finished changing into tights and a leotard, I walked into Studio A.

PRIMA RIDING THE ROBOT FLOOR SWEEPER

Barbara, Jasmine, John, and the other older dancers were already there. A playpen was set up in one corner for Prima and her puppies. Barbara could no longer leave them at home since they made such a mess when unsupervised. They were very rambunctious, wanting to greet everyone who walked through the door. One of the younger dancers had placed Prima on top of the robot vacuum used to keep the dance studio clean. It was so adorable to see her riding along, making circles. The dancer had tied some old pink pointe shoe ribbons decoratively around the dog's head.

I walked over to Prima, picked her up, and placed her back into the playpen while giving a stern look to the younger dancer. When placing Prima into the playpen, I petted the heads of all the dogs. They wouldn't let me go until I acknowledged each of them. They had so much energy.

Peter immediately came through the door, ready to go.

Barbara took control of the room. "We don't have much time. We need to give the understudies one more chance to practice. Jasmine, you dance with John and Marie with Peter. All the other dancers take your usual partners. Let's go now."

The couples paired up. Jasmine was displeased. As the 'star,' she did not see the need to rehearse with John.

Barbara reached over to turn on the music. The *Intrada* to *The Nutcracker Pas de Deux* sounded beautiful over the room's built-in speakers. Unfortunately, Jasmine stumbled and fell out of *arabesques* while supported by John.

Jasmine screamed at John. "Hold your arm up. Get it up. Stop being such a weakling."

The scream made Prima and her puppies stop playing and look toward Jasmine.

Jasmine and I held our extension in the competition.

Barbara spoke up, "Come on girls, a little higher."

Both of us wobbled.

Peter looked directly in my eyes. "Relax. Just relax. It'll go higher if you don't think about it."

I listened but, instead, tensed up more.

Jasmine again screamed at John, "You, clod."

Prima and her puppies whined a bit at the ugliness.

Jasmine lowered her leg and said to everyone in earshot, "I can't dance with amateurs." She walked away toward her dance bag, leaving John looking demolished.

"What now," asked Barbara?

"I can't waste my time with such amateurs," Jasmine said insolently. She picked up her bag and walked out the door. Prima and her puppies hid their heads while she walked by. They sensed her negativity.

Barbara turned off the music and rubbed her face looking very tired. She turned to John and said, "I'm very sorry for Jasmine's outburst. It's very unprofessional, but the performance is in just a few days. We can persevere." Barbara walked to the center of the room, speaking to all the dancers. "I'm sure we are all very tired. Final dress rehearsal is in a few days. Why don't we call it quits?"

John was almost in tears and quickly walked over to his dance bag.

Peter spoke to me, "If you like, we could go through it once more."

I brightened up and nodded 'yes'. I always appreciated dancing with Peter.

Peter caught Barbara's attention. "Just leave the music. Marie and I are going to rehearse for the last time."

"Oh, OK. Remember to bring Prima when you're done. I'll be in the office."

Barbara and all the other students vacated the studio leaving Peter and me alone.

"I'm glad that we have this time to work together, alone." Peter was good at taking control. "Here, let's take it from the supported *pirouette*."

I took position, and Peter placed his hands over my waist. "Now… 6, 7, 8, go."

I spun but lost balance. Peter had to save me.

I slumped and complained, "I'm just not good enough."

Peter stepped up to the challenge. "Here, use Prima as your spot. Look at her."

181

I wound up for the spin but was stopped before I could go.

"No, not yet. Just look at Prima. Relax. Enjoy looking at her."

I looked at Prima. Prima and her puppies looked back and were so cute; their eyes would make anyone's heart melt. I finally relaxed. Peter could feel the change in me.

"Now," commanded Peter.

I spun perfectly and in balance to the ending position in *arabesque* with no hesitation or wobble.

Peter encouraged me along, "Let's keep going... Feel the safety of my hands."

I danced flawlessly. I soared to the end of the routine.

"That was excellent. I would gladly perform this number with you on stage," Peter complimented me.

"It was you."

"No, it was you... being dance."

"But ... but, I just don't know."

"That's the point," reassured Peter. "When you transcend out of your body, you become the music... you become the dance... you dance better."

"I must try harder if I'm going to be a ballerina," I lamented.

"You are just as good, if not better than Jasmine. You just don't believe it and struggle. Try letting it be and just dance... dance with me."

Prima and the puppies were anxious from the lack of attention and let out small yelps.

"You know, you sound just like Roland."

Peter smiled. "I've learned from the best."

"Roland?"

"He's my uncle," Peter revealed. "Didn't you know?... He's in town for the greenscreen shoot for the *Nutcracker* movie."

I was flummoxed. How did I not notice the association, yet it made so much sense?

Bill, Barbara, and Nick entered the studio, looking ready to go.

Bill spoke up, "Hey kids... we have an idea. Let's do something really different, something to get our minds off the show."

Prima and her puppies became very excited at the arrival of the entire family and bounced around in their playpen.

"A bunch of us are going ice skating. Want to come?"

I really liked the idea and was skilled as a skater.

Peter spoke up, "Ah, sorry, but I don't think it is wise to take such a risk just before the show. Also, I'm from California... I've never ice-skated."

"Good point Peter. We can't risk our male star with a possible injury," added Barbara.

"But Mom," I implored, "we'll be careful... I'll take care of Peter."

Barbara looked toward Peter and said, "I'm not worried about Marie. She considered being a professional skater at one time and won many competitions. It's you I'm concerned about."

"I'm fine not skating. I'll just watch."

"It'll be fun. Come on. It's like roller skating, just smoother," I implored as I grabbed at Peter's hands to drag him along.

"We'll see," conceded Peter.

With that, Bill picked up the dogs and handed them to the others while he folded up the playpen. We carried everything to the front desk for Tom to babysit the dogs. Peter and I put sweats on over their practice clothes, and the family walked out the door. It was going to be fun.

*

24 — Filming *Waltz of the Snowflakes*

At the center of the mall was a large, very long ice-skating rink anchored at one end by a jewelry store. Brightly decorated storefronts surrounded the rink. At one end, a cluster of pine trees and other bushes and benches made a park-like setting for mall shoppers to rest and enjoy a pretzel or other goodies found at the surrounding food court. The filming of the *Nutcracker* took over the end of the rink nearest the park and jewelry store, along with the food court park. A dance floor was assembled just next to the edge of the rink in front of the pine trees. Scaffolding to hold lighting and cameras were installed around the rink and dance floor. A very large and very high scaffolding about thirty feet off the ground and just above the treetops held additional lighting, the artificial snow equipment, various three-to four-feet in size snowflakes, and a six-foot-long boat designed to look like one-half of an acorn shell. This outdoor forest setting was going to be used that evening for filming the *Waltz of the Snowflakes*. Dancers arrived to conduct a dress rehearsal in the late afternoon light before the final filming that night. They wore long coats over their costumes to help stay warm.

The other end of the rink was still open to the public. My family and many dancers from the studio, along with their families, were there. Some were already out on the ice, whereas others were still checking out rental skates.

My family, along with Sheila and Peter, paid our entrance fee, rented skates, and sat on the benches to put on their skates. It was cold out, and everyone was bundled up in heavy jackets. The storm the night before left a crispness in the air that made everyone even more excited about skating on ice for the first time that year. Of course, being from out of town, Peter still had his oversized jacket that made him look like a polar bear.

While lacing up the skates, Peter complained, "I know I'm going to be a klutz."

At that moment, Roland showed up. He walked directly over to Peter and Barbara and gave them deep hugs.

"Tom at the front desk said you were here... thought I'd join in," Roland said with a big smile. "I haven't skated in years." Roland walked over to the admission booth, bought a ticket, and rented skates.

Nick and Sheila bolted for the ice and zoomed fearlessly to the center. Barbara and Bill were more adult about it but still excited at the prospects of skating for the first time this season. They took little steps on their skates but glided along the edge not too far from the hand railing.

Peter was a different story. He stood up in his skates and froze. Dancers develop a finely honed sense of where their bodies are in space. Part of that sense is knowing where the foot is in relation to the floor. The inch or so of distance the metal blade added to the bottom of the boot was disconcerting to Peter. As he took each baby step, it was obviously very awkward for him.

Roland jumped in to give Peter an arm. "Here, we'll help you." Roland waved me over, and the two of us gave Peter support; me on one side and Roland on the other. It was a sight to see; Peter, in his oversized coat, was helped like a fragile older man to the ice's edge. Once there, Peter gingerly stepped on the ice. Immediately, his feet slipped out, and he headed for a fall. Roland and I effectively blocked the fall— the last thing we needed was for the Nutcracker Prince to be injured.

"Woooo," Peter let out a cry.

"We got you, boy," Roland reassured.

"Don't worry, we got you," I added. "Here, think of roller skating. Try sliding your feet out in a 'V.'" I let go of Peter and took a few slides forward to demonstrate the move.

Peter stopped. "To be honest, I haven't been on roller skates either since I was a kid. You know, dancers can't engage in physical activities that may injure us. If we can't perform, we don't get paid... so, I haven't done much of this in my life."

Roland firmly held Peter up by one arm. "Don't worry. We won't let anything happen to you... and have fun." I came back and took Peter's other arm. Peter took a few more slides, slowly building confidence.

186

MARIE HELPING PETER ICE SKATE

The rink was crowded with kids zooming by. There always seemed to be a few boys who make a point of weaving in between the slower skaters as though it was a slalom race between human cones. A few girls were in the center of the rink practicing turns, *arabesques*, and other balletic steps. It looked like Nick and Sheila were skating around the rink in a competition. Sometimes he would be ahead; other times, she would be. Barbara and Bill seemed happy to simply skate slowly in a large circle while holding hands and talking between themselves.

It didn't take long for Peter to get the basics of ice skating. Roland could feel his confidence grow. "You're doing much better now, Peter. I'm going to leave the two of you alone." Roland skated off over to join Bill and Barbara.

I kept hold of Peter's arm. It felt like he was going down a few times, but he recovered before hitting the ice. After a while, he needed a break and skated, no, more like walked, over to the railing to simply stand, hold the railing, and take account of what transpired.

"Sorry to be ruining your afternoon," Peter said to me. "You should go on and skate with your friends. I'll be OK. I don't want to be a bother."

"No, bother." I enjoyed the time I had with Peter, and, for once, he was dependent upon me. "I've skated my entire life. At one time, I thought about being a skater. It's very much like ballet."

"Really... like those girls in the middle of the rink?" Peter glanced to the center where a girl had just completed a *tour jeté* gliding away in *arabesques*. "Skate for me!"

On that cue, I skated a few feet away and performed a short series of steps, jumps, glides, and turns with a back *attitude*. When done, I skated back to Peter.

He couldn't control himself and gave me a rousing round of applause. "That was great... just great... I never suspected."

"EVERYONE INTO POSITION. WE'LL START IN FIVE," a bullhorn announced over at the film set.

188

Peter and I turned our attention to the other end of the rink, where the dance floor was installed in front of the pine trees. Paul was up on a stepladder using the bullhorn to get performers in place.

"THIS IS A TECHNICAL AND COSTUME CHECK. NO NEED TO DANCE IT FULL OUT BUT MAKE SURE YOU MAKE POSITION. SAVE YOUR ENERGY FOR TONIGHT'S FILMING."

Sandra walked over to the stepladder and conversed with Paul.

"Oh, let's go over and watch," I implored Peter. I grabbed his arm and guided him to the end of the rink, where others of the public gathered along the barrier to watch the rehearsal. I brought Peter up to stand next to Roland, Barbara, and Bill. Roland helped Peter get a good hold of the barrier to stabilize himself. Nick and Sheila were too busy skating to be bothered, as were many other kids.

"OK. POSITIONS... MUSIC... ACTION," Paul called to the performers.

The beautiful Tchaikovsky score of the *Waltz of the Snowflakes* came over the speakers. Ice skaters emerged from the jewelry store, sliding from the store entrance to the real ice rink.

"How'd they do that?" asked Peter.

Roland piped in, "See, they put down some plastic panels on the ground from the door to the rink. Never thought about skating on plastic."

The women skaters wore white and silver-trimmed short tulle dresses with large gossamer wings. They wore crystal crowns and carried clear plastic wands that shone bright white light from their centers. The men wore complimentary costumes with traditional long-tail white and silver tuxedos, large crystalline wings and crowns, and carried transparent plastic wands that were brightly lit. I had never seen the *Snowflake* number begin this way. What a brilliant idea— to start the number with skating male and female ice fairies emerging from a jewelry store like precious diamonds!

189

WALTZ OF THE SNOWFLAKES

191

About a minute into the music, there is a change in the base, with oboes taking over the theme. Many large three- to four-foot diameter snowflakes slowly lowered from the overhead scaffolding to the dance floor. As each snowflake touched the floor, the fairies pointed their wands at the stage, and the snowflake magically transformed into a live dancer. The snowflake dancers wore longer knee-length white tutus with silver trim. The top layer of the tulle was cut into a six-sided snowflake pattern. It was very traditional snowflake costuming. The ice fairies in the foreground and the snowflakes in the background complimented each other in steps and formation. Sometimes the ice fairies danced by themselves; other times, the snowflakes danced by themselves; many times, both groups danced and skated together.

I found myself to be very cold and began shivering.

"Cold?" asked Peter.

I didn't respond at first. I just smiled but kept shivering.

"Here, my coat is big enough for the two of us," added Peter. He opened his coat and pulled me inside, with both of us facing out. He closed the coat to keep us warm, placing his arms around my waist. He was tall enough to see over my head.

About four minutes into the music, there are clashes of cymbals. The choreographer used more magic to have the ice fairies use their wands to build a throne made of ice on each musical clash, piece by piece. In many ways, it was reminiscent of Elsa in the animated Disney film *Frozen* when she built her castle by throwing ice jets from her hands. It was very spectacular. Another minute into the music, there is an abrupt change from the loud orchestra and voices to quiet flutes.

At that moment, the large half-shell acorn boat carrying the Stewart twins playing the Nutcracker Prince and Clara, along with their Mouse sidekick, floated down from the top of the overhead scaffolding flying from side to side, landing in the middle of the stage. The audience *oohed* and *aahed* as the boat floated to the stage. Once the boat touched the stage, the Nutcracker Prince jumped out and pushed and spun the boat around the stage, making it glide. Clara's nightgown flowed in the wind, and the Mouse jumped up and down with joy. The snowflakes danced around them. After a short interlude, the ice fairies used their wands to make the snowflakes disappear, one by one, in a puff of ice crystals that flew back up into the pine trees.

The background of pine trees twinkled with more and more colored lights as more ice crystals from the transformed snowflakes hit their branches. The Nutcracker Prince escorted Clara to the ice throne for both of them to sit silhouetted against the wall of twinkling-colored lights in the pine trees. All the while, the Mouse tumbled and danced. During the last minutes of music, the large mechanical tumbler at the top of the scaffolding was turned to allow artificial snow to float down to the stage. The ice fairies bowed to the Nutcracker Prince and Clara in their final tableau. It was truly a unique and magical combination of ballet and ice skating with many traditional story elements.

"CUT," Paul yelled out.

Nick yelled, "Wow!" He had snuck in from behind the people to peek his head between Bill and Roland.

"Yes, double wow!" added Peter and me. I poked my hands through the spaces between the buttons of Peter's coat to clap my hands. Peter clenched his arms around my waist tightly. I was delighted but also surprised by Peter's increased affection.

The crowd broke into spontaneous applause and cheers. For most ballet companies, the *Waltz of the Snowflakes* is their biggest dance number. This production was ten times more impressive, with ice-skating fairies, dancing snowflakes, a flying acorn boat, magic, snowfall, and twinkling trees.

"THANK YOU ALL. TAKE THIRTY. WE NEED TO RESET. ONE MORE TIME UNTIL TONIGHT'S FILMING," Paul called on the bullhorn. He climbed down the stepladder and conversed with Sandra.

"Anyone hungry?" Bill asked the group.

Bill and Barbara looked around at the kids. Nick spoke up, "Pizza?"

*

25 — Pizza

"Why don't we rendezvous at the pizza place in about 20 minutes? That'll give you time to get your skates off and walk over the food court behind the trees," Bill told the group.

"Great," Nick exclaimed as he darted away with Sheila to take a couple more laps around the rink.

"Uh oh, is that snow I feel," Roland said while looking upwards toward the sky. "Real snow?"

Everyone looked up. Very light ice crystals landed softly on faces. Being twilight, the sun shone between dark clouds, but the sky was mostly clear. The small crystals twinkled in the almost horizontal light.

"I doubt it," Bill answered. "Maybe a bit more, but there aren't enough clouds to worry about."

"I wish it would snow," Peter piped in.

I turned my head toward him while unbuttoning his jacket to let myself out.

"Why?" I asked incredulously.

"It would be so cool." Peter was being honest. The group didn't respond. "I mean, I've never seen it snow."

"Oh," murmured the group. Barbara stepped in, "That explains it... trust us, once you live through a winter full of snow, you'll learn it's not the wonderful clean white stuff that you think it is... sorry, but I don't think it will snow tonight."

"Shucks." Peter was genuinely disappointed.

"Shucks!! Who says that anymore," I teased? Peter smiled at the exchange of endearments.

"Are you warm enough?" asked Peter.

"I'm fine. Now, let's all go eat," I reassured Peter. I grabbed his hand to help guide him back to the benches at the entry. It was slow going since Peter was still unsteady. There were times when he leaned in so close to me that I thought he would kiss me, but I was unsure. The mist of ice crystals influenced my romantic feelings for Peter. More than anything, I was hopeful from my growing feelings for Peter.

After checking their skating boots in at the front desk and leaving the rink, the group walked behind the pine trees to the restaurant. Bill led the way to the hostess, who sat the large group near the back. Bill, Barbara, Peter, Roland, Nick, Sheila, and I took up a large booth. The restaurant was empty since it was off hours, yet the warm smells of pizza, pasta, and sauce filled the air.

Roland spoke up to the group. "This has been a wonderful experience. It has been so many years since I've been so involved with ballet. And it has been great working again with you Barbara," he turned to Barbara, "… and with my Nephew," he turned to Peter, "… and at the same time. It's been fun."

The waiter came over, and Bill placed an order for us all. "The usual."

Roland seemed surprised.

"We come here often… and it's my treat."

"That is so kind of you to feed the herd," Roland joked.

Barbara buried her face in her hands for a brief moment, then lifted her face. She had tears in her eyes.

"Tired?" asked Bill as he placed his hand on her upper back to give soft rubs.

"I keep telling myself that everything will work out." Barbara looked exhausted.

"It's OK—same thing… every time this year. Months of rehearsals, some catastrophes, you think it won't come together, and then a glimmer of hope. I want to thank Peter for being so steady through all this and Roland… I want to thank you for helping so much. It's so good to have you back."

Bill lifted his water glass to begin a toast. Everyone raised his or her water glass in support.

"To the *Nutcracker*," Bill began.

"To the *Nutcracker*," everyone replied.

"… and God bless us, everyone," chimed in Nick, citing the famous line said by Tiny Tim in Dicken's *Christmas Carol*.

That got a laugh out of the group.

Barbara turned to Peter to give her deepest thanks. "Really, I want to thank you. You have been a rock through all the drama."

"I got that from my uncle," Peter looked to Roland. "He taught me that, yes, I must have technique, but I'll have a longer, more satisfying career if I'm a solid partner... 'Always make the ladies feel special, and they'll perform,' he says."

Bill almost gagged on his water while Barbara shook her head in disbelief.

Roland piped in with a sly smile, "I don't think I said it quite like that."

I felt I needed to give support. "I want to add that I think this year's *Nutcracker* will be the best." I turned toward Barbara. "Thank you, Mother."

Again, the entire group raised their water glasses in salute. "To Barbara."

We sipped our glasses of water and laughed. Sheila and Nick poked each other and often giggled.

Sheila spoke up. The group was surprised because she rarely spoke. With her tiny soft voice, she said, "We decided... "

Barbara couldn't hear, "What was that, Sheila?"

Sheila continued while not looking up from her water glass, "We decided that it... "

Nick joined in, "would be in our best interest...

Sheila continued, "to form a collaborative arrangement... "

Nick had to explain "of shared interest and goals as anthropologists... "

Sheila couldn't hold back and said, "I'm Nick's girlfriend."

Nick clarificd, "I'm Sheila's boyfriend."

Without missing a beat, they both finish using their straws to noisily slurp water out of their glasses.

Everyone at the table looked amused without being condescending.

Nick had to add a clarification, "And don't worry, you won't see us engage... "

Sheila finished his sentence, "in any courtship rituals or other forms of public display of affection."

"Where do they get this stuff?" asked Bill.

The adults at the table broke into belly laughs as the waiter delivered the food. With no hesitancy, the group dove into the food—obviously, everyone was hungry. Music played over the restaurant sound system.

"Gosh, we can't get away from it... hear... " Barbara pointed to the ceiling, "it's the *Nutcracker*."

The group laughed some more and finished every scrap of food. They say dancers don't eat but get them going and stand back.

"So, what did you all think of the *Waltz of the Snowflakes?*" asked Roland.

"Great," "Superb," "Outstanding," "Cool," said everyone at the table.

"I was at some of the planning meetings for this *Nutcracker,* and the waltz was discussed many times. Don't know if you noticed, but there is no CGI; no computer graphics were used. It was decided that we wanted a full stage look for the number since it is so traditional and central to the ballet. We called in a professional magician who figured out how to make things appear and disappear, shoot ice crystals, and more. Also, we wanted something truly different that would appeal to both boys and girls. That's why we have the ice-skating fairies with their magic wands. This way, we could have both male and female ice skaters shoot out ice crystals to transform the snowflakes and build the throne. We also contacted a company that makes plastic sheets that allow ice-skating without ice. What a great idea for getting the skaters from the store to the ice rink."

Roland paused to let this all sink in. "Disney's *Frozen* was such a big hit, we thought we needed magic like that, and our magic consultant really pulled it off. Don't you think?"

"Definitely," Barbara and Bill agreed.

"The dancers came from New York City Ballet, and the choreography was adapted from Balanchine's original steps. He was a master at moving groups of dancers around the stage. Paul helped blend the ice skating with the ballet."

"I thought I recognized some of the steps," added Peter. "Balanchine was a master of the corps de ballet, although, do I dare say, I don't think he was very good with couples. I've never liked his *Pas de Deux* in the *Nutcracker*. There's no focus."

"What an insightful observation for someone so young," Barbara complimented. "Most critics were in awe of Balanchine, but many thought he did not truly understand the *pas de deux*."

Nick and Sheila were bored with dance talk and were using breadsticks to build a Christmas tree decorated with pepperoni pieces for the ornaments and grated parmesan cheese for the snow.

"Well, I liked it," I said, "and I appreciate that so many of the dancers were of mixed nationalities and races."

Roland spoke up. "That is one of the major goals of this *Nutcracker*. We want to appeal to all kinds of people. Too often, ballet is viewed to be limited to only white girls. Instead, we want it to appeal to all races and to both boys and girls. We have gone to great lengths to have as diverse a group of dancers as possible."

Barbara gave a sharp look to Nick to tell him to stop playing with his food. "That's admirable, Roland... this should be a *Nutcracker* for the ages."

The waiter came up to the table, and Bill paid the receipt.

"Thanks, Bill, that was so gracious," commended Roland. Roland stood first and extended his hand to Barbara to help her up.

"Why, thank you, Roland, always a gentleman," Barbara gushed.

"M'lady."

Bill rolled his eyes. By now, he should have been used to Roland's use of compliments. Barbara, Bill, Sheila, and Nick rose, and they all walked away.

Peter turned to me. "After tomorrow's greenscreen filming, it's just a few days until our performance."

"Aren't you nervous?" I asked.

"No, not in particular." Peter rose to his feet and extended his hand to me. "M'lady."

I giggled, placed my hand in his, and stood up. "My prince."

Peter and I had to walk fast to catch up with the rest of the group as they headed out the front door into the cold.

*

26 — Filming the *Pas de Deux* on Greenscreen

The *Waltz of the Snowflakes* evening filming was a success. The weather held, and the Director obtained the footage needed to complete the number. Workers immediately broke down the sets, and most of the trailers were out of the mall by opening time in the morning. The mall was returning to normal.

The dance studio was also returning to normal. With dancers and ice skaters departing immediately after the filming, the professional class shrunk to only a few people. A few acrobats and actors scheduled for the day's greenscreen filming attended class, but they were not professional ballet dancers. New to the class were some male folk dancers hired to dance an authentic *prisyadka* in the *Russian Dance* and a married couple from American Ballet Theater to film the *Pas de Deux*.

Mark and Gigi were considered two of the world's best ballet dancers of this generation and had danced the *Nutcracker Pas de Deux* many times for ABT. The movie production was lucky to get them, particularly at this busy time of year. They traveled with their ten-month-old toddler, Henry. Gigi was amazing in class. Considering it had been less than a year since the birth of her child, she was in great shape and extremely strong. I was duly impressed by the two of them. Of all the professional dancers passing through the studio over the past few weeks, Mark and Gigi stood above the rest. Gigi's resiliency after giving birth laid to rest the myth that pregnancy was the end of a woman's ballet career. I thought that maybe Roland was right when he said mother used her pregnancy with me as an excuse to retire from being a professional ballerina.

The past few weeks have been exceptional for me. Meeting so many dancers from all over the United States and other countries was exciting. I found the whole environment instructional, and it gave me a glimpse into the world of professional ballet dancing. While representing my mother's dance studio, I learned to be gracious and talked with many dancers in a deeply personal way. I was not naturally outgoing and gregarious like Peter, but I still found ways to meet new people and actually care about what they were saying. I heard many stories and encountered many different personalities.

Peter, John, and I were due over at the warehouse at noon to film the short sequences requiring a greenscreen. Luckily, the warehouse was not far, so we could finish the professional class. We drove over together to the non-descript drab building. The industrial park contained many similar cement slab buildings with employee cars parked around the periphery.

Inside the building was a different story. Once past the reception office, it opened into a large space like a typical sound studio with high ceilings, lights, support scaffolding, and a computer center, but with a large defined area painted bright luminescence green. The walls and floor glowed like a radioactive green sapphire under the bright lights. There was no false ceiling over the filming area, which allowed overhead cranes to carry pieces into and out of the set. The idea behind the greenscreen special effects is that once filming of the actors in front of the greenscreen is completed, computers remove all the green leaving the actors by themselves. The picture of the actors then can be layered over a background scene— like a photograph of the mall or a three-dimensional model made by a computer— like a crystal palace.

Off to the side was a separate area for costumes, changing clothes, makeup, and a ballet *barre* for the dancers to limber up, besides refreshments and restrooms. Technicians bustled about adjusting lights, checking camera locations, and initializing computer-operated booms. Gigi and Mark were already in ballet costumes for the *Pas de Deux*. They were regal and exquisite and stood in the middle of the green set. Their baby's playpen was set up nearby, being attended by Mark's mother, who traveled with them.

Roland greeted the boys and me. "Glad you're here. Please check in over at wardrobe for your mouse costumes. You have about forty minutes."

202

Paul stood in the middle of the camera equipment with the Director and used the bullhorn. "QUIET ON THE SET. WE ARE FILMING THE PAS DE DEUX FIRST. RUSSIAN DANCERS WILL BE UP NEXT. PLEASE BE READY."

Paul walked over to Mark and Gigi and showed the marks on the floor to help space the shots. Unlike most filming, with greenscreen, the cameras are operated by computer and move a prescribed path. The dancers need to hit certain marks to stay within the frame. The computer paths are used to synchronize the background inserted later.

The boys and I checked into wardrobe and picked up our mouse costumes. The changing area was an open space, so we could still see all the action on the green set. Several folded room dividers were used to separate some of the changing areas from the studio's open space.

"SPEED... ACTION," called the Director.

The *Nutcracker Pas de Deux* is one of the loveliest pieces of music ever composed by Tchaikovsky. I had to stop dressing and watch. Mark and Gigi were exquisite, and baby Henry stood in his crib holding onto the vertical bars watching mom and dad dance. Soon it dawned on me that we were dancing to a version similar to what Peter had taught us.

I leaned over to Peter and whispered. "Isn't that the same choreography as yours?"

"I think so. The Russian ballet dancers Valery and Galina Panov created a stunning and logical *Pas de Deux* that builds to a spectacular climax. Many of us have adapted it for our use."

"Logical?" I asked.

"Well... yes. Good choreography is well planned and a skill. Contrary to popular belief, 'Art' is not just your 'feelings.'"

Some of the other dancers turned toward Peter and me to listen in.

"Are we talking too loud?" I was concerned and muffled my mouth.

"Don't worry. There are no live mics on the set. The music is piped directly to the cameras... but you don't want to disturb the technicians," one of the actors in mouse costume commented.

John, Peter, and I silently watched the rest of the *Pas de Deux*. It was stunning. Gigi and Mark were world-class professionals. The one-hand lifts were spectacular. Splits were easy for them making every extension and jump effortless. And they could both perform multiple turns— *pirouettes, fouetté*, and more— completely centered, ending with a light landing. Maybe five people in the world could pull off what they did. I was awestruck. It was odd and somewhat disconcerting, though, to see cameras moving about and zooming around the set on cranes without any human assistance.

"CUT... PLAYBACK."

At a number of places in the warehouse and above the computer workstations were placed very, very large LCD TV screens. Roland stood next to Paul, the Director, and the two dancers to review the recording. What came up was surprising. Not only did it show the dancers, but they were placed inside an ice palace. It looked like they were dancing in the grand entrance of the ice palace Elsa created in the movie *Frozen*. It was beautiful and elegant in ways few productions of *Nutcracker* achieved. There was a moment or two when the dancers were out of frame. Roland and the dancers discussed what they saw and walked to the center of the set. Roland moved some of the tape markings on the floor. I thought, 'so this is what Roland does. He helps with the CGI when there is dance involved.'

Sandra walked into the room and over to Peter, John, and me. She directed her comment to Peter. "Interesting to see your uncle at work, isn't it? Wait until you see what he has in store for the Battle of the Mouse King."

"Really?"

The Director ran the *Pas de Deux* two more times, tweaking small changes here and there to keep the dancing centered. Surprisingly, or maybe not surprisingly, Mark and Gigi were flawless each time. It shows that years of practice and repetition produce reliable and sturdy performers.

When filming the *Pas de Deux* was over, Mark and Gigi walked off the set and immediately headed for the playpen to check on Henry. Henry was a happy child. He couldn't walk yet, but he could stand and bounce. Seeing his parents made Henry bounce even more.

"How's my little boy," cooed Gigi as she picked up the child.

Henry smiled and made some unintelligible sound. Peter, John, and I walked over to congratulate the couple on their performance.

"That was truly wonderful," Peter said to Mark and Gigi.

"Yes, that was perfect," repeated John.

"Thank you... it takes lots of work," Mark replied.

Peter reached out to Henry. "May I hold him?" asked Peter. Henry was already reaching out to Peter.

"Well... sure, he already likes you," responded Gigi.

Henry easily transferred to Peter's arms, placing him securely on his hip. Immediately Peter started bouncing him and singing a quiet little song.

"You have a natural talent with children," stated Gigi.

John and I were surprised. Yet, at the same time, we were not. Peter was personable with everyone— it makes sense that he would have an affinity for children.

"There is an honesty with children... and potential that I admire," added Peter.

I felt I needed to ask Gigi. "Weren't you afraid you couldn't dance after getting pregnant?"

Gigi could see that I was genuinely concerned. "I've heard that myth all my life. But I think it harkens back to the old days of ballet portrayed in overly dramatic movies like the *Red Shoes*... what was that like in the '40s or '50s? Those days of women dancers having to be as a nun to be morally pure to be a ballerina are over... actually, they never existed. I dance for the joy of dance. I wanted a child... and he is everything that I wanted. If having a child ended my career... so be it... but it would not end my joy of dance."

Mark joined in the conversation. "Gigi is a determined woman. She has to be, to be a world-class ballerina. I stand by her... ah... our... decision to have a child. We will be at the top of this game for only a few more years. Then some younger dancer who can do tricks we haven't even thought of will come and replace us." Mark looked exasperated when he said, 'tricks we haven't even thought of.' "Once the ballet career is over, we can still keep dancing and teaching and doing choreography... and we will have a family... forever. I think we, right now, have the best of both worlds."

"WE NEED THE RUSSIAN DANCERS ON SET. RUSSIAN DANCERS TO THE SET," called the Assistant Director over the bullhorn.

Most ballet companies do not have dancers trained in *prisyadka*— the Russian folk dancing style where men squat low sitting on their heels and perform a variety of kicks from this difficult position. In many *Nutcracker Ballet* productions, sometimes they try to simulate *prisyadka* with modified ballet steps or simply substitute something else for the dance, such as dancing Christmas trees. *Prisyadka* is a style of dance most people are familiar with when the words 'Russian folk dance' are said. Typically, the men wear flowing red pantaloons and a white blouse with a tied sash that bellows in the wind giving a very Asiatic look to the costume, or a military-style costume of a heavy red jacket with a black felt or fur headpiece. Because of Nutcracker, Ltd.'s much larger budget, they could hire the best Russian dancers from all over the United States and not settle on an imitation.

Eight men emerged from the dressing area and approached the set. I had not noticed them before. They did not attend the professional dance class that morning. Perhaps they arrived that morning just for the filming. The costume designer decided to go for a mixture of costumes. Half the men were in billowy red pantaloons and white blouses, whereas the other four men wore military-style uniforms, all wearing black boots. The costumes were of high quality and detail and were very smart in their design. Like everything else associated with this

206

production of *Nutcracker*, money was obviously spent on the costumes.

Gigi reached back for Henry. "It was so nice meeting you. And thank your mother for putting up with us all at the studio."

Before I could respond, Mark jumped in and said, "Yeah, we have a plane to catch tonight, and it takes a while to pack up everything. It's amazing how much *stuff* there is when you travel with a baby."

Everyone smiled while Mark and his mother folded up the playpen, and Gigi reached for the baby bag. She pulled out some cookies that Henry had grabbed. "They're his favorite... sugar-free, and he can gum them to mush."

Mark laughed, "I call them dog biscuits." Gigi swatted Mark's arm in play. Mark continued, "... and they taste like them too... but Henry likes them, and that's all that matters."

*

27 — *Prisyadka*

Roland worked with the eight male dancers in Russian costumes on the set. There were eight green boxes on the green set along the back wall. It was hard to see the boxes as they totally blended in. Roland had the men stand on the boxes and then jump or leap to the floor. It wasn't far, just two or three feet. Roland gave them directions about moving their arms while falling and their final position on the floor. I had no idea what that was all about.

Peter shook the hands of Mark and Gigi. "Hope to see you in New York... Bye."

Gigi, Mark and his mother, and Henry walked toward the door. Sandra stopped them to chat. She shook their hands as they left and then walked over to Peter, John, and me.

"OK. WE'RE GOING TO FILM FIRST THE JUMP, THEN THE DANCE. QUIET ON THE SET," the Assistant Director yelled out.

A camera was placed in front of the first dancer, who jumped off his box and held position. The camera was adjusted to the second dancer, who did the same but with a different flair. One by one, the dancers jumped, did a flip, performed some kind of turn from their box to the ground, and held the position until all eight were filmed jumping. Roland came on set and had all eight men return to the top of their respective boxes, the camera pulled back, and all eight were filmed jumping at once. Right then, Tchaikovsky's *Russian Dance* music came on, and the men continued the dance.

They were glorious. I was not familiar with Russian folk dancing, but I could tell it was a skill developed over years of training and every bit as much demanding as ballet. What was surprising was that the music was doubled in length. I was perplexed by the change.

"CUT," called the Director. "RELAX. IT WILL TAKE A FEW MINUTES TO REVIEW THE TAKE WITH THE SPECIAL EFFECTS LOADED."

Sandra spoke up. "I could see you are confused, Marie. We decided to extend the length of three of the numbers. The

Russian Dance, *Chinese Dance*, and *Spanish Dance* are only one minute long. In updating the *Nutcracker*, we decided to make them twice as long. They were so short that they are over before the audience even notices they are happening. Lengthening them better matches all the other numbers."

The overhead monitors flickered to life. Everyone looked up to watch while Paul, Roland, the Director, and eight dancers viewed the screen at the computer station. First, the bottom branches of a Christmas tree came onto the screen, along with a few storefronts from the mall and the bench where Clara fell asleep. The tree extended from side to side, and the branches were large enough to support a human. Eight very large candy canes were positioned over the branches. Next, the eight canes dissolved into each one of the dancers who floated, jumped, or did a flip to the ground. Once they were all on the ground, the music and dance began in full.

"Ah," said John to Peter, Sandra, and me, "the Russian dancers are candy canes that jump to the ground to dance. How inventive."

"This is why we had to shoot this dance on greenscreen," added Sandra, "we needed the special effect of the large tree. Remember, Clara is supposed to be the size of a doll or mouse for the entire second half of the *Nutcracker*. We're going to be using this special effect tree for the Mouse King battle."

At the end of the dance, the Russian dancers made *tours en l'air* that special effects augmented and had them fly back up into the tree and become candy canes again.

"I'm starting to feel bad for my mother. Our little *Nutcracker* can't compare with all these special effects," I pouted.

Sandra wanted to reassure me and said, "You have a nice production for a small local ballet company. I've seen your rehearsal with Peter and John and the rest. Your mother should be proud."

RUSSIAN DANCE

She really did mean it. There is no way a big-budget Hollywood production with added special effects should be compared with a small local ballet company. Each has its merits, and the local shows give many aspiring dancers a chance to perform and hone their skills.

Roland and Paul moved the dancers to the stage, where they discussed some minor changes for spacing. Roland repositioned some of the tape marking the floor.

"QUIET ON THE SET. THIS IS A TAKE," yelled the Assistant Director.

Like before, the men took position on their boxes, jumped, or flipped down to their mark. The music began, and the men danced up a storm kicking their legs and jumping in ways that did not seem humanly possible. Russian dancing has a vibrancy that is so upbeat and lively. Shame that the history of Russia is full of pain and tragedy.

"I can't imagine doing that a couple of times a day. That kills my knees just watching it," Peter said as he screwed his face up to indicate pain.

"What's hangin'?" blared someone from the reception area. It was the unmistakable voice of Whitney. She walked, better yet, burst into the room, followed by her entourage of hair and makeup artists, bodyguards, some unknown admirers, and Jasmine. Sandra immediately sprang into action and stopped Whitney before she could progress too far into the room to disrupt filming. I looked back and saw her bodyguards close in on Sandra. Sandra held her ground and herded Whitney and her group to the dressing area filled with actors and gymnasts putting on mouse costumes.

"Please keep it down. We're filming," Sandra asked politely.

"You chirping at me?" demanded Whitney while she gave an insolent smile to her group.

"Yeah, don't diss my girl," jumped in Jasmine.

Whitney was disturbed that Jasmine felt the right to join in the conversation imitating teen lingo. She raised her arm to push Jasmine back but caught Jasmine on her nose. Jasmine screamed and fell back in pain, pushing over one of the actors in his mouse costume. Like a comedy routine seen in fun movies, the mouse pushed over another mouse who pushed another who hit the folding room divider that fell over onto Whitney's bodyguards and Sandra.

BAM!!!

Down they all went onto the floor exactly in time with the final notes of the Russian Dance. A moment or two passed while people assessed if they were hurt. Once they realized there was no harm, a soft laugh spread between them. What a sight! Mice were scattered everywhere on their backs, with legs and tails flailing and Whitney still standing in the middle of the pile unscathed.

"CUT... WHAT'S THAT RACKET?" cried out the Director into the darkened studio space.

Sandra yelled out from under the wooden divider, "We're OK. Please ignore us."

"LUCKILY, THAT'S A TAKE. RUSSIAN DANCERS, THANK YOU. PLEASE LEAVE THE SET. WE'LL FILM THE BATTLE OF THE MOUSE KING NEXT. EVERYONE REPORT TO THE SET IN FIFTEEN," announced the Assistant Director.

Peter, John, and I ran over and lifted the room divider. The bodyguards and Sandra stood up unharmed. The mice helped each other up. Jasmine, however, was sitting on the floor holding her nose. It was bleeding. A mouse soon appeared with a towel and wet compress for Jasmine to hold against her nose. Whitney helped Jasmine stand up.

"I'm bleeding... I'm bleeding," Jasmine cried as she grabbed the towel from the mouse.

Whitney and Sandra looked closely at Jasmine's nose, applying and reapplying the cold, wet compress.

"Just a small bloody nose. I'm sure it will be fine in a few hours," said Sandra while she dabbed some of the tears from Jasmine's eyes.

"I'm going to have black eyes... I'm going to have black eyes... I can't have black eyes for the performance in a few days."

"Here, let's go into the reception room where it will be quieter for you," Sandra said while placing her arms around Jasmine. She gently guided Jasmine out of the studio to the reception area. What more could happen to Jasmine?

*

28 — *Battle of the Mouse King*

Without a word, all the mice left the dressing area and reported to the set. Peter, John, and I also reported to the set carrying our headpieces. Whitney was left alone but soon, a cadre of makeup and costuming surrounded her to prepare her for filming her song later that day. I looked back and saw how dejected and sad Whitney seemed.

Besides the mice and Mouse King, about ten actors on the set wore greenscreen suits used for motion capture. These suits look like scuba diving wet suits covering the body from ankle to neck and headpiece made out of black stretch fabric. At every joint— ankles, knees, hips, waist, shoulder, elbow, wrists, neck, and smaller joints of the hands— were placed small white dots about the size of a dime. Basically, the movements of the white dots are replaced, by the computer, with animated figures moving just as the actors do. Looking at them, there was no way to know if they were clowns, dinosaurs, robots, or whatever. That would come later in the computer processing stage.

The Stewart twins and their Mouse companion were also on stage. I had not noticed them before. They had a special trailer outside the building for their preparation and use. Such are the perks of being a star. Bonnie, as Clara, wore winter clothes. Under the jacket was a soft flowing summer dress that she would wear throughout the rest of the *Nutcracker*. Jim, playing the Nutcracker, was in white tights and bright red jacket adorned with gold epaulets and trim. During the Battle of the Mouse King, he wore his headpiece. Once the King is defeated, his headpiece magically disappears, revealing the handsome prince.

Paul came out to the set along with Roland. Roland busied himself, placing tape markings on the floor for the new number.

Paul directed the dancers, "I know this is new for some of you… " he looked in the direction of Peter, John, and me, "but just do what we choreographed and rehearsed. Ignore all the green walls and just concentrate on your steps and where you are supposed to be in relationship with each other. Luckily, Roland is here so that we can quickly review the number with the special effects added... OK, take position."

The set was emptied with everyone off to the sides out of camera view. All the mice put on their headpieces. Bonnie, as Clara, laid down on some green boxes near the center of the set.

"... ACTION," called the Director.

Clara and the Nutcracker music played through the sound system. About three minutes into this musical section is when small mice should appear scurrying across the set, yet nothing was happening on the set. A minute later, the Christmas tree should grow larger to indicate Clara is shrinking to the size of a mouse or doll. But, again, nothing happened on the set. I figured all of this was special effects done in computer rendering. Finally, five minutes into the recording, Jim jumped onto the set as the Nutcracker with his headpiece on. Bonnie woke up and moved from the boxes, looking confused. The musical sequence ended and, without a pause, immediately began the *Battle* music. That was Peter, John, and my cue to enter the set.

Wow, I was disoriented. The mouse headpiece made it very difficult to see out. Now I had a better appreciation of what Nick and the other kids at the studio went through playing mice. Plus, when looking out, I was overwhelmed by the bright green; it was everywhere and blinding.

I danced the choreography as set. During the dance, I realized that the mice characters wore real costumes, whereas the army headed by the Nutcracker was all in greenscreen suits. That would mean that the entire Nutcracker army would be computer animated. I wondered what that would be like. In the traditional ballet, the army is made up of toy soldiers. However, the original story by E. T. A. Hoffman and Tchaikovsky's score did not specify soldiers. Instead, the scene is a battle between the mice and *toys*, meaning any toys.

I scurried around like a mouse. One-by-one, actors in greenscreen suits arrived at the other side of the set. The first one entered by walking very funny— rotating from one foot to the other. The next actor stamped around stiffly like a robot. The third actor imitated some large creature. The next was a combination of two guys acting like they were part of a horse or other four-footed creature. I had no idea what they were supposed to be. The Mouse King wore an elaborate crown and regal jacket and looked comical. The Nutcracker, carrying his sword, led a couple of charges toward the mice. Jim, the actor playing the Nutcracker, was not a dancer, so he was staged through some mock battles with the Mouse King. The rest of the actors also engaged in mock battles and wrestling but without weapons. For me, this wasn't as much dancing as it was staging and moving. It was fun, though.

I was aware that there was a major change in the usual plot. Instead of the Mouse King being killed, he would be trapped and allowed to live. Maybe the producers wanted to downplay the violence. I wasn't sure how that would work, but I was open to the new interpretation. Now, near the end of the battle, the Nutcracker army built some kind of cage around the Mouse King. The men in greenscreen suits sometimes carried poles and boxes that were arranged around the set. Eventually, the Nutcracker's army corralled the mice around the Mouse King, and they hunkered down in fear. A small Mouse begged the Nutcracker to let them go pleading that they could be of help. The Nutcracker let them out, and many mice picked up brooms and dustpans to show they could help keep the mall clean. Now, the Nutcracker's compassion breaks the spell, and his headpiece disappears and is transformed into the Nutcracker Prince. The small Mouse befriended the Nutcracker and Clara and guided them through the mall for the rest of the story.

Without hesitation, the music continued into the *In the Pine Forest* sequence. A boat made out of half an acorn shell is supposed to magically appear. On the greenscreen, this was a small box to sit on. The small Mouse took Clara and the Nutcracker Prince by hand into the boat. The other mice and toys waved goodbye while the three of them flew away. One of the actors in green suit was on wires and flew away next to the acorn shell boat.

BATTLE OF THE MOUSE KING

"CUT. WELL, DONE. WE'LL SEE THE RENDERED VERSION IS A FEW MINUTES. PLEASE MOVE BACK TO POSITION ONE," yelled the Director.

Roland was busy at the computer center working with some technicians to quickly blend the recorded action with the animation. Everyone surrounded the monitors with anticipation. All the mice took off their headpieces to relax. Peter, John, and I anxiously waited to see the final result. Even Jasmine returned to the studio, still holding the cold, wet compress against her nose, and stood with Whitney, watching a screen.

"OK, here we go. Remember, this is a rough idea. Full rendering will be done later," Roland announced.

Everyone looked at the video monitors. As expected, the scene began with Clara falling asleep on the bench, but Roland had inserted the mall center showing the bench and pine trees. Soon, several small-animated mice added by Roland scurried about the floor. They looked very lifelike but with bright beady eyes. Next, the Christmas tree behind her grew very very large, and many storefronts were visible to one side. Again, it looked surprisingly real.

Peter, John, and I were the first three mice to enter the set. We were tickled by how we looked like mice. Soon more mice and the Mouse King joined them. The Nutcracker appeared and called in his army. Then a gingerbread man ran in from the housewares store, and some of the mice proceeded to chew on him.

John piped in, "Oh, so that is why the actor in green suit moved so funny... Kinda like one of the playing cards in Alice in Wonderland. Rotating on one foot, then the next—he's a gingerbread man.

The second of the army to appear was a yellow robot similar to the ones seen in the *Transformers* movies. It entered from the toy store.

"So, that explains why he was stomping around," John realized about the second actor to enter wearing the greenscreen suit. "Wow!"

Next, a dinosaur and astronaut similar to the ones from the *Toy Story* movie entered from the Disney Store. The dinosaur gave a simulated roar.

"Double wow!" added Peter.

The two guys who entered together from the toy store made up a slinky bug.

"Triple wow!" I added.

Slowly, the Nutcracker army was made up of a collection of well-known toys, including soldiers made up of LEGO-like pieces. The battle between the toys and mice was remarkable. I was surprised by how well the choreography captured the differences in size and action between the various characters.

"Cool, isn't it... I had no idea." I couldn't contain myself.

"None of us did." John was very surprised.

The battle continued. The Nutcracker army brought out poles and other items like a bathtub placed high up on the pole and a large basket-shaped net and swimming pool. It looked like they were building something, but what? I wasn't sure. The mice and Mouse King were backed against a pole in the center of the set, surrounded by the Nutcracker and his army.

I spoke up. "Is that... is that the trap from the board game... Ah."

Just then, the dinosaur threw a ball into the bathtub situated ten feet off the stage. The ball fell through a hole that hit a teeter-totter, which sent a diver into a small pool, which set the large circular net ratcheting down— *snick snick snick snick snick snick snick* — capturing the mice and Mouse King under the cage.

No one in the room could resist yelling.

"MOUSE TRAP," echoed through the room as people threw their hands up over their heads simultaneously and began laughing, just like they did when they were children and played the Hasbro board game.

"Oh, no, they didn't." Peter laughed so hard.

MOUSE KING CAUGHT BY MOUSETRAP

The room broke into applause. Roland, somewhat embarrassed, stood up and took a bow. Roland looked around the room and spotted Peter. Peter gave him the thumbs-up salute and a big smile. Roland was pleased.

The video continued to the end with Clara, the Nutcracker Prince, and the small Mouse flying away in their acorn shell boat. The astronaut flew next to them and escorted them into the clouds. The screen went blank.

Another round of applause and cheers filled the room. Everyone was excited; even Whitney had a large smile. It was hard to tell what Jasmine thought because the cold compress covered much of her face and nose.

Sandra took over the bullhorn. "I want to thank Roland for all the novel ideas. We see it will be a hit. Thanks, Roland."

Peter was proud of his uncle's inventive ideas. Who would have thought of using the Mousetrap board game to capture the Mouse King?

The Director took over the bullhorn, "THAT'S WONDERFUL AND WHAT GREAT IDEAS. WE NEED TO MAKE A FEW ADJUSTMENTS AND RUN IT AGAIN... PLEASE GET INTO FIRST POSITION."

Paul, Roland, and the Director met on the stage and moved around some of the marks on the floor. They called over the various dancers and actors to review the changes needed to keep them in frame. A bit later, a second and third run was filmed. For being such a complex scene, the Director was satisfied by the third filming and dismissed the actors. Sandra, ever the pro, personally thanked each actor and dancer as they left the set, regardless if they were well-known celebrities like the Stewart twins or an actor whose face wasn't even seen under a mouse costume. As the representative for the administration of Nutcracker Ltd., her job was to maintain professional relationships between all parties, and she did it well.

Just one more number to film on the green screen.

*

29 — *Cheese Cheese*

Sandra walked over to Whitney and escorted her to the set. It was time for her to film her two songs.

"ALL UNNECESSARY PERSONNEL NEED TO LEAVE THE BUILDING. THIS IS A SECURE FILMING," called the Assistant Director over the bullhorn.

Security swept through the building to ensure only set technicians and Whitney and her team were left inside the building. Since the two songs would not be released until the movie came out much later in the year, every effort was made to secure the filming and avoid any unauthorized release onto social media.

Peter, John, and I were changing out of our mouse costumes, getting ready to leave, when Sandra came up to them.

"Whitney would like for you to stay. She wants you sitting with her when she sings. OK?" asked Sandra.

"Ah, sure," we all answered.

"Please leave your costumes on and carry your headpiece with you."

The three of us followed Sandra to the set. The building was much quieter, with fewer people working on the equipment. Jasmine tried to follow, but Sandra instructed the bodyguards to keep her back. Jasmine felt miffed that Whitney kept her isolated.

In her stylized mouse costume, Whitney was already in the center of the set with three other actors in mice costumes. As I approached, I got up and gave her a big hug, as big as possible, reaching around the bellies of the mouse costume.

"Cool, how swaggy my mains are with me," Whitney perked up with teen slang.

Roland stood by while Paul gave some instructions. "In '*Nutcracker, the Musical*' Whitney plays one of the mice in the *Battle of the Mouse King*. At the end of the number, a couple of the other mice will pull her offstage when they all, as actors, goof around and sing 'Cheese, Cheese.' We're still going to keep the three mice pulling Whitney onto the set, and you will begin the song as rehearsed. Now, soon after the song begins, all of you will take off your headpiece and stand behind Whitney doing backup vocals. The new mice will come in with their headpiece off and sit at Whitney's feet and listen. That is where you three," Paul pointed to Peter, John, and me, "come in."

It seemed easy enough, but I was apprehensive. I wasn't used to being in the background. Not that I thought anything was wrong with being a supernumerary, but I was uncertain what to do, how to genuinely look interested. Holding a smile too long often results in cheek muscles quivering and looking fake. At least with dance, you were always moving, and there was generally an understanding that a serious face or expressionless face was expected.

"OK, this is a run-through. We're going to have cameras running to estimate spacing, but don't worry about talk over."

"Talk over," I asked?

Paul demonstrated the infinite patience he learned growing up in the south and working as a professional dancer. With his smooth drawl, he explained, "The Director or someone else yelling directions to the actors while on the set and camera's rolling. Take directions and don't worry that we are filming."

"Oh," I replied.

"Whitney, please go upstage and be prepared for the other mice to grab you by your hand. Do it like we rehearsed," directed Paul. "We're going to let the camera run, so start when you are ready."

Surprisingly, Whitney looked good in the stylized mouse costume. Although it had a rounded belly and looked like all the other mice, the headpiece was not to be used but rather her hair and makeup styled to look like a mouse. The other two male mice and one female mouse wore standard makeup and nothing special. The three mice grabbed Whitney's hands and arm, pulled her downstage, and said, "Come on. Aren't we hungry?"

Whitney responded with, "Well, we could eat some cheese." Her three companions lined up behind her. The music started, and Whitney waved Peter, John, and me to join in. The three of us danced in and sat at her feet. Whitney sang, 'Cheese, Cheese.'

(4/4)
Cheese, cheese, cheese, cheese, we all love cheese cheese
Yellow cheese, white cheese, hard cheese, soft cheese
Why we even love moldy cheese!
Round cheese, brick cheese, sliced cheese and melted cheese
There's nothing better than cheese cheese

(3/4 waltz)
Slice some Cheddar on sourdough bread
With a layer of pimento olives
Mozzarella, with Ricotta spread
Grilled, cheese, sandwiches for all to give

Roland explained that halfway through the song, he would animate a large body-size wheel of cheese that would be rolled in next to Whitney and the mice. We were given over-size triangular shape pieces of cheese to continue the song.

(4/4)
Cheese, cheese, cheese, cheese, we all love cheese cheese
Swiss Cheese with holes, Blue Cheese with mold
Why we even love Cottage Cheese!
Monterey Jack or American Processed
There's nothing better than cheese cheese

(march)
Munster, Gouda, Port Salut
Gruyère, Colby, Camembert
Feta, Roquefort, Halloumi
Edam, Herve, Gorgonzola
Brie, both sliced and oven-baked
Grated Parmesan makes it shake

Cheese, cheese, cheese, cheese, we all love cheese cheese

I laughed to myself at the silly song. Whitney and the other singers looked absurd, singing and dancing in mouse costumes. The six mice swayed to the music, and the chorus sounded good. Whitney sometimes walked to one side and then the next, with the backup chorus providing some steps. Often, we made little mouse moves and simulated eating cheese. It was a delightful and playful routine. That was the point—simple fun.

While Whitney was singing, various technicians moved about the set, adjusting microphones, lights, and camera angles. Only the Director, Paul, and Roland gave them any attention but often looked at monitors for spacing issues. During the song, Jasmine slipped out from the dressing area and stood just a few feet away from Whitney and the others, holding the ice compress against her nose. Her lips protruded into a pout, and she looked like she was on the verge of yelling. At the end of the number, Jasmine walked up to Whitney, grabbed the piece of cheese she was holding, and threw it to the ground.

"This is beneath you. You're much better than this," yelled Jasmine at Whitney.

It was hard to understand her since her nose was still swollen from the accidental hit earlier that day, and it sounded like she had a stuffy nose.

"Stop being a hater... just chill girl," Whitney's slang came out.

"... and, and, you choose Marie to be with... why... " Jasmine choked up, and tears glazed her eyes. "I'm pure for my art." She looked around the group. "I live for ballet... the highest art... that's better than some cheap song."

"Hey, stop boosting... that's hurtful," Whitney responded.

The Director turned away from the monitors and toward the commotion. He motioned to one of the security guards. "Hey, get that girl out of here."

Jasmine couldn't take it anymore and ran through the studio out the front reception area to the outside; tears ran down her face and swollen nose.

Whitney stood up, thinking that she should do something but was uncertain about what to do.

I spoke up, "Don't worry about her... she lives just three blocks from here; so if nothing else, she can walk home... I know you care... but..."

Paul came to the group to demonstrate the new markings on the floor. He walked Whitney and all the actors and singers through the revised positions.

"LET'S TAKE THIS FROM POSITION ONE AND SEE HOW THE SPECIAL EFFECTS OVERLAY," directed the Assistant Director.

Peter, John, and I moved offstage. Whitney moved upstage, and the other three mice took their position.

"... ACTION," yelled the Director.

The second run-through was similar to the first, but Whitney seemed distracted. Perhaps the altercation with Jasmine hit a nerve. At first, she seemed shy, then partway through, she began blocking the other singers and actors in an unprofessional way— very much like she was arrogant. At one point, she pushed one of the mice, who was slightly off-point, with too much force. The mouse almost fell.

"CUT... WHAT ARE YOU DOING OUT THERE, WHITNEY?" called the Director.

The Director brusquely removed his headset and walked directly up to Whitney to confront her actions. "Remember your character. You are a young girl, insecure about your career. Everyone loves an underdog. The other mice are your friends and compatriots. I need you to act."

Whitney looked down at the floor. Being a major superstar had inured her to public admonishment. But the Director was correct. She needed to act the part she was being paid to play. She couldn't let her emotions get the best of her, but Jasmine's words had tripped her up. Maybe she was selling herself short just for the money.

"AGAIN. POSITION ONE... SPEED... ACTION."

I noticed how on edge Whitney had become. This time she acted very shy, almost frightened. Often the Director yelled at her to laugh, have fun, and show some teeth. But each yell only made Whitney tense up more. The Director let the scene run all the way to the end. That allowed Roland to lay in the special effects, giving us a better view of the final product.

'Cheese, Cheese' was sung right after the *Battle of the Mouse King* when all the actors relaxed after the filming. Roland used the images of the mall center with bench and pine trees in place as the background animation. Since it was a three-dimensional space, the camera rotated around Whitney and showed the mice from different angles and close-ups. It was a lovely overall scene, but Whitney truly lacked joy.

"CUT," yelled the Director. "TAKE TWENTY."

He turned his attention to Whitney. "You straighten up and get this right next time. I don't care what is going on; I need you to act."

Everyone was deeply concerned about Whitney's ability to pull off the scene. Sandra felt she needed to take action and walked over to Whitney.

"Honey, what's the matter?" asked Sandra as she brushed a lock of hair off Whitney's forehead. "You can tell me. We're all worried."

Whitney didn't hold back and broke into full-body sobs. "I'm such a fraud... who cares about what I do?" Her teen slang melted away.

"We do... we care."

"But I'm singing about cheese... no one cares about that."

Sandra let some time pass and then reassured her. "It's a fun song... and that's the point. It makes people feel happy. Think of all the children who will sing 'Cheese, Cheese'... Why I bet this song will last for decades, being sung around campfires, youth events, and even church choirs. You bring joy to children... and your voice will always be associated with it. What an honor."

"Honor?" repeated Whitney.

Peter jumped in and said, "Yeah, honor... although I'm sure a bunch of parents could kill you for introducing their kids to a song they sing over and over, every day, annoying everyone around them... ha, ha."

That put a smile on Whitney's face, including everyone else nearby. The image of small children playing the sing-a-long version, day after day, driving their parents nuts, seemed amusing.

"But what does it all mean? Why should I sing this or that? How do I decide? I've lost my moral compass," pleaded Whitney.

John felt he had to jump in and said, "I know I'm only a kid, but I think about why I dance all the time. All I know is that I love it; more than anything. But the kids at school tease me mercilessly... and sometimes threaten me... about dancing ballet and listening to classical music. I can't tell you how often someone will say something like, 'hey, I hear football players take ballet,' implying that since jocks take ballet, it must be OK for me to dance ballet. I don't need their validation. If anything, it should be the opposite; that if a ballet dancer plays football, it makes it OK for boys to play football. Both ideas are whacked! Why are either of these related and doesn't change my respect and love for ballet? It takes courage to stand up for what you believe and want."

Just as John finished, Roland and Paul sat down in the circle formed by Whitney, Sandra, and the mice. It was obvious that a deep discussion about motivation was necessary to address Whitney's concerns and get her back on track for the day's filming.

Roland joined in and shared, "For me, I was trained in a very conservative dance company. This was before I met Barbara and Bill. The director was very anti-sex. She impressed upon both the boys and girls that classical ballet required them to stay 'pure' and refrain from dating, or sex, or bad language, or bad thoughts, and so on. She tied classical ballet to personal morality. That bred a culture of secrecy and gossip that eventually tore the group apart. It took me the longest time to understand that ballet and sex and ethics are separate things. I danced because it was beautiful... in so many deeply satisfying ways. If I dated or had sex, which I put off until I was almost thirty years old, it was not related to ballet. Tying them together screwed with my head for so long."

231

Roland waited to see if Whitney made the connections. "For you, Whitney, I suggest that you separate your public persona and your career choices from your original love of singing. When you can, sing for the love of singing. Otherwise, keep all the other stuff related to being a star separate."

This circle of friends quickly became a consciousness-raising sharing of deeply held emotions.

Sandra next spoke to the group. "I struggled with being an average ballet dancer. I didn't have great skill. I knew that. I made it into a corps de ballet but never as a soloist. I, too, wrapped up my self-worth by attending ballet classes seven days a week and working hard, and thinking that the ultimate goal of being a dancer was to be a star. Somehow having perfect attendance, in my mind, made me think I was better than the other girls. I was the 'good' girl."

Sandra shuttered and looked deeply into the dark space extending past the floor. "I was about twenty-nine years old when I fractured my left ankle." She looked around at the other people. "No, not from jumping but rather from turning... I saw an orthopedic specialist who worked with athletes and dancers. I was immediately put into a cast for six weeks. I returned, and the x-rays showed the bones had not knitted, so I was put into a second cast for another six weeks. After twelve weeks, the bones were fine. I asked the doctor if I really needed a cast. He looked at me and asked if I had danced while I had the cast on." Sandra turned to everyone and nodded, "of course I did... I told the doctor that I did because I still had to teach, and, besides, I had a show coming up just three weeks after the cast came off. The doctor looked me directly in my eyes and said, "no, you didn't need a cast, but I know you dancers—you are insane. I can tell a professional athlete to lay off, and the team managers will see that they do, but you dancers are impossible." Sandra paused. "I remember feeling pride... yes pride... that I, as a lowly paid ballet dancer, was willing and able to withstand more pain than athletes paid millions of dollars a year... It wasn't until a few weeks later, when I injured myself again, that it dawned on me. I was gaining self-esteem from pain. In fact, I was trying to injure myself to prove to the world that I was committed more to dance than anyone else… wow, was that messed up." Sandra took a deep breath. She was sad but invigorated at the same time. "I'm glad I had that insight. In my mind, I had transformed dance from the purity and beauty that first attracted me into a quest for martyrdom to gain self-worth."

Tears came to Sandra's eyes. I reached out to hold her hand.

Sandra had more to say. "In order to keep dancing, I had to reach into my soul to allow ballet to be itself regardless of my effort or commitment or how I was rewarded with money or status. I had to be on guard against martyr behaviors and know when to stop. I had to recognize that my little world as a corps de ballet dancer meant that the soloist and stars would probably not even acknowledge my existence. I was completely invisible." Sandra turned to Roland. "I bet you don't remember me?"

Roland was caught off guard and hesitated. He didn't know what to say.

"You and Barbara were hired to dance the *Nutcracker* with the ballet company I worked with so many years ago. You were there for six weeks. We had class and rehearsal together every day. I often stood next to you. You lifted me many times during *pas de deux* class."

"Uh, sorry… " Roland was embarrassed.

"I'm not trying to put you on the spot, but once we lay our own values or hopes onto an activity we love, we ultimately will be disappointed. If I expected Roland or Barbara to remember me because we shared something special, I'm setting myself up for disappointment. I cannot expect everyone I danced with to remember the experience exactly the way I did, nor hold the same personal values. I've learned that, in many ways, it is our differences that bring richness to dance. I'm fortunate to be able to continue touching the world of dance through this Nutcracker project."

A long, silent pause filled the room. You could hear breaths being taken— in and out, in and out. In some ways, the talk was an absurd situation, with each person sharing deeply personal experiences and insights while sitting around in mouse costumes.

Sandra turned to Whitney. "You have a truly lovely voice... truly lovely. Years of singing in your mother's choir gave you great skill. Each song you sing touches someone: whether it is a couple hearing a love song, or singing a song to your mother on Mother's Day, or children singing your song about cheese."

That put smiles on Sandra's and Whitney's faces.

"Find the joy in the song. Imagine that child, playing alone in her room, singing 'Cheese, Cheese.' They will be happy... now keep that image in your mind and let's film this perfectly. Have fun!"

Whitney and others involuntarily clapped their hands. Sandra dabbed at her eyes with a tissue and reached over and wiped the remaining tears from Whitney's eyes. A makeup artist came and touched up her face.

"For whatever reason," Sandra continued, "Jasmine is hurting right now, and she lashed out at you—actually all of us. She needs to find her own path. Right now, we need to finish this shoot. Find that joy that drives you to sing and bring that joy to the world."

Roland hugged Sandra. Not just a hug, but one expressing thanks and hope. They had been friends for so long. Paul joined in for a group hug.

Paul turned to Whitney, hugged her too, and said in his heavy southern accent, "Honey, we don't want you doing a Lindsay Lohan, or Miley Cyrus, or Britney Spears. No crash and burn. Be true to yourself and have fun. Your audience can tell when you are true."

The Assistant Director yelled out, "OK, EVERYONE TO OPENING POSITION."

Whitney took a moment and seemed to pull herself together. The next take went extremely well. Whitney seemed to find the truth inside her and beamed. She was joyful and playful at the same time. Her interactions with the mice seemed authentic. I could see the joy in her eyes, making the filming process fun. The Director was pleased and thought it would be well received by children and parents. After Roland laid in the special effects, the cast gave it a big cheer. Whitney was relaxed and happy. 'Cheese, Cheese', would be a hit.

Sandra thanked the actors and singers for their time and escorted them to the dressing area. Whitney exited to the trailer just outside the building to change her costume and makeup. Whitney had one more song to film by herself. *There Are No Real Princes* would explore the disappointment with the promise that a prince would ride in on a white horse and save the day. It was going to be a solo performed in front of the greenscreen, and Roland was filling in the back with the 3-D special effect of the ice castle used for the *Pas de Deux*.

Peter, John, and I went to the dressing area to change out of their mouse costumes. It had been a few hours since we last ate, and we were feeling hungry. I pulled out my cell phone to call Barbara.

"Mom," I asked excitedly, "we're done with the filming today... Yes, it was great... I was thinking about asking Peter, John, and Whitney, oh, and Paul and Sandra over for dinner... do you have enough for all?... Probably in about an hour and a half. Whitney has to sing one more song... Great, I'll ask and call you back... Thanks, Mom, you're the best."

It didn't take Whitney long to change into a long dress similar in style to what Elsa wore in *Frozen*. The mixture of deep blue fabric extending into silver edging and rhinestones complemented the cold backdrop. Whitney looked stunning. Her hair was kept simple to not look like one of those girls who get too dressed up for their first prom. The Director, Paul, and Roland directed her through the set. It would be a simple effort, with her walking only a few feet along with a few slow spins. The rest of the effect would be supplied by the special effects Roland created. The building was very quiet, considering only a handful of people were still present.

"... ACTION," called out the Director.

This was Whitney at her best. She concentrated on her voice, harmony, and syncopation with no one else to think about and no complicated choreography. She knew when to make the sound small and when to let it grow. Years of singing in her mother's choir and now as a world superstar were evident in her poise. I was learning to appreciate Whitney more and more, considering that I had never listened to pop music before and didn't know who Whitney was before the filming of the *Nutcracker*.

The playback was beautiful. Roland's 3-D rendition of the ice palace had many more details than the one used in *Frozen*. That gave him greater range in where Whitney was placed, including viewing out over the mall and the ice-skating rink, the pine trees, and all the storefronts. It was very colorful and fun, yet meaningful at the same time... and Whitney's voice captured the song's sadness.

The Director insisted on two more takes. He wanted additional footage for editing purposes. Whitney was perfect each time.

"THANK YOU ALL. THAT'S IT. WE CAN SHUT DOWN," yelled out the Director.

That was it. Filming of *The New Nutcracker* and *Nutcracker the Musical* was over, and all the singers, dancers, actors, makeup, technicians, and others would be leaving town. I was both excited by the events of the day but also sad to realize it would all be ending. I went up to each of them and extended mother's invitation for dinner. The Director was too busy shutting down the set, but Paul, Roland, Sandra, Peter, John, and, to my great delight, Whitney all agreed. I was elated that we would all be together in a social setting with no pressures to distract them. I called Barbara and confirmed the extra people for dinner. It would be a night to remember.

*

30 — Dress Rehearsal of Act 1

The dinner was a success; it was very informal and a chance for Barbara to thank everyone for their collaboration with her dance studio. Most everyone was leaving her small northeastern town to return to their own lives. Paul left for New York to continue teaching and creating choreography. His knowledge and genteel manners would be sorely missed. Sandra returned to the headquarters of Nutcracker Ltd., located in Los Angeles. There would be many more years of work editing the films and promoting the products. She was grateful to still be involved with ballet. Whitney, too, was leaving for Los Angeles. She had to prepare for a New Year's Eve concert that she was singing at in Las Vegas. Many high rollers would be there, and she would be showered with adoration and money. Although she was leaving, Whitney was in regular contact with me by text. Whitney and I formed a surprising yet strong bond over the past few days.

The only person to stay from the *Nutcracker* film was Roland. He committed to Barbara to play the role of Godfather Drosselmeier in her production of *Nutcracker.* However, he needed to telecommute with the office to refine the special effects he created for the filming. Roland also appreciated spending time with his ex-partner Barbara and his nephew Peter.

The next day professional cleaners hired by Nutcracker Ltd. came and conducted a deep cleaning of the dance studio, which was cleaner than it had been in years. Barbara now had complete access to all four studios, which was important because her own *Nutcracker* was opening in one day, and she needed every square inch for classes, rehearsals, costumes, props, and sets. Having all the people involved with Nutcracker Ltd. use her studio for ten days was very disruptive, especially at this time of year. But it was a big honor and financially beneficial for Barbara.

Since her *Nutcracker* was opening with a Saturday evening performance, the dress rehearsal was held Friday afternoon and evening at the local city auditorium after school when kids and families could attend. The auditorium anchored one end of the mall near the ice-skating rink and held about a thousand people. It had fairly new stage equipment and sound and was the right size for her local production.

By about four o'clock in the afternoon, the student dancers, parents, and many volunteers filed into the auditorium. Several adults were assigned to direct children to the dressing rooms and bathrooms. Most of the older dancers were already in costume, warming up on stage. To control the problem with 'stage mothers,' parents were expressly forbidden from the dressing rooms once their child was dropped off. Parents were resigned to sitting in the front row seats of the auditorium. One of the long-time parents who had participated in many *Nutcrackers* was stationed to keep control of the parents.

Barbara and I walked down the aisle of the auditorium carrying several costumes. Beatrice followed closely behind, carrying more costumes and props. Behind her were Bill and Sheila carrying Prima, her puppies, and their playpen. Nick was last, pushing a cart containing many radio-controlled drones. Barbara was trying a new idea for a special effect in the *Waltz of the Flowers* that included drones. She had been influenced by what she saw during the filming. She hoped it would work.

Bill set up the playpen near the front of the stage where Beatrice was stationed to keep watch over them. The dogs were gently placed in the playpen with their blankets and toys. They seemed fine with the arrangement, although Prima was standing on her hind legs stretched against the bars, really wanting to be out with people. Over to the extreme side of the stage, but down in the audience walkway, was a photo station. Here, a professional photographer set up lighting and a backdrop to take individual and group photos of each performer in full costume.

Barbara walked up onto the stage and talked loudly. "I need your attention. There isn't much time for the dress rehearsal. All of you should be in costume. Those of you here for the publicity shots, go over there," Barbara pointed to the photo station off stage. "The rest of you, get into positions. We are starting from the beginning. We may stop every now and then to correct something. But dance it full out. Act like this is a real performance."

The children took position, the curtain was closed, and Barbara walked back to the audience area and sat near Beatrice and the dogs. She put on a headset to communicate with light and sound technicians and the stage manager. Barbara worked out all the lighting and set cues with the stage manager earlier in the week, who then took many days to set the stage and more. Putting on a production of the *Nutcracker* requires hundreds of hours of set preparation time.

Barbara spoke into the headset, "OK, to start when you are ready."

After a moment, the *Nutcracker* music swelled out of the auditorium speakers. The crisp, sharp tones of the strings and horns for the opening march announced the beginnings of the festivities. No one can resist feeling good and getting excited when hearing the *Nutcracker Overture*.

Each number proceeded smoothly. From the families' entry to the children playing; to the opening of the presents, it went smoothly— months of rehearsals and counting on so many to help bring it all together. Although there were minor mishaps, there was nothing an audience of parents and friends wouldn't forgive and, in fact, find endearing. Jasmine did well, although it became obvious to Barbara that she was getting a bit old for the part. This was the third year in a row she played the role of Clara, and it would be her last. Barbara reviewed in her mind who could be her replacement, but no one, in particular, stood out. She had specifically not given me the role of Clara to avoid charges of nepotism. Barbara expected both Jasmine and me to move on to better dance opportunities in the near future.

Roland entered the stage. Barbara perked up. He was dashing, and the years of dancing together brought a fondness that can only be kindled by best friends. His skill on stage— even when not dancing but just walking and acting— far surpassed the usual Drosselmeier played by the father of one of her students. He commanded the audience to watch him, which is important in this role since he is the mysterious force that makes the magic of the *Nutcracker* happen.

For a moment, Barbara became very melancholy. She missed being a famous ballerina. She missed being partnered by Roland. She missed learning new choreography and moving in new ways. She missed the excitement. She looked closely at the backdrops and sets and noticed how old and worn they seemed. Most of the costumes were fresh because many had been made for specific dancers, but still, none of her production compared to what she saw with the *Nutcracker* that was in town filming over the prior few weeks. They had fresh ideas, fresh costumes, the world's best dancers, new settings, and professional technicians. She was glad they came into town and used her dance studio, but it only reinforced the rut her life had become. She loved her husband, Bill, and her children. In many ways, her life was enviable— to spend it all day making beauty and art— but it was still a rut and not the exciting life she used to have.

She reached over to the playpen and picked up Prima. She needed to see her happy grin, pet her soft fur, and hold her tight. Of course, that excited the puppies, and they began to yelp. Barbara gave Beatrice a look to do something. Beatrice reached into the bag next to her and pulled out some dog treats. She opened the package and gave some to each of the puppies and Prima. After their first sniff, they gulped the morsel down and looked for more. That calmed them down for the moment.

Barbara laughed but also sighed at the situation. Prima perked her up but thinking of what had been and comparing it to what is, with what it could be, just brought her down. She righted herself and focused on the rehearsal at hand. There was nothing she could do at the moment to improve her life.

Jasmine had just laid on the bed on stage, and the dream sequence began. The smallest mice entered as the tree grew larger. Barbara always held her breath when the Christmas tree mechanism was used. She didn't need another incident like what happened in the studio when Nick got caught and carried fifteen feet up into the air. Luckily, there was no mishap.

The Mouse King appeared as Jasmine woke from her sleep. The Nutcracker entered with a series of *grand jeté* in *attitude*. The jumps were magnificent. Barbara was pleased with the choice to hire Peter for the role of the Nutcracker, and it was a pleasant surprise and added bonus that he was Roland's nephew. Peter was stunning in his white tights and red vested jacket. Barbara noticed the headpiece was looking a bit tattered. She made a mental note to rebuild it for next year. Still, Peter took it all in stride and ate up the scenery with his physical presence. The mice and Mouse King stood no chance against his skill.

The Battle scene went as choreographed, and the Nutcracker killed the Mouse King, allowing for the Nutcracker's headpiece to be quickly pulled off with a hidden wire to magically transform him into the handsome prince. Jasmine and Peter exited in a small sleigh in front of the curtain to allow for the set change for *Waltz of the Snowflakes*.

The scene went smoothly, and Jasmine and Peter looked good together as Clara and the Nutcracker Prince. But it was nothing compared to the special effects-laden version created by Roland for the *Nutcracker* film. Still, it would have to do. Barbara resigned herself to her limited budget and limited talent.

Waltz of the Snowflakes went smoothly; even the falling snow special effect went without mishap. Too often, the snow either comes down in clumps, or very little of it comes down at all, or there is a major dump. The turning drum up above the lighting was a simple contraption but prone to being inconsistent.

I looked good in the corps de ballet and my small solo. There seemed to be something different about me in how I danced and performed over how I was just a few weeks ago. I seemed much more *confident* and mature.

Ballet companies always put an intermission after the *Waltz of the Snowflakes*. First, it is about halfway through the music, and second, time is needed to sweep the floors and change sets to *Land of the Sweets*. Barbara put Prima back in the

241

playpen with her puppies so she could go on stage to give some last-minute directions.

Many children who were in Act 1 but not in Act 2 rushed the photographer. A long noisy line formed. Luckily, the break between acts would take twenty minutes for the set change and sweep of the snow-covered floor. Barbara walked the stage, making eye contact with many adult coordinators and dancers. There were few directions to give since she had been mounting the *Nutcracker* for decades, and every detail was documented. It ran like clockwork with so many volunteers. She gave big hugs to Jasmine, Peter, John, and me. The performance rode on the success of the stars and understudies, and so far, everything was flawless.

The stage manager called out, "Places everyone for Act 2 in five minutes."

Barbara returned to her seat in the audience. Bill joined her since his part in Act 1 was over, and he was not returning to the stage. The dogs were quiet for the moment, and Beatrice was busy making a quick alteration to a costume. In Barbara's production of the *Nutcracker*, Clara dances with the Nutcracker in the *Pas de Deux*, which includes the *Sugar Plum Fairy* variation. Everything was set for Act 2.

*

31 — Dress Rehearsal of Act 2

The curtains opened with *Clara and the Prince* music playing. The backdrop showed a large candy cane palace with cotton candy and chocolate bonbon accents. Peter pushed the sleigh around, with Jasmine standing at the crest of the sleigh, allowing her dress to billow in the wind. Once they came to rest, Clara stepped off the sleigh, and many of the dancers and children for Act 2 entered from the wings. Immediately Peter used dance to retell his battle with the Mouse King through pantomime. It was thrilling. Jasmine was dancing well, and none of the drama from the past week seemed to affect her performance. Barbara was impressed by Jasmine's expressiveness and technique. Still, Jasmine didn't come across as the innocent girl required by the part of Clara; she was too womanly.

After the two dances, Peter and Jasmine walked off stage. In many productions of the *Nutcracker*, Clara and the Nutcracker Prince stay on stage for the entire Act 2, sitting on thrones and being entertained by the other dancers in the specialty dances. Since this production required Peter and Jasmine to dance the final *Pas de Deux*, it would be unfair to ask them to sit for a half-hour, get cold, and then jump into a major dance. So, Barbara had them exit the stage to return later for the *Pas de Deux* at the end.

Peter and Jasmine used this break to be photographed by a professional photographer. She had finished taking photos of the children and could now spend some time with the stars. Twenty minutes would be sufficient to get the photos she wanted, and the bright spotlights would help Jasmine and Peter stay warm.

The next couple of dances proceeded without incident. The *Spanish*, *Arabian*, and *Chinese Dance* were good; not spectacular or inventive, but good nonetheless. The *Russian Dance* was always a challenge to mount. Like with so many small companies, Barbara did not have access to any local men or boys who knew *prisyadka*. So, she had to improvise. Instead, she had six Christmas trees dance entertaining patterns on the stage. The costume was a large cone-shaped net about seven feet tall that a boy or girl could fit inside and hold the frame. Being netting, the dancer could see out reasonably well— not great, but acceptable on a well-lit stage. Plastic ornaments, garlands, and decorations were sewn on the netting, all topped off with a multi-pointed star. The costumes looked great on stage, and audiences seemed to find it fun and accept them as a good replacement for skilled dancers capable of true Russian folk style.

Nick and Sheila were two of the six dancers inside the Christmas tree costume. The music was so infectious.

Rat ta la tat ta la tat ta la tat da da da
Rat ta la tat ta la tat ta la tat da da da
da da da da da da tat la da

The parents in the front row of the auditorium started clapping to the music as the trees slid across the stage, then up and down with small hops and bows. It was very cute. Even Barbara found herself clapping along. In many ways, the dance was reminiscent of the dancing mushrooms in Disney's *Fantasia*. During the last seconds of the dance, some elves skipped onto the stage, ending up behind the trees. This hid the fact that the elves were plugging an electrical extension cord into each tree. The plan was for the strings of lights on the Christmas trees to be turned on at the last note of the music while the stage plunged into blackness. It was a moment audiences looked forward to.

The trees began to spin on the last strains of the music. Nick couldn't keep it together. This was his first year as a Christmas tree, and he couldn't see well; neither could Sheila wearing her glasses. The two of them lost their position and spun into each other just as the final notes played, and the stage went black, and the trees lit up. It was an ending that always brought cheers but seeing two of the trees first bouncing together and then falling onto their sides didn't help.

The parents in the front row let out a laugh. Even Barbara and Beatrice chuckled. It seemed like a comedy sketch. Barbara spoke into her headset. "We need to stop for a moment and check on the dancers." The stage manager stopped the music and turned up the stage lights. Barbara stood up to walk to the stage.

"We're all right," Nick and Sheila said in feeble voices. "We're all right."

Some stagehands came out from the wings and helped Nick and Sheila stand up and lift the costumes off.

Barbara spoke out to Nick, "Spin a little slower next time, honey."

"OK, Mom," replied Nick.

Barbara couldn't resist another chuckle. The stage was cleared, and Barbara gave the OK to continue. Barbara turned to Beatrice, "Good thing little boys and girls bounce."

The next dance was the *Dance of the Reed Flutes.* Tchaikovsky did not specify who the dancers were to be in the number, so Barbara turned this into a *pas de trois* for John and two of the older girls. That would give the more experienced dancers something to highlight their achievements.

The three of them were lovely. John made an admirable partner. They wore peasant summer costumes, with John brandishing a reed flute. Barbara prided herself in providing ballet training for both girls and boys. Too often, there are very few boys in ballet school, and they get overlooked in their training. Barbara created a special library of DVDs and brought in male teachers to advance the skills of the boys. She was confident that John would be capable of handling the Nutcracker part if necessary.

Many of the younger girl dancers from Act 1 were seated in the audience next to the playpen containing Prima and her puppies. While *Dance of the Reed Flutes* played on stage, the dogs became very agitated. All of them were on their hind legs, paws against the playpen side. Sometimes they would scoot a few inches right or left to the musical beat. The girls picked up all the dogs and cradled them in their arms. As if on cue, the girls made a line and danced a mock *pas de deux* with the puppies. As John lifted his partner on stage, the girls lifted the dogs in the air.

When John and his partners *pirouetted*, the girls spun around with their dogs. It was amusing and cute. One girl pulled out her cell phone and recorded the dancing dogs for social media. Even Barbara had to smile. When the number ended and John and the dancers left the stage, the girls took bows with their canine partners and placed them back into the playpen. The dogs seemed happy and not as restless as before. I'm sure the short video would go viral.

Barbara returned her attention to the stage just in time for the *Waltz of the Flowers*. After seeing the special effect-laden version filmed by Nutcracker Ltd., Barbara thought it was time to spice up her number. In the studio, with Nick's help, a few radio-controlled drones were modified to lift straight up, unfurling a banner painted with a very large ten-foot-high flower. Her idea was to have one of the clowns from the previous number throw some small flowers at the ground, and a group of six drones lift the banner flowers during the first couple of seconds of the music. It would give the impression that magical flowers were planted and grew into dancing flowers. The drones would fly around the stage in formation, stopping next to the wings, at which point girl dancers in flower costumes would emerge and finish the six-minute dance. In the dance studio, the idea worked. Today would be the first time to try it on stage.

Dancers dressed as clowns finished the *Dance of the Clowns* by placing the six drones on stage. Of course, they didn't look like drones but rather the top of large flowers. The *Waltz of the Flowers* began, and, as planned, a clown threw artificial flowers at the ground where the drones were located. Six teenagers in the wings controlled their own drone. Nick was one of the drone drivers. The drones turned on and began to rise in unison. Barbara thought it looked magical and a good change over the traditional opening. Being electric-driven drones, they were virtually silent. The drones reached the prescribed height above the stage and began a slow rotation in a large circle. At one point, they broke off from the circle and went down the center of the stage before moving over to the side curtains. Once there, the corps de ballet stepped out from behind the banner to begin their waltz. The drones moved upstage in a line and held their position while the girls danced.

During this time, Peter and Jasmine went over to the photographic station to have their pictures taken in various poses. Even though I was on stage dancing as one of the flowers, I could see what transpired at the photoshoot. Jasmine was giving it all she could. Many of the pictures had her cozying up to Peter. From my distance, I couldn't really see their expressions, but I could see how much Jasmine was draped over Peter in every shot. This disturbed me. Although I reminded myself that he was not my boyfriend, it still hurt. I really liked Peter. I wanted the number to be over and go backstage.

Jasmine went in for the kill. She pinned Peter against the backdrop and gave him a long hard kiss. I saw it all and stumbled. I became disoriented and spun out of position, catching one of my arms in the banner of the center flower supported by the drone. Before I knew it, my other arm got caught in another banner. My turning motion caused me to fall gracefully to the ground pulling two of the drones down with me. I lay flat on the ground, face down, with the banners lying across my back, my tutu standing straight up in the air, and the drones bouncing up and down.

Barbara stood and yelled, "Stop. Stop. Everyone stop." She ran toward the stage.

The stage manager stopped the music and pushed up the lights. Peter and Jasmine rushed to the edge of the stage to see what had happened. The parents in the audience were hushed with anxiety.

I took an assessment of my situation. I could tell nothing was injured, just my pride. While facing the floor, I cried out, "I'm OK... I'm OK."

Barbara rushed up the stairs to the stage and over to me. She placed her hands on my back.

"Are you OK?" she asked.

"I said... I'm OK," while lifting my head and rolling over onto my back. I was angry with myself for making the blunder and embarrassed at the same time.

"I didn't do it... I didn't do it," Nick pleaded while running to center stage. "She wasn't in the right place."

Barbara gave me one of those stern motherly looks.

I took responsibility for the mishap. "I wasn't in the right place. It's my fault... I'm OK. Let's do it again."

By then, Peter had reached me and helped me up. I was so embarrassed. After helping me stand, I brushed him off and straightened my costume.

"I'm OK... just leave me alone... can we please just go on," I pleaded with an icy voice.

Barbara called out to the stage director. "Let's reset and start from the beginning of the *Waltz of the Flowers.*" She turned to Peter, "... and Peter, you and Jasmine should be in the wings since you go on next."

Peter tried to get an acknowledgment from me, but I was fuming too much and not receptive to anyone. In all the commotion, I failed to see that Peter forcibly pushed Jasmine off him when she kissed him. He wanted nothing to do with her.

Barbara returned to her seat in the audience; the drones were reset on the stage, and music backed up to the beginning of the number.

"Whenever you are ready, let's take this to the end," Barbara gave directions to the stage manager over her headset.

This time around, the number went as planned. It looked like the revised *Waltz of the Flowers* would work, and Barbara hoped it would give an added boost to the show. Peter and Jasmine walked onto the stage as the last of the dancing flowers left. The unmistakable opening strains of Tchaikovsky's *Pas de Deux* came over the speakers. The couple looked dashing. When the *Nutcracker* was staged for the first time in the nineteenth century, choreographers complained that the big pas de deux came at the very end of the ballet, which was not typical. As such, choreographers often changed the sequence of dances to the consternation of Tchaikovsky. Still, the entire ballet builds to

248

the *Pas de Deux,* making it the perfect capstone to the evening's magic.

The *Pas de Deux* was also Barbara's favorite dance in the ballet. Of all her partners, Roland was the best. The way he carried himself. He was regal and strong without being obnoxious or overbearing. Barbara saw many of the same elements in Peter. Roland taught him well. Jasmine was a different story. Although she was skilled, something was missing that she tried to mask with her womanly manners. That got Barbara thinking about past *Nutcrackers* that her dance studio put on. There had been many Claras, each unique and beautiful in her own right. But to Barbara's knowledge, none went on to become world-class ballerinas. She wondered why that was. Maybe she wasn't as good of a teacher as she thought. Waves of self-doubt washed over Barbara.

Roland, sitting nearby in the audience since his part was over in Act 1, sensed something was wrong with Barbara. He left his seat and sat next to her. She stoically stared at the stage, watching Peter and Jasmine in the *Pas de Deux.* Roland reached over and took her hand. Small tears coalesced under her eyes and trickled down her cheeks. She turned her head momentarily to glance at Roland. He squeezed her hand and gave a small smile— so many memories, so many good times. Letting go of something so beautiful and bigger than yourself is hard.

Peter nailed the one-hand lift finale, which sent the audience of parents into a frenzy of applause. Standing in the wings with the other dancers, even I broke into applause. I wished it was me flying high above the stage in Peter's hands.

The stage manager was instructed to stop the music at the end of the *Pas de Deux* to allow for bows if needed. That would vary from performance to performance. Since this was a dress rehearsal, the music continued directly into the *Final Waltz* and *Apotheosis.*

Barbara bolted from her seat when the curtain closed and walked onto the stage. Everyone was pumped up and flush-faced. The stage manager and Barbara spoke for a while. She thanked all the dancers, parents, volunteers, and workers. "That was excellent. Thank you all. Be here tomorrow night by 5 PM for our first show… excellent… excellent," yelled Barbara to the crowded stage while she applauded them. "It will be the best show ever."

The older girls and I in the dressing rooms were taking off makeup and packing up costumes. Jasmine sat off by herself, acting very much like a prima donna. She slowly wiped the makeup off her face with long, slow, sensual strokes. It was meant to be self-indulgent and to establish privilege over those watching. I couldn't wait to get out of there and stuffed my dance bag quickly.

"I feel like a hippo. I mean, I can still feel that blueberry muffin I ate yesterday. I'm such a pig," stated the redheaded dancer to no one in particular. "There's no way I can lose another five pounds by tomorrow night. I'll never be as pretty as Jasmine."

"Did you see what Jasmine did?" asked the brunette dancer to the redheaded dancer sitting next to me.

"Did I?… girl… she has some chops," replied the redhead.

"Yeah, she's the star… and she has Peter. Mmm, mmm. The way she zoned in on him and kissed him. I thought she might suck his teeth right out of him," said the brunette while doing her best ghetto-girl side-to-side head swing.

The two girls laughed. I felt very uncomfortable with the talk about Peter and Jasmine.

"I hope the photographer caught that smooch on film," continued the redhead.

"I'd pay money to see those shots," replied the brunette.

The girls laughed again and slapped a high-five.

Peter entered the room at the door closest to Jasmine. His shirt was off, showing his chiseled bare chest. He was still in his white tights but rolled down to his waist. She reached out and grabbed his arm. He wrestled his arm away and walked over to me.

"What are you doing after rehearsal tonight?" asked Peter.

I slumped my shoulders.

"I thought we could get a bite to eat or something," continued Peter.

"No... no, it's been a long day, and I'm sure Mom wants to get home."

"Sure?"

I was tired and annoyed. I rose up with my dance bag slung over my shoulder and a costume in my other hand and walked toward the door.

The redhead caught my hand and pulled me down for a private conversation. She whispered, "I think he likes you. If you leave now, Jasmine will for sure get him."

All this talk of Peter and Jasmine was exhausting. I just wanted out. Besides, I made a fool of myself getting tangled in the *Waltz of the Flowers*. Who could possibly want me now?

"I'm sorry... sorry," I said while walking out the door.

*

32 — Opening Night

It was the opening night of the *Nutcracker Ballet* for Barbara's dance studio and local dance company. The weather turned decidedly cold. Snow was in the forecast. I loved the snow and hoped that once it came, it would persist a few weeks through to Christmas. It is always special when there is snow on Christmas Day.

Barbara and the entire family were at the auditorium hours earlier than the 5:00 PM call time. There were so many details to clean up for the evening performance. She also wanted one more run-through with the drones used in the *Waltz of the Flowers*.

I was in my costume for Act 1, sitting by myself on a bench just outside the dressing rooms. I always had stage fright before a show, and it was best if I didn't hang around the other girls. The other girls became so loud and talkative that it irritated me. It is well known that the backstage of professional companies tends to be calm and quiet, whereas the backstage of school productions is chatty and noisy. Professionals know the need to be centered before a show, requiring a serene environment backstage. School kids are the worst by broadcasting their anxiety to all within earshot.

More and more dancers arrived, and the halls filled with boys and girls and adults in costume for Act 1. Peter wore grey sweatpants and a sweatshirt over his tights and tank top while he warmed up at the practice *barre* placed off to one side of the backstage. Since he didn't come on until the middle of Act 1, he had plenty of time to get dressed. He stretched easily into full splits. More than anything, he wanted to stay warm and limber. He showed no signs of stage fright.

Once he was done, he walked down the hall and plunked himself next to me.

"Are you OK?" asked Peter.

"Just a bit nervous," I replied.

"I used to be that way... but got over it."

"Really!"

Peter turned his head to give full attention to me.

"A dancer friend of mine got me over stage fright a few years back. He said to realize that when it is time to go on, you go on, and when it is time to go off, you go off. It is all set-in motion, and there is nothing you can do about it. The determinism of the situation sets you free. There is nothing you can do in the next fifteen minutes that will make you a better dancer. Is there? So, just go out there and do what you've spent months of training."

"But what if I mess up?"

Peter took my hand into his. "The second thing my friend said was, it really doesn't matter. The audience is rooting for you, especially the younger and less experienced you are. I mean, think about it. Does it make any sense that people applaud at movies? Yet some do. There are no actors there to hear them. No, people applaud to reinforce they had an enjoyable time. In a sense, they are applauding themselves and their experience. The best thing to do is relax. Let it happen and have a fun time. The more fun you have, the more the audience will enjoy it. They will forgive your mistakes, but they won't forgive being bored."

The two of us stayed silent. I mulled over what he had said.

Barbara walked around the stage and into the dressing rooms announcing, "ten minutes... ten minutes to curtain... it's a full house."

John walked by Peter and me and gave us a thumbs-up. Jasmine also came out of the dressing room and saw Peter holding my hand.

I stood up and said, "Gotta go."

Peter held onto my hand. I was self-conscious of his affection. I had to state, "You... but you kissed Jasmine."

Peter looked fed up with the constant pairing with Jasmine. "No, Jasmine kissed me... and if you watched long enough, you would have seen me push her off."

"Oh." Then it dawned on me what he really meant. "OH."

"You'll do fine, trust me," Peter reassured me as I walked away. His eyes followed me until I was out of sight.

Jasmine walked by and sarcastically asked, "What was that all about?" She was very curt with her question.

Peter limited the conversation and said, "Nerves." He wanted her to leave, but the show was to begin in just a few minutes. This was no time to tick Jasmine off.

Jasmine pressed her importance. "You're with me; don't you forget that. You were hired to dance with me... me. Dance well tonight. I have agents out there watching me."

Roland walked down the hall announcing, "Places everyone."

The dancers scrambled to their assigned spots for entry. The house lights dimmed, and the music began. The curtain could be heard opening, and children dancers rushed out onto the stage. The audience applauded enthusiastically. There is something quaint about small-town citizens applauding when a stage curtain opens, revealing sets and backdrops at the beginning of *Nutcracker*. It would take a spectacular set to obtain a similar response in a big city.

Barbara stood off to one side of the stage with the Stage Manager to oversee any potential problems and give answers when needed. The Stage Manager wore a headset facilitating communication with lighting, sound, and props.

Act 1 proceeded better than during dress rehearsal the day before. More children hit their marks. There was better energy from the dancers and actors. Maybe the excitement of performing helped. Roland controlled the stage when he arrived as Drosselmeier and gave Clara her Nutcracker doll. Jasmine seemed to have toned down her acting to reflect a young Clara better. And the Christmas tree grew without incident at the beginning of the *Battle* with the Mouse King. Barbara was pleased. When Roland left the stage, he would not be needed through the rest of the ballet and took up station next to Barbara to act as backup.

The mice scurried out of the wings and onto the stage. Jasmine, as Clara, woke up and acted frightened by all the hairy rodents. The Mouse King made his entrance to some boos from the audience. That is always a good sign, as it indicates the audience is engaged in the show. All the small mice took formation for a short, choreographed dance. Something seemed amiss. Barbara could swear there were one too many mice, but it all happened so fast it was hard to tell. Maybe one mouse was simply out of position.

I stood in the wings next to Barbara and Roland. It dawned on Barbara that that was unusual. She spoke up to me, "Honey, shouldn't you be changing for the *Waltz of the Snowflake* number?"

Too much was happening, with mice and soldiers exiting and entering the wings as the battle between the Mouse King and Nutcracker continued for me to reply. Jasmine ran to the prop man waiting in the wing to get the shoe she was supposed to throw at the Mouse King.

The prop man gave her a wand instead. Jasmine exploded and threw the wand at the prop man. "I've had it with this amateurish company. You can't even get me the right prop."

Barbara stepped in and handed the shoe to Jasmine. "Here, here is the shoe. Now get back out on stage."

At that point, Jasmine was out of position and missed her cue. She turned around to face the stage just as one of the mice flew into the wing. They collided in what could only be called a calamity.

SMASH.

Jasmine grabbed the curtain to break her fall but caught her foot under the light tree. The mouse fell back onto the floor, and its headpiece came off. It was Whitney. Jasmine cried in pain. Whitney looked astonished.

"Whitney!!!" said Barbara. "Whitney!!"

With no time to think, Barbara directed Roland to help Whitney while she reached to help Jasmine up.

"Jasmine... Jasmine, are you OK?" asked Barbara.

"No, you idiot," Jasmine said while being helped up. "It's my ankle." She grabbed for her ankle and winced in pain.

"Can you dance?"

Jasmine tried to take a step but collapsed into Barbara's arms. She turned to face Whitney. "I'm going to get you... you... you."

I stepped between Jasmine and Whitney and said, "I can explain."

Barbara was confused by all that had happened and not thinking of their immediate needs.

Roland took command. "Jasmine, take off the dress. Marie needs to go on."

"No, no. It's my part," yelled Jasmine. "Besides, it won't fit her." She had to get in one more cut at me before she lost her starring role.

Roland unhooked Jasmine from her costume and slipped it over her head. Barbara continued to help support Jasmine standing in her leotard and tights.

"Here, Marie put this on," directed Roland.

"But... but... "

"No time for *buts*; you are taking over for Jasmine."

I was in Jasmine's costume in less than fifteen seconds and handed the prop shoe. The entrance was already missed, and Peter, on stage, saw the confusion in the wings. Not knowing what was happening, he just continued with the battle and killed the Mouse King. Not to frighten children, the Mouse King died comically lying on its back, legs up in the air, occasionally twitching. The audience laughed at the scene.

Roland took the prop shoe out of my hand and pushed me onto the stage just as the Nutcracker was magically transformed into the Nutcracker Prince. Barbara handed Jasmine off to Roland to escort her back to the dressing room. She moaned with each step. Whitney followed along, very humbled.

I walked directly to the Nutcracker Prince. Peter said under his breath, "I wondered when you would be my Clara." He gave me a big smile while deeply bowing. When he rose, he placed a tiara on my head. I radiated joy even in a dress a bit too big for me. The sleigh was brought onto the stage, and Peter promenaded me into the sleigh as choreographed. Peter also climbed into the sleigh, and some toy soldiers helped pull it off the stage into the wings. The set was changed to the *Waltz of the Snowflakes*. Peter and I would not be needed until Act 2.

In the wings, Peter asked, "So, what happened?"

"There was an accident... Jasmine twisted her ankle. It looks bad."

"Accident?"

"One of the mice ran into her and knocked her down... Actually, it was Whitney... Whitney was playing one of the mice. Mother didn't know."

"Whitney... our Whitney?"

"I didn't tell anyone. She really wanted to do it anonymously."

Peter laughed. "Jasmine so much wants to be her friend, yet she keeps getting hurt by her; I mean, first her nose last week, and now twisting her ankle. Kinda ironic... Intermission is after the Waltz, so we have about twenty minutes before we go on. Let's go to the ballet *barre* and get some stretches in? It will be quieter there."

Barbara showed up. "Marie, Jasmine won't be able to go back on tonight. Go to the dressing room and put on your Clara costume. It will fit better."

I looked at Peter, smiled, and walked away with Barbara to the dressing room. It didn't take long to change and adjust my hair and tiara. I really did fit the part of Clara better than Jasmine.

In no time, intermission was over. Peter met with me in the wings.

Peter took a double-take. "You are a princess," Peter flattered me.

I smiled but was very nervous.

"Remember what I said about letting it all go. The audience will love you if you love to dance."

The music for Act 2 began, and the curtain opened. Peter escorted me into the Land of the Sweets. Peter whispered in my ear, "Enjoy the music. Be playful." They danced the small variation. I danced OK in the number, but it was not spectacular.

I didn't make any mistakes, but I seemed too cautious. I had a forced smile that was obvious to all.

The rest of Act 2 went well. The audience always enjoys the specialty dances, especially the *Spanish, Arabian, Chinese,* and *Russian* dances. John was truly 'on' when he and his partners danced the *Dance of the Reed Flutes.* Good for him. Luckily, the revised *Waltz of the Flowers* went well with the new drones, which revved up the audience. Finally, it was time for the *Pas de Deux*— the climax of the *Nutcracker.*

Peter and I were in position on opposite sides of the stage. The *Intrada* music began, and we both took a few steps in and bowed. We walked toward each other and met center stage. Peter offered his hand and promenaded me downstage. He turned to me, and I stepped into right *arabesque en pointe.* Peter slowly slid his back foot out to allow me to take a deep *arabesque penchée.* I wobbled. Peter could feel how tense I was. He went off choreography and tilted his head into my hands as though he was cradling my hand while placing it on his cheek. He slowly rose, allowing me to stand up. He took both of my shoulders in his strong hands and gave me a light kiss on the lips. I was stunned.

Peter said softly, "Dance for me."

My face softened from the forced smile, and I relaxed. A new vitality reinvigorated my stride. I trusted Peter and found that we danced as one. It was lovely. For once, I attacked the more difficult steps with confidence. My *Sugar Plum Fairy* variation sparkled. Even in the spectacular one-hand lift finale, I felt I was Peter's equal.

The two of us were brilliant. Barbara had to stop the music to allow for the thunderous applause from the audience. Even Barbara was taken aback by the intensity and joy of the *Pas de Deux.* A star was born that night.

The ballet wrapped up with the *Waltz Finale* and *Apotheosis.* I was not cognizant of time passing. It all seemed a dream, very much like Clara's dream in the *Nutcracker.* Curtain calls brought out the entire cast, from the youngest child and parent in Act 1, to the older boys and girl dancers in the later numbers. Jasmine would not miss the applause and had herself wheeled out on a rolling chair to join the cast. When the mice came out, they took off their headpieces for the bow. When Whitney took off her headpiece, an audible gasp was heard in the audience, with people whispering, 'Whitney Smith?' Whitney smiled and waved to the audience, which elicited even more applause and picture-taking. Finally, Peter and I took center stage. The applause rose to a deafening roar. I was overwhelmed. When flowers were brought out for me, I took one from the bouquet and handed it to Peter. He accepted it graciously and kissed my hand. No one could hear it, but Peter said, "M'lady." The audience went nuts over the ritual.

The curtain closed, and house lights were brought up. The dancers on stage were excited. There's nothing like a good *Nutcracker* performance to get worked up and flush-faced and happy. Crowds of family and friends flooded the stage to congratulate the dancers. John had a good crowd around him. Peter and I were slowly separated by the groups of well-wishers. Being opening night and the surprise save by the understudy caused a good hour of backstage congratulations. Eventually, the auditorium emptied, leaving just my family, Peter, and a few workers. Most of the lights were turned out with just overhead work lights still on.

I was finally able to go to the dressing room to take off my makeup and change out of my costume. Whitney had just finished packing her bag when I entered.

"I want to thank you so much... I like being anonymous," Whitney said excitedly.

I smiled. "I'm glad we became friends."

Whitney paused and gave me a big hug. "You are my only truthful friend. I appreciate it... it was so much fun... I've got to do this every year."

We both laughed.

"See you at tomorrow's show?" Whitney asked while walking out of the room.

"I won't tell."

I was dead tired but a good tired. It was nice to have the dressing room all to myself. I took off my makeup, put on sweats, and let my hair down. By the time I stuffed my dance bag, Peter had shown up at the door and leaned against the doorframe. He was ever handsome, even out of costume.

"You did very well tonight," praised Peter.

"Well, thank you... so did you," I smiled.

"Come on. Everyone is gone. Your family is waiting in the van. Nick is really tired."

I walked to the door. Peter offered his arm. I was touched by the gentlemanly behavior and put my arm through his. We walked to the stage door. Roland pushed the door open for us while holding the Nutcracker doll.

"So, what nut did we crack tonight?" asked Roland.

"Marie's insecurity... I think we have a budding star on our hands," added Peter. He reached over and gave my arm another squeeze.

Just outside the stage door, my parent's van was parked. Light snow was falling. Barbara, Bill, and Nick opened the van door and let out Prima and the puppies. Each dog was dressed in a sweater and bow tie— way too cute.

Barbara spoke up to me. "Honey, you were great tonight. I'm really proud of you. You showed yourself to be a real professional." Barbara reached over and gave me a kiss on the cheek.

Bill added, "So am I." He, too, reached over to kiss me on the cheek. "Now, everyone in the van. It's getting very cold." Bill looked up in the sky to see the snow getting heavier, his breath making a large cloud.

Peter turned to me and asked, "Want to go for a short walk. I'm too worked up to go home yet."

"Yes." I turned to look to my mother, who nodded 'yes'.

Peter looked to Bill, "Go on without us. I'll drive Marie home."

"OK." answered Bill.

Barbara and Roland offered their goodbyes. "Thanks, Peter... for everything."

Bill, Barbara, Nick, Roland, and the dogs got into the van, started up the motor, and pulled away, crunching snow under the tires.

Peter and I were alone and walked arm-in-arm to the front of the auditorium. The mall was vacant, but all the lights were on. The ground and ice-skating rink were a sea of white foam. The trees twinkled with colored lights, and all the storefronts were ablaze with holiday decorations. The snow created a white blanket that reflected the multicolor lights. It was a winter wonderland.

Peter asked, "I was wondering... if you would be interested in visiting me in New York?"

"New York?"

"Yeah, you could take classes where the professionals work out, you know, at Paul's studios and elsewhere. I could introduce you to many of the schools that would prepare you to audition for the larger companies like ABT or New York City Ballet."

"I've done summer camp before. It was fun but didn't lead to anything."

"No, no, not summer camp. One of the strategies for getting into a ballet company is to take company classes for a while and then approach them for a job. That way, they know you instead of being just a dancer off the street."

"Dancer off the street... that's attractive," I said sarcastically.

"You know what I mean. It would be good for you. You could stay with me... as long as you want." Peter's eyes were filled with hope.

At that moment, the mall sound system began playing the *Nutcracker's Waltz of the Flowers*. We both smiled. Peter put out his hand into ballroom dance position. I took form, and we began to waltz, feet kicking up freshly fallen snow. Peter picked me way up on one of the crescendos and brought me down slowly until our lips touched. We kissed—a real kiss. A meaningful kiss. I looked into Peter's eyes with kindness and love. I had never felt this way about a boy before.

262

"To live is to dance," Peter pontificated.

"To dance is to live," I added.

We continued to waltz in the light snow, highlighted by Christmas tree lights twinkling around them, warmed by their growing love.

MARIE AND PETER ALONE IN THE SNOW
*

33 — Epilogue

More than a year had passed since I became a star, not a big star but rather a big fish in a small pond. I was at the top of the class in my mother's dance studio and recognized it was time to move on. With Peter, Roland, my family, and Paul's encouragement, I moved to New York to continue my study in ballet classes. Importantly, I <u>was not the best dancer</u>. The struggle was hard, and there was so much competition from girls with extraordinary talent and similar ambitions.

Peter landed a contract position with ABT in the corps de ballet. He was elated by the possibilities.

Peter and I lived as a loving couple in New York. We enjoyed each other's company and, at the same time, were honest about our future prospects. I may never land a position with a prestigious dance company. And even though Peter currently had a paying job, all dance positions eventually end someday, usually sooner than later. Both of us needed to plan for a future when we would not earn a living by dancing. Luckily, we were of similar minds and supported each other. We sought joy in our dancing and in life. We never wanted to lose sight of what was important. Each Christmas, we returned as guest dancers in Barbara's production of the *Nutcracker*.

Roland encouraged Peter and me to attend special effects and computer modeling school. That way, we could, as Roland had, continue expressing our art in movement once the body was gone. Roland also returned each December to perform in Barbara's *Nutcracker* as Drosselmeier. It was a wonderful tradition of family coming back together for the holidays.

Barbara continued with the dance studio, and Bill still worked as a psychotherapist. As older dancers left the studio, the younger dancers were able to move up to lead positions. Such is the cycle of dance. Barbara was concerned about me moving to New York, but she knew it was important to do so at this stage in my development. Barbara continues to mount the *Nutcracker* each year with a bit more joy and a new crop of eager faces.

Nick is still a nerd and is taking more classes in anthropology. Sheila is still Nick's best friend, and they attend museum events together. They are not boyfriend/girlfriend since that would not make sense to either of them.

Prima's puppies all found loving homes.

Jasmine quit dancing and moved to Los Angeles to work in Whitney's production company. It was rumored that she became pregnant by one of Whitney's bodyguards.

John also left the studio as soon as he graduated high school. With 'courage,' he could not wait to leave his 'small provincial town.' He auditioned during the summer for a couple of regional companies and landed a position with the Oregon State Ballet Company. He hoped that a few more years of training surrounded by better-quality male dancers would prepare him for the big leagues. He also hoped to find a boyfriend who shared and respected his love for ballet.

Whitney released a new album that was a bigger hit than before. At age twenty-two, she was transitioning from "teen" heartthrob to adult sexy superstar. Deep inside, she was not pleased and felt manipulated even more. The joys of singing were quickly vanishing. She hoped that when *Nutcracker the Musical* was released later that year, it would help transform her career from being a pop singer to an adult entertainer and actress focused on her talent, not sex. She often texted or called me to talk on the phone. I seemed to provide a sensible, quiet perspective on the whole entertainment merry-go-round that Whitney didn't get from her "yes-man" employees at the production company. When Christmas comes around, Whitney longs for the time she spent in the little northeastern town. She often takes a "private" vacation in December and disappears for a few weeks to an unknown location. It is sometimes said that, if you look closely, during the *Battle of the Mouse King*, you can see Whitney playing one of the mice.

End

*

Let's Make A Movie!!!!

We hope you enjoyed *Marie's Nutcracker*. Some recent film productions have tried to put a dark spin on the *Nutcracker*— which is not true to Tchaikovsky's vision. It is time to make another *Nutcracker* movie focused on fun and dance.

It also needs to be updated. Today's kids are smart consumers. Placing the *Nutcracker* in the nineteenth century alienates the youth market. For example, how many kids even know what a 'hobby horse' is? They know iPhones, computers, electric cars, skateboards, hip-hop, and more— and they know malls.

Placing the *Nutcracker* in a mall setting offers more unique advertising opportunities than any other advertising outlet. Advertisers pay large fees to place their products in movies for a measly ten seconds. With the *Nutcracker* situated in a mall, advertisers could receive 1-2-3- up to 15 minutes of advertising exposure depending on the dance number they sponsor. Imagine the advertising revenue this new *Nutcracker* could generate!

Come, and be part of the effort to produce *Marie's Nutcracker* film. Talk about the idea with your friends and family— and at your dance studio or company. Do you know a film production company willing to take on this task? Do you know a mall owner looking for an exciting new media campaign? Please turn them onto *Marie's Nutcracker*. Lend them a copy of your book! Have them contact SES Publishing.

Once production begins, we will need lots of talent—dancers, musicians, designers, costumers, and more. You can help! Contact us at info@NutcrackerLtd.com.

It will be fun and should be financially rewarding.

*

Made in the USA
Middletown, DE
09 December 2022

16383907R00156